BABY DOLL

Hollie Overton is a television writer who has written for ABC Family, CBS and Lifetime.

Overton's father was a member of Austin, Texas notorious Overton gang, and spent several years in prison for manslaughter.

Raised by her single mother, Hollie, an identical twin herself, draws on her unique childhood experiences to lend realism and compassion to her depictions of violence and complicated family dynamics.

Praise for BABY DOLL

'What a compulsive read! A brilliant first novel that kept me transfixed and entertained until the very last page.'
Tess Gerritsen

'Moves at breakneck speed . . . a really good read.'
Stylist

'A compelling psychological thriller.'
Daily Express

'This compelling first novel opens where most thrillers end . . . Overton throws in enough twists, turns, and surprises to keep the reader wondering what on earth can happen next.'
Publishers Weekly

BABY DOLL

HOLLIE OVERTON

arrow books

1 3 5 7 9 10 8 6 4 2

Arrow Books
20 Vauxhall Bridge Road
London SW1V 2SA

Arrow Books is part of the Penguin Random House group of companies
whose addresses can be found at global.penguinrandomhouse.com.

Penguin
Random House
UK

First published in Great Britain by Century in 2016
(First published in the USA by Redhook in 2016)
First published in Great Britain in paperback by Arrow Books in 2017

www.penguin.co.uk

A CIP catalogue record for this book is available from the British Library.

ISBN 9781784753467
ISBN 9781784756994 (export)

Typeset in 12/16pt Bembo by Jouve (UK), Milton Keynes
Printed and bound in Great Britain by Clays Ltd, St Ives Plc

MIX
Paper from
responsible sources
FSC® C018179

Penguin Random House is committed to a
sustainable future for our business, our readers
and our planet. This book is made from Forest
Stewardship Council® certified paper.

LILY

A dead bolt has a very specific sound. Lily was an expert at recognizing certain sounds—the creak of the floorboards signaling his arrival, the mice scurrying across the concrete in search of food. But Lily always braced herself for the sound of the dead bolt, listening as metal scraped against metal. The lock was beginning to rust, so it always took him several tries. But inevitably, she would hear the click, the sound that meant they were trapped for another week, another month, another year. But tonight, she heard nothing. Only deafening silence. Hours passed, and she couldn't stop thinking about the lock.

Beside her, Sky stirred in her sleep and sighed. Lily stroked her daughter's jet-black hair, her gaze lingering on the stupid yellow stuffed monkey that Rick had given Sky for Christmas. Lily despised that monkey, but she couldn't deny her daughter a toy. Not when they had so little to begin with.

But the lock—why hadn't she heard the lock?

Stop obsessing and go to sleep, Lily told herself. She couldn't be tired when he returned. She knew how angry he would be if she were tired. Obsessing was foolish. But tonight she couldn't seem to stop. She'd been on edge these past few weeks. She hoped that it was just the aftermath from the stomach flu she'd been battling. But that didn't explain why she hadn't heard the lock.

The problem was, Rick didn't make mistakes. He was too precise, too meticulous. Maybe he was testing her again. There were so many tests in the beginning. But she'd proven herself. He believed she was his. She'd made him believe.

Maybe that's why he'd forgotten. What if he'd finally trusted her? What if this was their chance at an escape? There were so many what-ifs they left her paralyzed. She was still weighing the odds when Sky stirred again, and that was all Lily needed. She summoned every ounce of courage and gently slipped out of bed. She inched up the steep wooden staircase, her stomach clenched in a million knots. What if he was on the other side of the door? She could already picture his Cheshire cat grin, wagging his finger, eyebrows curled in that calculated manner. *Tsk, tsk, Baby Doll. Didn't I tell you what would happen if you disobeyed me?*

Lily hesitated at the top of the staircase. What was she thinking? Her last attempt at freedom had nearly gotten her killed. Could she really defy him? She almost made her way back down the stairs but her gaze landed on

Sky, radiating innocence, and Lily realized that she couldn't fail her child. *Do it for Sky*, she told herself. Lily turned the knob and just like that, the door swung open. She tentatively stepped into the perfectly preserved winter cabin. Plush fur rugs lined solid oak floors. An ornate vintage desk tucked into the corner, a well-stocked bar on the opposite wall: an ordinary room for a man who was anything but.

Lily held her breath. Nothing but silence greeted her. She glanced toward the windows, moonlight streaming in through the white silk Italian curtains, massive pine trees stretching out as far as her eyes could see. She forgot about Rick and his threats and raced toward the front door and suddenly, Lily was standing in the doorway, staring out at the vast, white, snow-covered horizon.

Outside. She was outside!

She hadn't been outdoors in so long. There was a different kind of silence now, nothing like what she'd grown accustomed to. This was peaceful and content. An entire world was unfurling around her, and somewhere out there in the distance was her family.

Run! We have to run!

Lily turned and raced inside, nearly tripping as she made her way back down the rickety stairs. Scanning the makeshift closet where their clothes hung, Lily knew nothing was appropriate for the winter conditions.

"My baby doll has to be beautiful," he'd said when Lily requested more-functional clothing. Their pajamas would provide almost no protection against the elements, but there were no other options. Lily would rather freeze to death than waste this opportunity. She moved toward Sky, who was still fast asleep. Lily wanted to scream, *Get up. Hurry. Move!* The clock was ticking, and her panic was rising. But she forced herself to breathe. She had to keep Sky calm. Lily knelt down beside the sleeping child and gently shook her.

"Baby, wake up, we have to go."

Sky bolted upright. She was an extraordinary child and had been since birth, displaying an innate understanding that life down here wasn't normal, and adapting to each and every circumstance. Sky wiped her eyes, blinking away sleep.

"Is it time for our adventure, Mommy?"

Lily always told Sky that they were so happy together, just the three of them, that they didn't need the outside world. But sometimes when Rick didn't visit, she would tell Sky about the magical adventures they'd take one day. She'd talk about trips to Paris, Morocco, or Indonesia. Places Lily had only ever read about online or in her high school geography class. Every child deserved to believe in a fairy tale even if Lily knew it was only make-believe.

"Yes, Chicken, it's time. But we have to be quick."

Sky grabbed that stupid stuffed monkey, clutching it tightly. Lily hesitated. She couldn't handle the thought of bringing anything Rick had touched with them.

"Sky, we have to leave your monkey here."

Sky's eyes widened as she shook her head emphatically.

"Mommy, I can't...He has to come with me."

"Mommy will get you a new friend. Cross my heart."

Sky hesitated but she would never disobey her mother. She bravely set the stuffed animal back under the covers and gave it a tender kiss good-bye. Lily layered Sky in several pairs of pajama pants, pulling three sweaters on until she was wrapped up tightly. She grabbed a fuzzy down blanket and draped it around Sky's shoulders.

"Hold on to this, okay? Don't let go."

"Okay, Mommy."

Once Sky was ready, Lily pulled on several pairs of tights under her pajamas. Her hands trembled violently; she worried that any moment he might return. But she just kept breathing, just kept telling herself if she stayed calm, they'd get out of here.

They were both ready but Lily had one more task to do. She hurried over to the corner of the room and worked open a loose floorboard. She grabbed a worn piece of paper, the note she'd written years ago, when she was still a child herself and the mother of a newborn. The pages were yellowed with age, but the writing still legible, each word painstakingly written. If this was a trap, there was no hope for Lily. She knew his punishment would be fatal. But she had to believe that Sky might have a chance.

Lily took the note and tucked it into the pocket of Sky's pajama pants.

"Remember Mommy's rules for the big adventure?"

"If you say run, I run. No stopping. No looking back. Find a policeman and give him this."

"And how will you know he's a policeman?"

"Because he'll be wearing a uniform, and he'll keep me safe."

"You're Mommy's perfect little angel; you know that, right?"

Sky gave a brave smile as Lily lifted her daughter into her arms. Sky's body was so tiny and birdlike; she felt weightless. As they slowly ascended the stairs, Lily found herself gazing down over the railing, studying this room that had housed them for the last eight years. No more than four hundred square feet, with its damp, dark walls...Hell on earth in every sense of the word. With each creaky step, she vowed she'd never return. She would never let him bring them back here. She pushed open the door again and they made their way through the main cabin. Seconds later, they were outside.

The cold air whipped Lily's hair around, her face burning from the frigid temperatures. Sky gasped, wiping her cheeks as if she might be able to swipe away the cold. She clung to Lily's neck, her body convulsing from winter's brutal assault. But Lily reveled in this moment. With the snow crunching under her slipper-clad feet, she could barely contain her joy.

"Chicken, this is it! This is the beginning of our great adventure!"

But Sky wasn't listening. She was gawking at the endless sea of white powder stretching out before them.

"What's that white stuff, Mommy?" The one request Rick indulged them in were books. They'd studied weather and season patterns. Summer. Winter. Fall. Spring. But how could dear, sweet Sky really understand what snow was when she'd never seen it? How could any child raised in that awful, windowless room truly understand anything about a world they couldn't see or touch or feel? Lily wanted to explain, to give Sky a chance to revel in these new experiences, but there wasn't time.

"No questions, Chicken. You have to do what I say, when I say it."

The sharpness in Lily's voice was uncharacteristic, but she couldn't worry about that. Sky grew quiet as Lily began walking. She forced herself to ignore the ominous, looming shadows the pine trees cast. With each step, Lily's pace quickened. She refused to glance back at the nondescript cabin. Her walk turned to a jog, and then she was running. Her legs ached, muscles weak from lack of use, but she fought through the pain. She'd endured so much that this was nothing. Lily's heart pounded so hard in her chest she thought it might explode. It had been so long since she'd been able to run, but her cross-country training came rushing back to her. She could almost hear Coach Skrovan's voice telling her to "Find a rhythm. Find your stride."

Lily ignored the cuts on her face from wayward branches and thick brush. She lost track of time as she made her way through the overgrown trail. She kept running until they arrived at what appeared to be the main road. Lily squinted, trying to make out the sign in the distance. As she grew closer, she gasped, stopping in her tracks. Highway 12. With growing horror, Lily realized she was less than five miles from home. Five miles!

The realization nearly derailed her. She wanted to drop to her knees and scream in anger and frustration. But she couldn't. *Focus on this moment.* This moment was all that mattered. *One foot in front of the other,* she told herself.

She focused on Sky, who was whimpering from the cold. "You're such a brave girl. Mommy is so proud of her brave little girl."

It was difficult, witnessing Sky's discomfort. But darkness was their salvation and she couldn't waste any time. In spite of the cold, in spite of Sky's distress, Lily realized that today was a spectacular day. She hadn't had one of those in over 3,110 days. It was a silly game she'd played with her twin sister, Abby. They'd started tracking their "spectacular days" in seventh grade.

Spectacular was a vocabulary word. *Definition: Beautiful, in a dramatic and eye-catching way.* Abby, older by six minutes, was obsessed with Oprah and her happy-go-lucky philosophies. Following the talk show host's

lead, Abby had created a calendar to track their spectacular days. And so it had begun: the day they both
made varsity track. The day they both passed their driving tests and sat on the hood of their Jeep outside the
Dairy Queen eating their banana split Blizzards, reveling in how grown-up they finally were. And then there
was the most spectacular day of all, when Wes asked Lily
to go to the movies. Lily was the first one to be asked
out on a date, but Abby helped her get ready, choosing
the perfect outfit and doing her makeup. When Wes
picked Lily up, she'd been worried that her spectacular
day was not meant to be. He was quiet and on edge, not
a trace of the carefree, goofy boy she'd been crushing
on for half the school year. She kept pushing him. "Are
you okay? Are you sure? What's wrong? You can talk
to me."

Wes had lost his temper and told her he was far from
okay. His father had been arrested for driving under the
influence. He tried to pretend it didn't matter.

"I don't know why I'm surprised. I should be used to
him acting like an asshole. It's stupid. I don't want to
ruin the night. C'mon, we're gonna miss the previews."
Lily had grabbed him before he could get out of the
truck.

"I don't care about the previews. And it's not stupid.
Tell me what's going on." An expression of gratitude
flickered across Wes's face. "Really?"

Lily had nodded. No movie in Hollywood could

compete with that moment. They sat in his pickup as Wes explained that his father's drinking had only gotten worse once Wes's mother had died. He was trying to keep the bills paid, make sure his father didn't miss work, but it was wearing on him. But he didn't just want to talk about himself. He'd asked Lily about her life, listening as she talked about Abby and how close they were and how she was so worried that their parents were planning to divorce. They were so busy talking they missed the movie, and Lily had nearly missed curfew. She couldn't believe it. She'd only ever felt this comfortable with Abby. Just when Lily thought the evening couldn't get any more perfect, Wes leaned over and kissed her. Before long, Lily's life became one spectacular day after another.

Lily kept running, adjusting Sky in her arms, but she couldn't stop thinking about that spectacular year she'd spent with Wes. Of course, that Tuesday in September had been as far from spectacular as one could get. In fact, the day had been totally shitty. She was still on crutches after spraining her ankle at her first track meet. She'd stayed up late talking to Wes on the phone and had forgotten to study for a chem pop quiz. She knew that she'd completely bombed it. Lily hobbled over to Abby's locker, prepared to vent about how she'd screwed up her GPA. Abby didn't bother hiding her annoyance.

"Where's my black sweater? You said you put it back in my locker," Abby said.

"I did. You had it on last week after practice."

"No. I didn't. You lost my favorite fucking sweater, didn't you? I knew you would."

Lily had adamantly denied losing the sweater. But Abby didn't believe her. She'd called Lily a liar. Face red, lips thinned to slivers and pursed in a way that always annoyed Lily, Abby had glared back at her. A fight had been inevitable.

"You're such a fuckup," Abby said.

"Right...and you're sooooo perfect, aren't you?" Lily retorted. She hated how Abby acted like she was the Second Coming just because she was six minutes older.

"Whatever. You're never borrowing anything of mine again."

"Abby, seriously...I didn't lose it."

"You can never accept when you're wrong. I swear, you're such a selfish bitch. Life would be so much easier without you."

Abby had stormed off. Lily knew Abby would take the car because it was her day to drive, but she didn't care. She'd rather get a ride with Wes or call her parents than listen to her sister's stupid tirade about a sweater that Lily knew she'd given back.

The things they said to each other might have sounded awful to an outsider, but that was how twins fight. Their arguments meant nothing. One minute they would be trading vicious insults; the next, they were curled up on the sofa in the family room, examining each other's Facebook pages and making plans for the weekend. Any other night, Lily would have come home and flopped onto the couch beside Abby, the entire fight forgotten. How could she have known that day would be the last time they'd see each other? She could never have predicted what lay ahead. No one could.

Lily's arms were aching now. She rearranged Sky, kissing her and whispering encouraging words. Lily was careful to stay off the main road, ducking anytime headlights grew near. They needed to get warm soon or they'd be risking hypothermia. Lily had no idea how long they'd been running, but they had to be close. She rounded the bend and suddenly gasped. There it was— the WELCOME TO CRESTED GLEN sign. For years, Lily had hated that sign. She hated what it meant—being stuck in suburbia for another day. She'd wanted skyscrapers and the frantic pace of a big city. She wanted coffee shops and hookah bars and tiny pubs where hipster bartenders served endless pints of Guinness. She'd dreamt of seeing off-Broadway plays and thrift shopping. She'd imagined finding a career she loved. She'd envisioned living in a loft in the West Village, with Abby, the two of them exploring New York City together. "The Riser Twins Take on Manhattan" was their childhood dream, the two of them making vision boards and daydreaming about decorating their loft space. Crested Glen was the opposite of New York. It was, Lily used to joke, where dreams went to die. She'd never imagined feeling such joy at being back here. But seeing that sign, that spectacular sign, meant they'd almost made it home. She picked up the pace, whispering to Sky that everything was going to be okay. *Keep going*, Lily thought. *Just keep going.*

RICK

Don't be a pussy, Rick told himself as he navigated the snowy back roads. *Don't let the stress get to you.* Stress made people careless, and Rick couldn't afford to be careless. Between his classes, his wife, and his girls, he'd overextended himself these last few months. But he could handle it. He simply needed to manage his time better.

Rick turned up the volume on the satellite radio, the Rolling Stones' "Get Off of My Cloud" filling the car. God, he loved this song. He'd hoped the music would soothe him, but he was still annoyed. He'd been having a blast, schooling Lily and Sky on the beauty of the Beat poets, and he hated leaving them. He considered staying overnight, but he'd already been gone for two days. The last thing he wanted was for Missy to come looking for him. She'd shown up at the cabin once before, and it had been a very close call. From that day onward, he'd promised himself he'd never give Missy a reason to be suspicious.

Almost as if Missy were reading his mind, Rick's cell phone buzzed. He didn't even need to look at the display to know that his wife was calling. He sighed but answered anyway.

"Babe," Missy whined predictably, her voice filling the car through his Bluetooth speakers. "It's almost three in the morning. You said you'd be back early."

"I know, Miss. But I got into the writing zone and didn't realize it was so late. I'm gassing up the car now. Please tell me you're warming up the bed?"

"It's already so late and we both have to work…"

"Are you kidding me, babe? You better be wearing something sexy or I'll be very disappointed."

"Love you, Ricky," she whispered breathlessly and hung up.

He could already see her pouring her third glass of Merlot, smiling as she planned her "seduction." God, she was so boring and predictable, and he hated when she called him Ricky. He'd told her that over and over again, but Missy never listened. Rick could feel his whiskey buzz wearing off and the beginnings of a headache forming at the base of his temples. Manipulating Missy was easy but terribly exhausting.

He entertained the idea of a divorce at least once a week. The prospect of getting rid of Missy, the idea of telling her uptight prick father to shove his money up his ass, was tempting. He'd spent many planning periods online searching for a bachelor pad, a place where he could indulge in all the things that made him happy. But it was too risky, having her out there, asking questions, following him around. Knowing her, she'd probably hire a PI, someone she'd seen on one of those inane talk shows she liked so much. No, the only way he'd ever be free of Missy was if she were dead. For now that wasn't practical, so he tolerated her.

Rick continued driving, drumming on the steering wheel as Led Zeppelin's "Black Dog" began to play.

Damn, this is a good tune, Rick thought. His phone buzzed again. He glanced down at the console and saw Missy's sex kitten pose.

Goddamn it! He felt annoyed already missing Lily. And then it hit him. Rick realized he hadn't bolted the lock at the cabin. He slammed on the gas and began searching for the next turnaround. He was so focused on getting back to the cabin that he missed the cop car patiently waiting on the side of the road. A siren began to wail and Rick looked up to see the flashing police lights. He fought the urge to slam his hand down on the steering wheel. There was no need to panic. He'd had close calls before. Surprise visitors, like his basketball buddies dropping by the cabin for a drink and news about his progress on the great American novel he was supposedly writing. There was that extended vacation to Hawaii with his in-laws that had made seeing his girls impossible. Or Missy's surprise visit where he'd barely gotten upstairs in time. He'd made it through all of those bumps in the road without a problem. This was some piece-of-shit local cop, and he was Rick Hanson.

Rick eased on the brake and pulled onto the side of the road. He reached into the console, took two pieces of gum, tore off the paper, and shoved them both into his mouth. He chewed quickly, hoping the spearmint would mask the smell of whiskey on his breath. He was well over the legal limit. If he got a DUI, the entire town would know. Missy would be all over him. His boss would be pissed. He could even lose his driving privileges. He still couldn't believe this was happening. If it weren't for Missy, he'd still be with the girls. It was all her fault. The stupid cunt.

Forget her, he told himself. *Focus, Rick. Focus!*

He rolled down his window and watched in the rearview mirror as the highway patrolman—a townie, from the looks of him, with his ruddy face and portly waistline—ambled over.

"License and registration, sir."

Rick gave an obedient nod and handed over his identification and vehicle information. The cop shined his flashlight on the documents, then shined it back at Rick, the bright glare forcing him to squint uncomfortably.

Fucking prick, Rick thought, but he kept his expression neutral.

"What's the trouble, Officer?" Rick asked.

"You know how fast you were going, sir?"

"Not sure. But from the looks of things, I'd say it was too fast."

The cop frowned, apparently not appreciating Rick's attempt at levity.

"You realize traveling at a speed of eighty-five miles per hour in these weather conditions is a disaster waiting to happen?"

Rick knew people. He studied them, understood their psychology, how to earn their trust. This was a no-brainer.

"I'm very sorry, Officer. You're totally right. It's just that my wife is waiting up for me and I guess I got careless."

Rick held up his phone, displaying the photo and Missy's impressive attributes. The cop paused for a moment, then his demeanor changed entirely. A smile spread across his wide, fat face.

"Shit, I'd break every speed limit in the state to get to her."

"I was a little overeager. But I understand you have a job to do."

The officer shook his head and handed back Rick's documents. "You're one lucky son of a bitch. I hope you know that?"

"Yes sir, I do. I'm a very lucky man."

"Be careful out there. We wouldn't want something to happen to you and upset the missus, would we?"

"No, Officer, we would not."

The cop smiled, shook hands with Rick, and headed back to his squad car. Rick wanted to do a victory lap. But he couldn't take all the credit. For once in her life, Missy was actually useful.

Rick slowly pulled away. If the cop weren't still parked back there, waiting on his next victim, Rick would have driven back to the cabin immediately and secured the lock. Not because he didn't trust Lily, but because his own carelessness bothered him. He had to maintain his routines, or everything he'd built could come crashing down. But he'd head to the cabin at lunch and check on the girls. Right now Missy was waiting for him, and he had class in the morning. Besides, there wasn't a chance in hell that Lily would ever disobey him. Rick cranked up the music even louder. Maybe he'd buy Missy something nice after work tomorrow. Hell, while he was shopping, he'd buy Lily something too. Both his girls deserved a reward for being on their best behavior.

LILY

Lily's lungs were burning, her thighs and calves on fire. Her arms felt like they might give out any second, and Sky was growing more and more restless, whimpering and moaning, "I want Daddy. Please, let's go home."

But Lily kept moving. They ran past the playground where she had spent endless hours with Abby. The colorful swing set, monkey bars, and merry-go-round were abandoned and covered in snow. But Lily could almost see Abby beside her, identical twins, the two of them in their matching pink snowsuits, running hand in hand, so in sync they almost appeared to be one person. Abby. All these years Lily had never stopped missing Abby. Her twin sister.

During the day, Lily forced herself not to think about Abby. She had plenty to keep them occupied. They did their lesson plans and their chores, cleaning everything they could to try to keep out critters and bugs. They'd spent the end of each day prepping for Rick's visits, never knowing when he'd arrive but knowing they had to be ready. Lily had to make sure they were properly dressed and in good spirits. It was only late at night, when Rick was gone, when Sky was asleep, that Lily allowed herself to think of Abby. Seeing the playground again, everything came rushing back. Her sister's smile. Her laugh. The bond they shared. Abby was no longer just a memory that Lily conjured up to get her through one of those endless nights. Soon Abby would be real.

Lost in thought, Lily's foot struck the edge of a rock and she stumbled forward. She caught Sky seconds before she hit the ground. They had been running for at least an hour, and Lily's arms were on fire. But she had to be more careful.

"I'm sorry, Chicken. I've got you. I won't let go."

Sky clutched Lily's neck even tighter. "Mommy, we're gonna get into trouble. Please...let's go back to Daddy Rick's."

Lily kissed her daughter's forehead.

"Just be Mommy's brave girl for a little bit longer."

Lily turned the corner and saw the house—*her* house—at the end of the cul-de-sac. The sky-blue shutters were faded with age. The old maple tree she'd spent hours lying under reading Harry Potter and *To Kill a Mockingbird* was gone. Snow covered the garden Dad had endlessly labored over in the spring, but otherwise, the house looked exactly as she'd left it. Eight years since she'd last seen her home, and it was as if no time had passed at all. Lily closed her eyes. She could almost hear the laughter of the neighborhood children. She remembered their endless snowball fights, the time Abby had helped her soundly defeat both their parents. She could picture herself lying on a blanket in the front yard with Wes, her first love, her only love, the summer sun beating down on them, his arm draped around her waist. She remembered him whispering, "I love you." The first boy who'd ever said those words, a promise of so much more.

Lily stood in the middle of the road gazing at the house, when suddenly a car horn honked, startling her from her reverie.

She froze.

It was Rick. It had to be.

She thought about running, but her legs were finished. No chance they would hold up long enough to get away. Her throat tightened and tears welled up. If he were this close, escape was impossible.

Slowly, she turned, savoring her last few moments of freedom. But all she saw was a gray-haired retiree, waving at her from the driver's seat of his faded Toyota. Concern was etched on his face and she knew he must be wondering what they were doing, wearing such little clothing in these freezing temperatures.

"You okay, Miss? It's awfully late and the little one looks cold."

Lily tried to speak, but her voice failed her. She

cleared her throat and tried again, forcing herself to sound calm and collected. "We're fine, sir. Just going home."

Before he could say anything else, Lily spun around and strode purposefully up the sidewalk as if she always walked around clad in her pajamas and blankets in the dead of winter. *Go away*, she thought. *Leave us alone.* A moment later, she heard the truck speed off. Lily put Sky down, then knelt beside her so they were eye to eye.

"I know you're scared, Chicken. But I need you to be brave for a little bit longer. Okay?"

"Okay, Mommy," Sky whispered softly.

Lily was constantly amazed by how sweet and obedient this child was. She hugged Sky tightly and stood up. Lily instinctively reached for the doorknob. She wanted the door to open. She wanted to be sixteen all over again, rushing in, sweaty and out of breath from her early-morning run. Abby would breeze past her, hollering, "Shotgun shower." Lily would act annoyed, but secretly, she loved having one-on-one time with her father before he rushed off to the hospital for his morning rounds. But that was wishful thinking. In real life, the door was always locked.

Lily knocked softly at first. There was a chance her family didn't even live here. They could have moved years ago, started over without her. Lily knew it was a possibility, but deep down, she didn't think that would ever happen. If the situation were reversed, Lily would never leave their home, not without Abby. She continued knocking, harder and harder until her hands ached.

"Jesus Christ, hold your darn horses."

The voice was so familiar that Lily's tears began to fall instantly. A moment later the porch light flipped on and the door swung open. There was an endless pause as the older woman gaped at Lily. Mouth open, eyes wide, she was staring at Lily as if she were a ghost. Lily realized that until that very moment, that's exactly what she was.

Crying was unacceptable. That's what Rick always said. But in that moment, Lily forgot everything he'd beaten into her, all the lies he'd told her. In that moment, the broken girl in the basement ceased to exist. With tears streaming down her face, Lily thrust herself into her mother's arms.

"Mom, it's me. I'm home."

EVE

Eve was trying to process what was happening. It wasn't possible that this young, pajama-clad girl, with her sunken features and hollow eyes, was crying and calling her Mom. Was it? Could this really be her Lily?

Maybe it's a dream, Eve thought. She dreamt every night. Some nights the dreams were an endless loop of horrific images: Lily's body, bloody, battered, and bruised, her eyes hollowed out, skeletal hands reaching for Eve. "Help me, Mommy! Save me. Please!"

Sometimes Eve's baby girl visited with hopeful eyes and kind words. "Mommy, I love you. I miss you. I'm okay." Those nights were the worst. The nights that Eve woke feeling hopeful, believing in the impossible, that her Lily might actually be alive. Maybe that's all this was, she told herself as she stared at this girl. Maybe it's one of those wishful-thinking dreams.

But the girl was still clutching Eve, holding on to her so tightly and weeping. Eve could feel the girl's sharp edges. She was flesh and blood and calling Eve Mom.

Eve wrenched herself away. She needed to get a better look, needed to make sure this wasn't some sicko's twisted ploy. There were cruel people out there, people who had, in the past, attempted to exploit Eve's weakness and vulnerability. People that sent letters, asking for money, promising answers that never came. She'd believed them before. This time she wouldn't allow herself to be duped.

She gazed into the girl's eyes—deep pools of green—and Eve was transported to the delivery room, the moment she met her two identical twin daughters. There was no denying it now. Those were Lily's eyes. A mother never forgets her child's eyes.

It was Lily. She was home. Lily was home.

For eight years Eve had waited for answers. Days passed. Weeks. Months. Endless years. Back in the early days, when Eve was still a sheep who believed in a higher power, she'd prayed for closure, begging God to bring her Lily back to her. Even a body was better than the emptiness or those ghastly images her subconscious conjured up. But this was real. Eve was standing here, on her porch, staring back at her long-lost child.

Eve heard a whimper. She'd been so focused on Lily that she hadn't noticed the child standing beside her. Maybe three or four years old, she was pale with bright green eyes and a matching expression of pure terror. God, the resemblance to Lily was uncanny. Lily was a mother? She'd had a daughter? Where had they been all these years? What in God's name had kept them away for so long? There were so many questions surging through Eve's brain she didn't even know where to begin. She opened her mouth but no sound came out.

"Mom, can we come in? Please?" Lily whispered.

Shame coursed through Eve as she realized how cold it was and what little clothing they were both wearing. What was wrong with her? She ushered them inside. As Eve closed the door, she whirled around. She had squandered that first hug but she wouldn't waste this one. She pulled Lily to her, holding on tightly.

In her dreams, when Lily returned, Eve was unbreakable. She said and did all the right things. But this was not a dream. Lily was alive. No, it was safe to say that Eve didn't keep it together. She didn't keep it together at all.

LILY

Lily had expected that her mother would know what to do. Cool, calm, and collected, Lily's mother was the one everyone turned to in a crisis. "Even-keeled Eve," her father called her. Dad used to tell the story about Mom working her entire shift at the hospital, a full eleven hours, before telling anyone she was in labor. No matter what happened, Mom had always been unshakeable. But that person wasn't standing in front of Lily. She didn't know who this was. Her mother was weeping, her body practically disappearing into her old blue robe. Her thin, veined hands kept pushing up dishwater-blond hair, as if by pushing up her hair she could make sense of the senseless. This was unacceptable. They needed help, but her mother was acting helpless.

She glanced out the large bay windows. It would be daylight soon. Rick would realize what he'd done. He'd discover they'd escaped and he'd come looking for them. Lily grabbed Sky's hand. "Follow me, okay?"

Sky obeyed, keeping pace with Lily as she moved

through the house. Lily could hear Mom trailing her but she didn't look back. She flipped on the light switch and brightness flooded the living room. Lily took in the pretty pastel decor, the colorful throw pillows, the cozy sofa she'd spent hours curled up on, reading or watching TV with Abby. For a moment Lily tried to convince herself that she was safe. But then she remembered his warning, his constant warning. *I will never let you go.*

Lily turned back to Mom.

"Are the other doors locked? The windows? Are they all locked?" Lily asked.

"Yes, they're locked. We always keep them locked."

Lily didn't believe her. Mom's lack of awareness when it came to home security had always driven Dad crazy.

"Bad things happen when you least expect them," he used to say. The irony wasn't lost on Lily. She would never make that mistake again. Never trust anyone again. She had to test them herself. Once Lily finished securing the downstairs, she stopped and looked around.

She was home. Lily was finally home.

The familiarity assaulted her. Lining the walls were dozens of photos of her and Abby, gap-toothed and grinning up at the camera, awkward phases, bad perms and baby fat on display. Lily searched the walls for new photos, hoping to catch a glimpse of her father and Abby—a glimpse of the future she'd been denied—but time had apparently stopped at Crested Glen. She wanted to see the rest of her family. Needed to see them. She knew that her father was probably at the hospital, but her sister, she had to see her sister.

"Where's Abby? Where is she?"

"She's at her place. Her house . . . it isn't far, maybe twenty minutes."

"Call the police. Make sure she's safe. Make sure she's safe, and tell them to come here."

Mom hesitated, staring at Lily as if she were speaking a foreign language.

"Goddamn it, Mom, call the cops. Do it now!"

Standing at Lily's side, Sky gasped and backed away. Shame coursed through Lily. She never raised her voice. She never used that kind of language. That was *his* way. She knelt down and wrapped her baby in her arms. Lily needed to remember who she was, not what he'd tried to make her. She stared up at Mom, her voice low and measured.

"Please, Mom. We need the police!"

Her words seemed to trigger something in her mother, who sprang into action. Mom disappeared into the dining room and a moment later, Lily heard her on the phone, speaking in a hushed but frenzied whisper to the 911 operator. Lily held Sky close, trying to keep her calm.

"It's okay, Chicken. We're good. We're safe now. We'll get warm and dry. We'll get some food. We're safe here. Nothing bad is going to happen. Not anymore."

Lily almost believed those words until she glanced up and saw the strange man standing on the landing that led to the upstairs. Tall, with salt-and-pepper hair and a matching beard, he was clad in only a pair of too-tight plaid boxers, his middle-aged spread on full display.

Lily opened her mouth and screamed, letting loose all the terror and desperation she'd kept bottled up. The man took a startled step back. Before he could gather his wits and come after them, Lily jumped to her feet. Dragging a wailing Sky behind her, she ran into the kitchen. She headed straight to the counter and opened all the drawers, tossing out spatulas and rolling pins, until she located the biggest, sharpest knife she could find. She rushed back to the living room, pointing it at the man, mentally daring him to come toward her. This was *her* house. *Her* home.

I'm in control now, Lily thought. *I'm in control.*

EVE

Lily's piercing scream startled Eve.

"Oh my God," she said as she leaned down to retrieve the phone, her panicked plea to the 911 operator interrupted.

"Ma'am, what's going on? Hello? Ma'am?"

Eve was cursing herself. How could she have been so stupid as to leave her child alone for even a second? She rushed back to the kitchen, still clutching the phone. She saw Lily standing in the center of the room beside the island, Eve's giant boning knife in one hand, her other hand protectively shielding the little girl. Eve gazed up at the landing and saw the man she'd brought here last night. She'd completely forgotten about him. Eddie? Or maybe Ethan? She couldn't remember. She stared at his fat gut sticking out, his eyes wide with surprise.

Eve was disgusted with herself. He'd told her she was pretty, plied her with Chardonnay, and listened patiently when she'd told him about her two daughters. All Eve's friends had grown tired of her sad tale. She had grown tired of it too. It was easier to go out, to find strangers who'd listen to her. She'd create elaborate stories about her twin girls and how picture perfect their lives were. In the end, all she really wanted was someone to hold her, to ease the empty ache inside her. Instead they'd had clumsy sex that she instantly regretted.

"Who is that? Who is it?" Lily shouted.

"Get out," Eve yelled at the man. "Get the hell out!"

He hesitated. Lily stepped forward, still clutching the knife. He held up his hands in surrender. "I'm going. I'm going. I just...I need my stuff." He turned and disappeared up the stairs.

"Ma'am, please, can you hear me? Is everything okay?" Eve remembered the operator was still on the phone.

"Please just send officers as soon as you can. And tell Sheriff Rogers to come to the Riser house. Please."

"We've got units on the way. Stay on the line..."

Eve ignored her and hung up the phone. She slowly moved toward Lily, stopping inches from the outstretched knife.

"I know you're scared, Lil. But the police are coming. You're safe. We'll keep you safe."

"You can't promise that. You can't."

Eve couldn't argue with her daughter. She didn't know where Lily had been or what she was running from. She didn't know anything. Eve searched for the right thing to say to her delicate, wounded child. But words failed her.

"Who is he? Who is that man?" Lily asked, still glancing up at the landing.

"He's no one. He's nothing."

"Where is Dad? Did you two split up? Where is he, Mom? Where is my father?"

Eve both hated Dave and ached for him.

"I'll tell you everything, but you have to put down the knife. Please, Lily, you're scaring the baby. Give me the knife."

"Where's Daddy?" Lily asked again, her voice raw with desperation.

Eve wondered if words could actually pierce one's heart. Abby was Mama's girl, or at least she used to be. But from day one Lily was Daddy's girl. Anytime Lily had a bad dream or a tummy ache, it was Dave to the rescue.

"He's gone. I'm so sorry, but Dad is gone."

"I don't understand. Is he at the hospital? Call him. Tell him to come home. Tell him I'm here."

"He died, Lily. A few months after you left. He suffered a massive heart attack and died."

Lily reacted as if she'd been punched in the chest, doubling over, a sob exploding from her mouth. She dropped the knife, and it clattered to the floor. Lily leaned against the sofa. Her outburst horrified the child, who tugged desperately at her mother.

"Mommy, don't cry. Please. We'll get in trouble. Please...stop it. Stop crying. Please!"

Lily seemed to understand her daughter's pleas. She

stopped crying, almost instantly, sucking in large drafts of air. She slumped to the floor and pulled the child onto her lap. She began to rock her, swaying back and forth, her words indecipherable to Eve, almost gibberish. Eve grabbed the knife, setting it on one of the end tables, and then lowered herself next to Lily and Sky, the three of them huddled together on the cold kitchen tile.

Eve needed to calm Lily, so she focused on the child.

"Lily, is this your daughter?"

Lily stared straight ahead, still trying to process the news about her father. She gave Eve a weak nod. "Yes. This is Sky. She's six. Sky, this is my mother. She's your grandmother."

Sky kept her face buried in Lily's shoulder. Eve still couldn't believe it. This was her granddaughter. She had a granddaughter.

"She's beautiful, Lil. Just like her mom." Eve meant it too. They were both so lovely. Light was streaming through the kitchen window signaling that it was morning. An hour ago, Eve would never have noticed the sunrise. She hated mornings, the dawning of a new day without Lily. But today everything was bright and clear, as if she were waking from an eight-year slumber.

"It's your mom, Lilypad," Eve said, her voice low and steady. "It's your mom. I know your heart is broken over Daddy. Mine is too. It's just... he loved you so much. I think he loved you too much. And I know you're scared but I'm here, Lil. I'm right here."

Eve held Lily's gaze, watching as Lily lifted her chin and straightened her shoulders in an outward show of courage. *So brave*, Eve thought. Her brave, brave girl. Lily took Eve's hand and clutched it tightly, staring down at their intertwined fingers.

Without warning, Lily wrapped her arms around Eve's neck and hugged her again, her grip so tight she thought her ribs might break.

So be it, she thought. Eve melted into Lily's arms. All those moments she'd forced herself to forget: Lily, eight months old as she tentatively crawled across the living room carpet, keeping pace with Abby by her side. Lily as a teenager—no longer awkward and gangly but a gifted athlete. Lily and Abby, making a mess as they baked cookies, arguing over who got to eat the last of the batter. Eve remembered seeing Lily that last morning, her backpack slung over her shoulder, munching on a Pop-Tart. So tan and full of enthusiasm, she'd waved good-bye and disappeared out the front door. Disappeared from their lives. And now here they were, inches away from each other, as if no time had passed at all. Neither one of them moved, not even when they heard the front door open as the nameless man slipped out of Eve's house.

Eve waited, fighting the shame, and then she knew she needed to get moving. The police were coming and she still had Abby to think about. She hated to leave Lily again but she had no choice. She stood up.

"I'll be right back, Lil. Stay right here. I'll be right back."

Eve grabbed the cordless phone and went into the dining room, still keeping an eye on Lily. She kept her voice low and nervously dialed, her fingers so clumsy she had to redial twice. Wes picked up his cell phone after two rings. Eve didn't even wait for him to say hello.

"Wes, it's Eve. Lily came home. You have to go to Abby's. The police are on their way to her, but you need to tell her that her sister is back. It has to be you."

"Eve, what are you talking about? What do you mean she's home? She's...I—"

"I don't have time for questions, Wes. Go get Abby!"

Eve hung up the phone and hurried back into the living room, where she returned to her spot on the floor beside Lily and Sky. She wrapped her arms around her daughter, rocking her like she had when she was a baby.

"Hold on, Lil. I'm here. Your mom has you and I'm never letting you go."

ABBY

Abby fumbled in the dark for her phone. She never turned it off. Never let it out of her sight. She always believed that one day she'd get a call with news about her sister. It's what kept her going. She frowned at the sight of Wes's name on her caller ID. Abby quickly silenced the ringer.

What the fuck was wrong with him? It was five o'clock in the morning. What did he not understand about needing space? Abby swallowed hard, closing her eyes tightly as she pressed one thumb to one pinky and slowly counted to ten. One of her shrinks had suggested this stupid exercise. She'd never admit it to him, he was a smug asshole with a God complex, but the trick worked. When the panic overwhelmed her, it was a lifesaver. She ignored the voice mail icon when it appeared, and sat up in bed. If she were smart, she'd go back to sleep before her shift at the hospital started. But Abby was too annoyed. She'd never sleep now. It was pointless to even try.

She wasn't entirely comfortable living alone. She'd found the silence since Wes moved out more unsettling than she'd anticipated. But it was her choice. She'd wanted him to go. She'd demanded it. And for the most part, she was glad that she was by herself, that she didn't have to try so hard. There was no pointless chatter about work or politics or any of the other mindless bullshit that fills the spaces when there's nothing else to say. She didn't have to make excuses about why she had two breakfasts, or why she stayed in bed until two o'clock on her day off. No, for her this was the only option. She was free to make her own choices, good or bad.

Abby got out of bed and grabbed her gray terrycloth robe off the back of the door. She caught a glimpse of her reflection in the full-length mirror and grimaced in disgust. Fat, round face, belly swollen to an unnatural size. One moment she'd been thin and sexy, the kind of girl that turned heads, and the next, she was this...this pig.

Whoever said pregnancy was a gift was a goddamn liar. Abby's body was being held hostage by this alien invader, and she despised each and every change. She kept imagining Mom's horror, or Wes's for that matter, if they knew her true feelings about this pregnancy.

The worst part: The entire world wanted her to be over the moon about this new life she had created. No matter where she went—work, the grocery store, the dry cleaner's—someone wanted to touch her belly and ooh and aah over each freaking burp, fart, and weight change. Abby didn't get it. Almost anyone with a uterus could pop out a kid. Thirteen-year-olds in the Ozarks. Strung-out junkies. Prison inmates. She wanted to tell them all how stupid they were. Pregnancy wasn't a blessing or a miracle. Getting knocked up was a result of reckless behavior and a major lapse in judgment. Even if you wanted a baby, bad things were bound to happen. Abby knew that firsthand.

She made her way into the kitchen, flipping on the lights as she went. She stopped, gripped by the incredible urge to have a drink. Five months and twelve days since her last drink, and it still happened all the time. In the middle of washing dishes or taking a patient's temperature, walking to her car... Some days she'd think about leaving work and hauling ass to the first liquor store she passed. Other times, she'd drive by Costco and pull into the parking lot, imagining herself walking in and loading her cart with enough booze to numb herself for days. But this town was so small someone would be on the phone to Wes or her mother before Abby ever cleared the checkout. So she shook off the feeling. If she couldn't drink, she might as well eat.

She opened the fridge and stared at the vast array of options. Mom insisted on doing her shopping now, as if Abby were some kind of invalid. It was like a goddamn Whole Foods exploded in her fridge. Baby carrots, hummus, cold cuts, fresh fruit. But she wasn't in the mood for any of that. Instead she grabbed the chocolate crème pie she'd bought at the market after her shift the previous night. She'd promised herself she would take it to work and share with the girls, but Abby knew deep down that was never going to happen. This was the other reason she'd given Wes the boot. He'd find it unacceptable, eating chocolate pie first thing in the morning. She considered warming up a slice, topping it with ice cream, whipped cream, and fresh strawberries— *see Wes, see Mom, I'm eating fruit*—but she decided to hell with it and dug in, eating straight out of the plastic container.

From the other room, she heard her cell phone ringing. Wes again. It had to be . . .

No, *this* was why she'd ended things. The baby wasn't even born, and Wes was suffocating her. A few weeks ago, things had come to a head.

"You should let me do that."

She'd glanced down at the basket of laundry she was carrying.

"What? You're joking, right? It's not heavy."

"Babe, I'm here. I don't mind doing it."

"Well, I mind. And I have a name, Wes. It isn't 'babe.'"

She'd seen that look, the petulant expression he got when he didn't get his way. He'd kept on, spouting baby book statistics, talking about miscarriages and ruptures, none of which she cared about. She'd given in and handed over the laundry just to shut him up. Then she'd

spent the rest of the day simmering. When he'd asked—
for the hundredth time—if she was okay, Abby lost it.

"I can't do this. I can't."

"Do what?" Wes asked.

"I'm not a house cat."

"A house cat? Abby, what are you talking about?"

"I'm fine. If I'm not, I'll tell you. But you have to give
it a rest."

Normally, when she tried to push his buttons, Wes
fought back, calling her out. But that day, he'd shrugged.

"Tell me what *you* really want, Abs, and I'll give it to
you."

"I want some goddamn space."

He'd packed his bags that night and left his house.
The house he'd bought for them. He'd gone to stay
with a friend, a frat buddy who still lived in town. But
now here he was, calling her at the ass crack of dawn.
Looking after her was *his* addiction.

The phone finally stopped ringing, and she hoped
he'd gotten the hint. Anxious and annoyed, she ate
even faster. She'd made a mistake, moving in with him;
she knew that.

"I love you," he'd said over and over again.

But that was the problem. Abby didn't want to be
loved, and she wasn't interested in loving him. Loving
anyone, for that matter. Sex she could handle. They did
that well. But a romance or—God forbid—a marriage
wasn't in the cards. Not now. Not ever.

Breaking up with Wes the first time had nearly killed her. She'd struggled when he left for college. She'd lost all her friends in high school. She wasn't the fun, happy-go-lucky teenage girl anymore. How could she be? Lily was gone, what did they expect? For her to carry on like everything was fine? She hadn't cared. She had Wes. When he'd been accepted to Penn, he was the one who wanted to try long distance. Abby knew that would never work, not with his classes and a part-time job.

"We need to be on our own," she'd told him. It was the right thing to do; she knew that. He was never supposed to be hers. Once he was gone, she realized how much she relied on him to help her through the endless days and nights, to calm her when the bad thoughts wormed their way in. Alone and left to her own devices, Abby did whatever it took to numb herself. Booze, drugs, sex, anything to keep from thinking about Lily.

Over the last few years, she'd gotten treatment and had even managed to earn her degree as an LVN. Thanks to her mother's connections (God bless nepotism) Abby had landed a job at Lancaster General as an LVN in the pediatric department. As far as anyone could tell, she was a functional member of society. Abby hadn't "moved on" or "gotten over the loss of Lily," but her life was orderly and structured. And then Wes walked back into it, at the TGI Friday's of all places. It was a busy Friday night, the after-work crowd and families all vying for a table. She'd been eating dinner with Mom when Wes showed up. Abby wanted to run away, to avoid him, but Mom had told her to stop being ridiculous, and when Wes approached, Mom had invited him to join them. Abby couldn't believe that he was back in town. The last she'd heard through the gossip mill was that he'd accepted a real estate job in New York City. Abby wanted to know what he was doing here, and Wes explained that his father had gotten prostate cancer and he'd returned home to look after him.

As much as Abby tried not to enjoy their dinner, she couldn't help herself. He'd always made her laugh, and that night was no different. And he looked so good, tanned and muscular from a summer working construction. But it was the ease in which they interacted that she'd missed the most. With Wes there were no awkward questions or backstory to fill in. Lily lived on in their silences. They could talk about anything. Though to be honest, after that first night, there wasn't a lot of talking. Abby loved those moments together, naked and weightless, his muscular arms wrapped around her, blotting out everything else.

But as time went on, Abby realized Wes wanted more. She saw the longing in his eyes when he kissed her good-bye. She could hear the neediness in his voice when he'd ask her why she wasn't staying over or why she'd left so early. She'd had to end things between them before anyone got hurt. He'd fought her because that's who he was, a stand-up guy. Or maybe he fought her because the idea of losing both her and Lily was too much, even for him. But she'd been adamant—this time, they were done.

Three weeks later, the alien invader made its presence known. Every day for a week, she drove by the Planned Parenthood, trying to convince herself that this was the right choice. She kept telling herself that she didn't care about the baby or about Wes. He didn't even have to know. She didn't want to trap him, and she knew that's what she'd be doing if she had his child. But in the end, she couldn't do it. She might be a total asshole in every aspect of her life, but she owed him the truth. She told him over pancakes at the IHOP, and Wes had done exactly what she'd expected.

"Let's make a go of this. Let's be a family," he said. For the first few months, Abby went along with Wes, moving in with him. Playing house, she thought. She'd been overwhelmed with the changes to her body but she'd tried. She'd really tried (and fuck anyone who said she hadn't). But they constantly fought. Or, as Wes said when he'd packed his bags, "All you do is pick fights."

He wasn't wrong. Anything he did seemed to set her off—his tone of voice, his morning breath, his constant monitoring of her nutritional intake. She should have never allowed him to get close. Keeping people away was Abby's only means of self-preservation, and then she'd gone ahead and screwed it all up.

After Lily vanished, Abby realized that she really

didn't like that many people. Most of them annoyed the hell out of her. They kept on and on about things that meant absolutely nothing. Prom and boys and college and the future. Her past, her present, and her future vanished that dreary Tuesday in September.

"Don't you see?" she wanted to scream at them. "It's all so pointless."

How could any of that crap matter when her sister was out there somewhere? She knew Lily was out there. They were twins. She would know if Lily had died. Abby kept saying over and over again that Lily wasn't dead, but no one would listen. Not Mom or Dad. Not the half dozen therapists she'd been forced to see.

"Until you accept your sister's death, you'll never have a normal life."

But that was it; Abby didn't want a normal life. A normal life was a lie. A normal life was the life she'd had with Lily. She called bullshit on a normal life. But the rest of the world didn't. They wanted normal. They'd moved on. Because people had a time limit on compassion. Not that they didn't care. The entire town had been devastated after Lily disappeared. They went into mourning. All of the schools closed. Grief counselors were on call 24/7. Police roamed the streets, vigilant in their desire to protect the young women of Lancaster, Pennsylvania. Agonizing months passed as the entire city held its collective breath, waiting for closure, for answers. But there were no leads. No matter how much they loved Lily, they had to move on. Before long, Lily was nothing but a memory, a face emblazoned on a memorial in the administrative office.

But Abby couldn't let go. That sweater. The goddamn sweater she'd accused Lily of losing. Why did she have to make such a big deal about it? Why did she have to take the car and leave Lily at school? Why couldn't she have been nice instead of acting like a total fucking bitch?

Abby took another bite of pie, trying to forget about the sweater, always trying to forget about the sweater and the choices she'd made that day. She had nearly devoured the entire pie when she heard the doorbell ringing.

"Abby, it's Wes. I know you're here. Your car is in the driveway."

What in God's name was Wes doing here? When would he learn?

"Abby, open the goddamn door."

Enraged, she raced to the entryway and swung open the front door, ready to tell him that enough was enough. Her mouth fell open as she stared at Wes and what appeared to be half the Lancaster Police Department.

"I've been calling you nonstop. Why didn't you answer your phone?"

Abby became very aware of her appearance. There was almost certainly chocolate on her face. She quickly wiped away crumbs from her T-shirt, hating herself for caring.

"I didn't hear the phone."

"So you're okay?"

"Other than the fact you're here on my porch at dawn? Yes, I'm fine. Seriously, Wes, what is going on?"

A weathered cop stepped forward, his hand on his service weapon as he peered inside. Several deputies stood behind him, watching, waiting for his signal.

"Is there anyone in the house, ma'am? Anyone else on the premises?"

"What? No. No one's here."

"Do you mind if my men take a look?"

He didn't wait for an answer; made to brush past her and go inside. She held out her hand to stop him.

"You can't come in here," Abby said.

Wes pulled her away from the door.

"Abby, for God's sake, shut your mouth and do what you're told."

This time Abby flinched. Wes never spoke that way. Not to her. She took in his ragged appearance. Hair uncombed, heavy stubble, and wearing his ratty Penn sweatpants and sweatshirt, the clothes he always slept in. But this wasn't like Wes. He never left the house without a pressed shirt. Hell, he ironed his goddamn jeans. She realized he must have rolled out of bed and showed up at her door. Abby stared past him. Several of her neighbors were eyeing them curiously. In an instant, she realized there was something seriously fucked up going on. She grabbed the doorframe to steady herself.

"It's Mom, isn't it? Oh my God, is she...? I have to call her. I have to talk to her. I heard the phone ring, but I..." Abby paused. What could she say? *I was stuffing my face with an entire fucking pie!*

She could feel herself beginning to spiral. That's how she'd always described it to the doctors. Heavy breathing, then the spins, and seconds later, it consumed her. Total blackness. Was it true? Was Mom really gone? That had to be it. But if that was the case, why were the police here? Wes stepped forward and wrapped his arms around her. Abby tried to fight him, but he held on tight.

"Breathe, Abby. Just breathe."

She was feeling nauseous, the pie threatening to make its way back up. Why did she eat the whole thing? She was disgusting, that's why. So disgusting... and now Mom was dead, and Abby was the bitch that had ignored the call. First the sweater and Lily. Now Mom! She swallowed again. *Inhale. Exhale.*

She leaned into him, her heart racing. He kept whispering.

"You're okay. You're okay, Abs."

He held on to her until her breathing slowed.

"Are you listening to me?"

His voice was so serious she had to look up at him, had to hear what he was going to say.

"Lily's back. Your sister came home."

A rushing, roaring sound consumed Abby. She froze, hearing the words over and over again. *Your sister came home. Your sister came home. Your sister came home.* It wasn't possible. That's what everyone said. Maybe this was a trick? Some punishment Wes had devised to get back at her for being such a bitch? But Wes wasn't the cruel one. Everyone knew that. He was still staring at her, waiting for the news to register. Abby pushed Wes away.

"You're lying," she said angrily.

"I'm not..."

"You saw her? You saw Lily?"

"No, but I spoke to Eve and she said that Lily's alive. It's like you always said, Abs. Your sister is alive."

After eight years—3,110 days—the darkness that had encompassed Abby seemed to evaporate. She didn't cry. She didn't scream. She didn't say a word. She simply turned and headed toward the nearest squad car, barefoot, wearing her chocolate-stained T-shirt and oversized pajama bottoms. Police radios squawked as officers seemed to spring into motion. She heard Wes talking in hushed, hurried tones with a cop. Someone wrapped a coat around her shoulders, but she ignored them, settling herself in the back of the squad car. She waited, keeping her breathing slow and controlled. Moments later, Wes joined her in the backseat, slipping a pair of boots on her feet. An officer climbed into the front and started up the engine.

Lily was home. Of course she was. Why had she let them doubt her or her sister? Abby wanted to stand on the roof of the largest building in town and scream at the top of her lungs, "My sister's alive. She's alive. I told you all!" But Abby had to be calm. She didn't want to give anyone a reason to worry about her, to medicate her, or try to manipulate this moment she'd spent years dreaming about.

The cruiser sped down the road, police sirens wailing. After a moment or two, Wes grabbed Abby's hand. She didn't pull away. His calm-in-a-crisis demeanor soothed her as she tried to prepare herself. Abby didn't know what Lily had been through, but Abby knew she'd have to be strong enough for both of them.

Thoughts of their reunion overwhelmed her. She stared down at her stained T-shirt and ran her hands through her short red hair. Would Lily see her and think she was a fat slob? Or worse, a loser? They'd spent their entire childhood planning their escape to Manhattan. Abby had done nothing really. She was no one. A small-town nurse and former addict who wasn't even allowed to dispense meds to her patients. Abby's face flushed with shame as she thought about all these years that she'd wasted. Why hadn't she done more to make Lily proud?

Just then, the alien invader kicked and Abby winced, her pulse quickening. For the first time since she'd gotten the news about Lily, Abby realized she'd have to explain this *thing* to her sister.

Hey, sorry, but while you were gone, I fucked your boyfriend, and he knocked me up. Jesus Christ, Lily would hate her. Trying to keep her composure, Abby let go of Wes's hand.

"She can't know about us," Abby said.

"What are you talking about?" Wes looked confused.

"Lily can't know about us. Not until I've talked to her. Until I can explain."

"Abby, don't start creating problems…"

"I'm telling you, I need time. We need time. After all these years, Lily and I deserve this. I won't let you ruin that."

That familiar flicker of hurt danced across Wes's face. Whatever. Abby couldn't worry about him. She had Lily to think about now. She would do anything to protect her sister. Maybe she could give Wes the baby, and he would go away. It was an idea, something she'd have to consider. All she cared about was seeing Lily again. *Hang on, Lil. I'm coming. Just hang on.*

LILY

"Jesus, Eve, we've got half the department here, and she's taking a goddamn bath?"

Lily could hear their voices. Men's voices. Her mother was clearly trying to manage the situation. Only this didn't sound like her mother either. This woman sounded nervous and hesitant.

"I know, Tommy. I know. But she insisted. She was terrified, freezing, and soaking wet. What was I supposed to say? 'No, you can't clean up'? God knows what she's been through."

Lily forced herself to block out their voices. When she'd heard the sirens growing closer, her only thought was of getting dry and clean. She'd needed warm clothes and a few minutes to think about what was going to happen.

She undressed Sky first and then slipped off her own wet clothes. Lily chucked all of their clothing in the trash can. Water gushed from the faucet in a heavy stream. Sky was staring at the claw-foot tub, her eyes panic-filled. Back home, they'd had a small makeshift shower but the plumbing was faulty. Lily had to fill buckets from the kitchenette and transport them to the bathroom. The water was never warm enough. Never. She couldn't wait to get into an actual tub, but Sky appeared on the verge of a breakdown, her lower lip quivering.

"Don't be afraid, Chicken. This is a bathtub. It's going to feel so good and we'll get all nice and clean."

"I wanna go home. Daddy Rick's gonna be mad if we're not there."

Lily's stomach dropped at the mention of his name. She hadn't considered how she would explain who Rick really was, what he was. Sky loved him as much as she feared him. He was her father, the only other person she'd ever known. Right now, though, Lily was too overwhelmed for explanations.

"Don't worry about Daddy Rick. We need to get clean and warm. Don't you want to take a bath with Mommy?"

Sky, it seemed, had reached her breaking point. She began to cry, her tiny body racked with sobs. Lily lifted Sky into her arms. Slowly, she lowered them both into the warm, soapy bath, her child wailing.

"The water feels good, doesn't it? Isn't it so nice and warm?"

She hummed and rocked Sky back and forth, the warm water and the motion hypnotizing them both.

Before long, Sky's sobs subsided. After a few moments, Sky wiped her eyes, glancing up at Lily with a look of wonder. It was a look Lily hoped to see over and over again.

"Mommy, it's so warm. I don't ever want to get out."

Lily didn't want to get out either. She leaned back against the porcelain tub.

"Chicken, we can stay as long as you want." She wasn't sure how long they stayed in the bath. The water grew cold and Lily refilled the tub again. They tried out the array of shampoos and bath gels that Eve was obviously still obsessed with—Lavender Dream, Lemon-Ginger Zing, and something called Twilight Woods, which smelled of pine trees. They stayed until Sky began to yawn and they both started to prune, and even then, Lily wanted to stay longer. But she knew no amount of soap and water could wash away what they'd endured. The voices were growing louder, and she knew that Abby would be here soon. Lily wanted to be ready when Abby arrived.

She climbed out of the tub and wrapped big, fluffy yellow towels around them both, marveling at how soft and clean they were. She tenderly untangled Sky's long dark mane of curls, then ran the brush through her own long blond hair and braided it. She ignored the mirror, not wanting to see herself like this, tired, gaunt, and ravaged by her ordeal.

Lily carried Sky back to her old room, the

room she'd once shared with Abby. Her mother had laid a pair of blue jeans and a worn gray sweatshirt on the bed. Lily pulled them on, thrilled by how comfortable they were, loving the feel of the soft cotton against her skin. With Rick she was only allowed to wear what he deemed appropriate attire. Frilly, girly summer dresses. Sexy cocktail dresses. Lingerie. He allowed nothing comfortable, no versatile clothing. But these clothes were perfect. Baggy and loose, they covered her figure completely. They made her feel invisible.

Lily dressed Sky in an oversized sweatshirt, and she wrapped a blanket around her. Sky fell asleep almost instantly. Lily cradled her daughter in her arms and headed downstairs. From the landing, she saw police officers milling about. Mom was in the living room, quietly talking with a tall, imposing man wearing a police uniform and a stern expression. Instinctively, Lily knew he was in charge. As if he sensed her presence, he locked eyes with her. His shocked expression mirrored the one Mom had worn when she'd opened the front door earlier, though this man did a better job of recovering. Mom hurried over, ready to make the introductions.

"Lily, this is Sheriff Tommy Rogers. Sheriff, this is my daughter Lily and her daughter Sky."

"It is very, very good to see you, young lady." But he kept a polite distance as if he could sense Lily's mistrust. She couldn't help herself. She gazed nervously at the other officers in her living room. Their probing eyes seemed to bore into her, their unanswered questions lingering. She fought her rising panic. Sheriff Rogers seemed to know exactly what she was thinking. He snapped his fingers, and like a well-choreographed army, the men stepped outside and closed the door behind them.

There was a moment of silence, her mother and Sheriff Rogers waiting for her to speak. For a brief, insane instant, Lily longed for that damp, cold hole she'd climbed out of. She knew the rules there. She knew what to think, what to expect, how to survive. Here, she knew nothing.

"Where's Abby?" she asked Mom, trying to keep her voice neutral, trying not to show how afraid she was.

"She's on her way. She'll be here any minute," Sheriff Rogers said. Lily's arms trembled violently, worn out from carrying Sky for so long.

"Maybe you should sit?" Sheriff Rogers said, clearly worried she might drop Sky. He gestured to the sofa, and Lily moved toward it. She gently set Sky on one of the cushions and then settled down beside her. She leaned back and closed her eyes. Mom and the sheriff moved away, but Lily heard every word.

"She hasn't told me anything," Mom said.

"We need to act fast, Eve. It's important."

"I don't want to rush her. Or upset her."

"I understand, but if there was an abduction..."

"If?"

Eve's voice rose, and Lily's eyes snapped open. His question echoed in her brain. Did he doubt her? Could he possibly think that she'd stayed away on purpose? That she'd had a choice in the matter? Maybe he knew Rick. Maybe he was in on it all along.

Lily stared at Sky. The pressure to keep her child safe was all-consuming.

Don't be weak, she told herself, but an uneasiness she couldn't shake was working its way through her bones. She was still studying Sky when the front door opened. Lily knew instantly that Abby was here. Lily turned and saw Abby standing in the entryway. The sight of her sister, alive and safe, was almost too much to bear.

"I knew it, I fucking knew it," Abby said.

Lily wanted to remember this moment. She wanted to replay it over and over again when the dark times with Rick came rushing back. If she had seen Abby before she sensed her presence, she might not have recognized her. Abby's features were heavier. She was carrying a good twenty pounds on her tiny frame. Her hair, which she'd always worn long, just like Lily's, was cut short in a bob, a deep vibrant red replacing her golden-blond locks. But her eyes were unmistakable. Green with flecks of gold. The same eyes that comforted Lily in her dreams each night for eight years.

Lily stood and slowly moved toward Abby, trying not to make a spectacle of herself. But Abby had apparently made no such promises. She let out a joyous yell or a wail, or a mixture of both, and catapulted herself across the room. They came together, clutching each other. In an instant, 3,110 days vanished. In the years following her abduction, after all those months spent with Rick teaching her "appropriate behavior," Lily had been convinced that she would never love the way she'd loved before. She became convinced that even her daughter would be shortchanged. That Rick had stolen that ability to feel real, genuine emotions. But holding on to Abby, Lily realized that in spite of all his efforts, he could never break their bond. Her twin was always with her. Always. *This* was unbreakable.

Lily cried loudly, her sobs matching Abby's.

"I told them, Lilypad," Abby said. "I told them you weren't dead. All these years. All these years, I knew it."

Was that what saved me? Lily wondered. *Maybe Abby's fire kept me alive.* Abby pulled away, stroking Lily's hair. "You're so pretty, Lilypad. Your face and your gorgeous hair."

Lily flinched. She hated her hair. She'd begged Rick to cut it, but he refused. He'd spent hours stroking it, braiding it, running his fingers through her long blond locks.

"It's your triumph, Lily. Your shining glory," he always said.

A worried expression flickered across Abby's face, and Lily realized she'd gotten lost, that she'd let him in. She forced herself to shut him out. He wouldn't ruin this moment. He wouldn't steal another second from her. What she wanted was to see Abby smile.

"Abs, you're gorgeous too."

"You're a shitty liar, Lilypad. You always have been."

Lily smiled, her gaze dropping to Abby's protruding belly, and in that instant, Lily realized that Abby wasn't fat. She was quite obviously pregnant.

"You're having a baby?" Lily said, touching Abby's stomach.

Abby cringed, and this time she was the one who pulled away. A million questions zipped through Lily's brain. *Who's the father? Why are you not happy about this baby? What have I missed?*

But Abby changed the subject.

"It's okay, Lilypad. It's okay. We have time to catch up. This is enough. You and me right here is enough," Abby said.

Lily hugged her sister again, needing physical proof of her existence, physical proof that she could experience human touch. That she loathed only *his* touch. Abby began to rub Lily's back, slowly in circles. This was confirmation for Lily. He hadn't destroyed her. She hadn't let him.

"It's okay, Sissybear. It's all going to be okay."

For some people, after experiencing what Lily had experienced, the idea that anything would ever be okay was impossible. But when Abby said it, hope bubbled up.

Their reunion could have gone on forever, but Lily became aware of the silence that had descended over the room. She was always in tune to moods and shifts in behavior. She'd had to be. The sheriff hovered nearby, impatiently waiting. Mom stepped forward.

"Girls, I'm sorry, but Sheriff Rogers has questions."

Obviously annoyed, Abby glared at their mother. "Jesus, can we have a goddamn minute?"

Lily was caught off guard by Abby's harsh tone, but Mom didn't appear to register it. Abby had always gotten a kick out of upsetting their mother with mumbled profanities. She apparently didn't mumble them anymore.

"It's okay, Mom, I'll answer his questions. Give us one more minute."

She took Abby's hand and led her over to the couch, where Sky was lying. Lily sat down and gently kissed her daughter's forehead. Sky woke up, her eyes sleepy. Lily lifted Sky into her arms.

"Chicken, there's someone you need to meet. Abby, this is my daughter. Her name is Sky."

Abby stared at Sky, and Lily held her breath. She wanted Abby to love her child as much as Lily did. She wanted her to understand what Sky meant, what she had given Lily all these years. Abby held Lily's gaze.

"She's incredible, Lil. Incredible."

A rush of relief flooded Lily. She needed Abby to love her daughter. She needed her acceptance. But Sky looked confused, blinking furiously as she gazed between Abby and Lily with wide and confused eyes. Sky finally spoke, her tiny voice tinged with disbelief.

"Mommy, she has your face."

Neither Lily nor Abby, it seemed, was expecting that, and they grinned. Lily tried to explain.

"Remember when Mommy told you that she had a sister?"

"Your twin sister?"

"Yes. This is my twin sister, Abby."

Sky was still staring, analyzing their faces.

"Sky. I'm your Aunt Abby. It's so nice to meet you."

Abby reached out to shake Sky's hand. Sky mirrored Abby's actions, put out her hand, and they shook.

"Are you back from your adventure now? Mommy said we couldn't see you or Grandma because you were on a big adventure."

Lily knew how difficult it must have been for Abby to keep smiling. But she never wavered. "Yes. I'm back from my big adventure, and I've never been so happy to see your mom and to meet you!"

"Mommy missed you a lot. She talked about you all the time."

"I missed her too."

Lily wanted to stay here, to tell Sky how amazing her aunt was, to find out everything there was to know about Abby's life, but there would be time for that later. Right now, she had things she needed to do. Lily turned her head, zeroing in on the sheriff. He sprang forward like a jack-in-the-box.

"I'm really sorry 'bout all this, Lily, but the clock is

ticking. If you were abducted...?" Lily saw the flash of anger in her mother's eyes. Abby's expression mirrored Mom's. She spoke up instantly.

"What does that mean, Sheriff? *If* she was abducted? Where do you think she was? A fucking day spa?"

Sheriff Rogers tried to backtrack but Abby kept at him, her words a steady stream of fury. Lily's attention drifted, an argument unfolding around her. If there was anything Rick had taught her, it was that losing your cool made you weak. Lily refused to give in to weakness. She looked down at Sky.

"Stay right here. Mommy will be back in a second."

Sky obeyed, laying her head on the pillow, her exhaustion overwhelming her. Lily moved away, out of Sky's earshot. Abby, Mom, and Sheriff Rogers followed. She spoke softly so that Sky couldn't hear her.

"It was more than an abduction," Lily said, silencing everyone. "A man held me hostage. He tortured me. For years, I was his captive. Today we escaped."

Abby squeezed Lily's hand. Eve gave her an encouraging nod, as if to say, *It's okay. We've got you.*

Rogers took Lily's silence as his cue to speak.

"We should get you and Sky to the hospital. Do you have this man's name? A description? Anything that might help us track him down?"

All Lily had to do was say his name, and the officers would rush off and make an arrest. But all those cops waiting outside were strangers. What if they knew him?

What if they played in his Tuesday-night basketball league? Or he tutored one of their kids? Maybe a few of them sat side by side with Rick and Missy Hanson at Sunday morning mass. A shiver raced up Lily's spine. What if she told them who he was and they didn't believe her?

"No way. Not Rick Hanson," they'd say.

"Guy's a saint."

"Wait, that Rick Hanson? Not in a million years."

Or worse, what if they were like him? Sadists disguised in state-issued uniforms.

Lily considered her options. What would happen after she gave them his name? They'd take her to a hospital, where doctors would poke and prod her and Sky endlessly. Doctors would document the abuse. Detectives and therapists would ask all sorts of invasive questions, while Sheriff Rogers and his men got to play hero.

"What's today?" Lily asked Abby.

"It's Wednesday, November 11, 2015."

Lily glanced at the hall clock. It was a little after ten in the morning. He would be regaling his second-period students with stories about his weekend exploits. Maybe he'd share a humorous anecdote about his writer's block.

"I can't crack the last chapter," he'd say.

Or maybe he'd tell his students about another one of Missy's failed kitchen experiments, or he'd lament the horrible Giants' defense. She bet he never once mentioned the hostages he kept locked away in his underground bunker.

"I know who he is. I'll take you to him myself."

Sheriff Rogers stared at her as if he couldn't quite comprehend what she was saying. Lily repeated herself, carefully enunciating each word. "I'll take you to the man who kidnapped me."

"Young lady, that can't happen," Sheriff Rogers said, speaking to her as if she were a child. He stopped himself, softening his tone. "What I meant to say is, not only is it dangerous, but that is completely against protocol."

"Fuck protocol," Abby said, glancing over at Lily, who was standing still, listening to everyone.

Mom stepped forward, joining in the chorus of disapproval.

"Abby, you're not helping. Lily, you and Sky need medical treatment. Not to mention food and rest. And whoever this man is, he doesn't need another chance to hurt you. To hurt any of us."

Lily tried not to overreact. How was it possible that even now she wasn't responsible for her own choices? Even after surviving Rick, after getting the luckiest break of her life, they were telling her what she could and couldn't do. She and Abby had always been allies. As children, there were constant battles to be waged against their parents. Lily could remember being furious with her sister over what was no doubt some minor childhood injustice, but the minute their parents turned on either of them, Lily and Abby had each other's back. That was part of the twin bylaws. They always looked out for each other. Lily was hoping that time hadn't changed that.

Abby stood by Lily's side.

"You heard what Lily said. She'll take us to him. And if I'm not mistaken, you're the cops. Your job is to protect us. Do your job."

There was that harsh tone again—the edge Lily had heard when Abby snapped at their mother. Abby didn't sound like herself, not the Abby she remembered, but her words were effective. Sheriff Rogers gave up and gestured for them to follow him.

Grateful, Lily hugged Abby again. She turned back to the sofa and picked up Sky, who barely stirred, nestling into Lily's arms. Adrenaline coursed through Lily's body as she moved toward the front door. An instant later, she remembered Abby. Her sister was still standing near the sofa, frozen, watching Lily, waiting to see what she should do. Lily stopped. She wasn't alone anymore. Her sister, her best friend, was here to see her through this. She held out her hand, and Abby surged forward and grabbed on tightly. Together, in perfect unison, they walked hand in hand through the open door, toward the beginning of the end of Lily's hellish nightmare.

EVE

This is real. This is real, Eve thought as she followed her girls outside. She watched them walking side by side, her heart about to burst out of her chest. Eve always said that having twins was like giving birth to three things: the two of them and their relationship. Losing Lily had destroyed all of that, and now here it was, reborn. Eve would never forget this day. For so long that miserable day in September haunted her. The day she'd gotten Lily's voice mail.

"Uh, Mom, it's almost six, and I'm still at school. That bitch . . . sorry, birch . . . Abby, left me here. Can you pick me up? And I'm starving. Let's get sushi tonight."

Eve had deleted the message, doing her best to fight off her annoyance. She'd been stuck in a budget meeting all day, and now she was going to have to spend her evening playing referee. The girls' constant bickering was a part of life, like traffic jams or plowing the driveway after a snowstorm, but that didn't make it less taxing.

She arrived at the high school a little after six. The

place was deserted. She'd wandered around, but there was no sign of Lily. She'd tried her cell, but in spite of her and Dave's pleas, the girls never charged their phones, and the damn thing went straight to voice mail. Eve figured Lily had gotten a ride from Wes or one of her track friends. She'd stopped at Yoshi's to pick up sushi, knowing that spicy tuna always brokered peace in their household. Dave was on call at the hospital that night, and Abby had been upstairs, in the bedroom she shared with Lily, laboring over her homework.

"Where's your sister?" Eve asked when she arrived at home.

Abby shrugged. "Her highness said she'd get a ride. I'm sure she's at Wes's."

Eve's motherly instincts hadn't been fully functioning earlier, at the school, but in that moment, they kicked into overdrive.

"Call Wes and make sure she's there."

Abby did as she was told and dialed Wes.

"Hey, can I talk to Lil?" Abby had paused, her nose scrunching up in concern. "So you haven't talked to her since last period? Okay, if you hear from her, tell her to call us ASAP." Abby hung up, staring back at the phone as if willing it to ring.

Eve had instructed Abby to phone all her friends. Anyone Lily might have gotten a ride with. Each call only seemed to confirm Eve's worst fears. Something bad had happened to Lily. She called Dave at the hospital, praying that Lily had dropped by to visit her father.

"Please tell me that Lily is with you."

"No. I haven't seen her since breakfast."

Eve's dread grew. "Lily. I think...I think she's missing."

She'd tried to keep the panic out of her voice, but he heard it anyway.

"I'll be there in ten. Call the police, Eve. I'm sure she's okay, but call them now."

Eve had tried to stay calm, hoping to counteract Abby's growing hysteria. She kept offering up suggestions. Maybe Lily went to a movie or out to dinner. Or she'd gone into Philly and forgotten to call. But that was ridiculous. Lily wasn't impulsive like that, and she never went anywhere without her sister by her side.

At some point, their house began to fill with cops. Neighbors showed up, along with a flood of tearful teenagers. The press arrived too, camping out on the front lawn. The FBI was next, and then the interviews began. Eve and Dave were questioned—no, grilled— for hours. Polygraphs. Police interrogations. They asked prying, probing questions. They wanted to know about her marital problems. About Dave's infidelity and Eve's subsequent visit to a divorce attorney. They were questions that had nothing to do with Lily being gone.

"She's my daughter. My goddamn daughter. Why would I hurt her? Why? It doesn't make sense," Eve had said over and over again. Dave did his best to console her, but they were at the point where everything about their partner annoyed them. Lily's disappearance only heightened that.

When it became clear that neither Eve nor Dave had anything to do with Lily being missing, the authorities cast a wider net. They questioned the entire school and faculty, interviewed transients and sex offenders. The police swept rivers and swamps. Hundreds of friends and family members searched the countryside. The story made national news. Usually, there were clues, but sometimes, the pundits on CNN said again and again, people simply vanish.

Eve had wondered if she would ever be whole again, but her devastation was nothing compared to Abby's. Her girls were a pair. Abby was the leader, six minutes older and bossy as hell. Lily happily accepted Abby's role as commander in chief. But Eve soon realized that Lily was the glue that held them together. Without Lily, the light in Abby vanished. Lily was Abby's light.

But now, after all these years, here they were, arm in arm. All Eve wanted to do was shut everyone out and hold on to her girls. She wanted to hold on to her grand-baby and swear that no one would ever hurt them again. But things were moving too fast for that. One second Eve was standing on her porch with Lily; the next she was sitting next to Sheriff Rogers in his police cruiser.

Tommy. That's how she knew him. They hadn't

been in the same room in over seven years. There were new lines around his eyes, his temples were graying, but other than that he hadn't aged. How was that possible when she looked years older?

Before everything with Lily happened, Tommy had been a complete stranger. Eve didn't even know his name. In fact, she was pretty certain she'd voted for his opponent in his first election. But she'd grown close to him in the weeks and months after Lily vanished. He'd been tireless in leading the search, assuring her they were doing everything they could, keeping her calm and listening to her desperate ramblings when Dave simply wouldn't do it anymore. After three weeks with no sign of Lily, he was the only one who had the courage to tell her the truth.

"I'm sorry, Eve," he'd said, her house dangerously quiet. "We're calling off the search. You have to accept the fact that Lily isn't coming home." This gruff, tobacco-chewing, deer-hunting man had broken down when he told her. She'd kissed him then, needing someone to hold her and tell her that things were going to be okay, even if she knew they never would.

It had been complete and total stupidity on her part to fall in love with him, but Lily's disappearance made her reckless in a way that she'd never been before. She'd pursued him with a single-minded determination. For three months, their affair continued. In seedy motel rooms, Eve's SUV, Tommy's patrol car—any place they could steal away. It was Dave's sudden heart attack that ended things for good.

"We can't do this anymore," Tommy said after the funeral. Eve knew he had a family, but she didn't care. She loved him. But Tommy had made up his mind.

"It's not who we are, Evie. We're good people."

Eve wasn't good. Or maybe she'd been good once. All she cared about was how he made her feel. She'd begged him not to leave her. He'd kissed her one last time, and then he disappeared from her life.

Eve told herself it didn't matter that he didn't want her. She was free. She focused on work and keeping Abby out of trouble, which was often a full-time job. She had one-night stands when she was feeling lonely, but she never got close to anyone, never let anyone in. She hadn't thought about Tommy until this very second, but now she found herself seized with an overwhelming urge to kiss him. How inappropriate, she thought. How awful. Eve looked out the window, hating herself for being so self-absorbed, for even thinking about him.

She felt his hand on her knee, squeezing gently as if to say he was here for her. Eve had never been more grateful for his kindness. Once they were all in the car, Tommy surveyed Lily in his rearview mirror.

"Lily, can you tell me where we're going?" Tommy asked.

Lily was staring out at the neighbors, who had gathered to watch the scene with unabashed curiosity. Eve's face flushed with embarrassment, knowing the neighbors were probably gossiping about what new tragedy had struck the Risers.

"The high school. We're going to the high school."

Abby gasped. Eve didn't even think. She grabbed Tommy's hand and squeezed it, feeling the bile rising up in her throat. She racked her brain for a list of suspects, but no one came to mind. It was a stranger. It had to be. All these years, she'd comforted herself by thinking some nameless monster had snatched her daughter away. Was it possible that it was someone they knew? Someone they trusted?

She leaned her head against the cold glass window, fighting her urge to ask Lily more questions. They drove through town in silence, arriving at the entrance of the high school in less than ten minutes. Tommy turned off the engine, waiting for Lily to speak, to give them a name. Eve could tell he was on edge. He was a man used to being in charge, used to having the necessary information to properly assess a situation. Lily had denied him that, and her actions didn't sit well with him. Eve didn't blame Tommy. She wanted answers too.

"We need a name, Lily," he said. "Whoever kept you prisoner, he's disturbed. We have to be prepared and—"

"He's only disturbed behind closed doors," Lily said.

"We need to do our job..."

Lily remained unmoved.

"I said I'd take you to him. And I will."

She climbed out of the car. Tommy muttered a curse under his breath. But there was no stopping Lily. Eve had seen that same expression on her daughter's face when Lily stood in the kitchen clutching that knife. Nothing anyone could say was going to stop her. All they could do was follow along.

LILY

Everything looks exactly the same. That was Lily's first thought when they'd pulled up at the entrance of Lancaster Day School. The American flag flying high above the building, the red brick and stucco and large airy open windows were all so... ordinary.

Lily thought back to the girl she'd been in high school. She'd loved coming here. She would have been a total dork if she hadn't been athletically gifted. She'd won top attendance her freshman and sophomore years. She always made the A honor roll. She was a member of every club her schedule would allow. She'd readily embraced high school's absurdities, all of its ups and downs.

Today there was a group of wide-eyed high school kids milling around the quad, laughing and teasing each other. Was it possible she'd ever been that young and hopeful? Lily wanted to scream at the top of her lungs, "You're wasting time. Don't waste it." But that would be pointless. That was the privilege of being young, she realized. Lily would have wasted her freedom too.

As she stood staring at the school, Sky slept in her arms. Lily realized that she had another decision to make. She had never let her child out of her sight. Maybe she should listen to the sheriff and let him handle it. But she knew Rick was here. She knew how close he was. This was her chance to make sure, to know with absolute certainty that he would be caught. Lily knew there was no other option. She had to finish this. But she wouldn't put Sky at the center of it. Lily knew her mother would protect Sky, that all these cops would make sure they were protected.

"Mom, can you stay here with Sky? Will you keep her safe?"

Without hesitation, Eve enveloped the sleeping child in her arms. "I'll take care of her, Lil. Just be careful."

Lily gave Sky one more gentle kiss. She took Abby's hand, leading her to the entrance of the school as Sheriff Rogers and an army of officers followed. As they neared the entrance, an older woman with salt-and-pepper hair, glasses, and a forceful gaze intercepted Sheriff Rogers.

"Sheriff, what's going on here? What's the problem?"

Lily assumed that this was the principal, but she didn't care. She pulled Abby inside the building before anyone could stop her. As they made their way into the school, a part of Lily wanted to tell Abby his name. They'd never kept secrets—Lily had told Wes as much when they'd first started dating.

"You mean, she knows everything about you? Like everything?" he'd asked.

Lily hadn't realized how strange that had sounded until he said it out loud. She'd racked her brain trying to think of an event or moment she hadn't shared with her sister, some deep dark secret. But there were none. With a flicker of sadness, she realized there were so many things she could never tell Abby. Things she couldn't share with anyone.

"If you want to wait with Mom, it's okay."

"No way, Lil. I'm here with you. All the way."

Abby's support kept her going as she moved through the halls. There was a time when they'd owned this school, identical and in total unison. Now they were complete opposites. Abby so much larger, her feet heavy on the polished tile floor, Lily nothing but bones, her steps hesitant and delicate.

Lily walked past the admin office, and a photo caught her eye. Her photo. It was her sophomore class picture. She'd worn her favorite lilac sweater and a matching headband, and she was laughing as if she'd heard the world's funniest joke. A simple gold plaque hung below, the words *In Our Hearts Forever* etched in a perfect cursive scrawl.

A tribute. A memorial. They'd thought she was dead, Lily realized. They thought he'd killed her. Lily's pace quickened. She passed the gym, the sound of sneakers screeching on the hardwood as gawky teenage boys did basketball drills. She passed several classrooms filled with bored students staring dully back at their teachers. She turned down the hall and stopped a few feet from Rick's classroom, where she could see him but he could not see her. He'd always bragged about the fact that he got the best and biggest classroom space. He prided himself on decorating it in a way that separated him from the other teachers. On the walls there were posters of Led Zeppelin, the Beatles, Jim Morrison—all "true artists," or so Rick said. He prided himself on being "cool," and his classroom was a reflection of those efforts.

The early-morning sunlight streamed through the windows illuminating Rick's casually tousled black mane (though nothing with Rick was ever casual). He was almost forty, but with his smooth, angular features, he could easily pass for early thirties. His jeans were designer, of course—and he wore a black button-down shirt with the sleeves rolled up, and a skinny green tie. He smiled back at his students, his chiseled features and dimples on full display, his eyes bright as if something one of his students had said was the cleverest thing he'd ever heard. Even now, Lily could understand why they worshiped him, how simple it was to fall under his spell. He knew the texts. His intelligence was indisputable as was his charm.

She stood frozen for a moment, simply staring at him. The decibel level in the hallway was growing by the second. Sheriff Rogers moved beside Lily as two deputies and a school security guard pushed their way to the front, the principal trailing them. Through the window, a student spotted them and interrupted Rick's lecture.

"Hey, look it's the cops!"

Rick stopped talking and followed his students' gaze. In a life filled with spectacular moments—and Lily intended to have many—this would go down as her favorite. His expression of confusion and disbelief faded and was replaced by a look of pure rage. She'd spent years avoiding that look, learning how to recognize the signs of his impending fury, knowing what awaited her when she miscalculated. But not today. Today she absorbed it, used it to fuel her. She turned to Sheriff Rogers.

"That man held me captive for three thousand one hundred and ten days. Rick Hanson is the man who kidnapped me. He is the man who raped me and impregnated me. He's the man you need to arrest." Lily's voice wasn't weak anymore. It was steady and strong, demanding to be heard.

As she'd predicted, the officers were obviously trying to reconcile the fact that this respected teacher could have committed such a horrifying crime. But she'd been wrong about their lack of commitment. They were professionals. They had a job to do, and they did it with startling efficiency. The sheriff and his men burst into the classroom and surrounded her abductor.

"Rick Hanson, you are under arrest for the kidnapping of Lily Riser. You have the right to remain silent."

They continued reading him his rights. Rick didn't resist or show any signs that he was in trouble. He didn't show any emotion at all. As they cuffed him, he spoke to his students, his voice filled with the same quiet confidence in which he taught his classes.

"Guys, get back to work. I'll be back in class soon, and I expect you to have read the last three chapters."

His students weren't listening. They were holding up cell phones, snapping pictures, and taking videos. Lily took great pleasure in knowing that soon everyone in the world would be aware of Rick Hanson's true nature.

They'll know, Rick. They'll all know what you are.

She was so caught up in this moment, in seeing Rick finally get what was coming to him, that she completely forgot about Abby. Glancing over at her, Lily found no joy on her sister's face. Instead, Abby's expression revealed a dawning sense of disbelief, then horror. Abby doubled over, an anguished scream ripping through her. For the first time, Lily wondered what she'd been thinking. Why was she so selfish? Why hadn't she considered her family? Her sister?

Lily moved forward to console Abby but her sister raced past her, descending into the classroom. Bursting past the cops, Abby flew at Rick like a street fighter, hitting and punching him as he tried to shield himself from her blows.

"You son of a bitch. You motherfucker. You stole her life. You stole our fucking lives."

It took both Sheriff Rogers and another deputy to pull Abby off him. She was inconsolable, slumped on the linoleum classroom floor, weeping from the depths of her heart. Seconds later, a handcuffed Rick Hanson was marched out of the classroom and down the hall. As he passed Lily, she heard him softly whisper, "You've made a big mistake, Baby Doll."

Lily should have known that he'd never let her have the last word. And as she rushed over to Abby, as she watched her sister come apart at the seams, Lily wondered if maybe, just maybe, Rick was right.

ABBY

Rick Fucking Hanson. His name didn't just rattle around in Abby's brain; it bounced off of her skull, exploding like cannon blasts. Over and over again, Abby kept hearing his name but she couldn't believe it. *Mr. Hanson? My English teacher?*

There was noise all around her but Abby couldn't focus on any of it. She saw an EMT, someone she worked with at the hospital, but she couldn't remember her name. She was kneeling beside Abby, asking her a barrage of questions.

"How far along are you? Are you on any medications? Abby, squeeze my hand if you can hear me."

The EMT kept talking, but Abby was overwhelmed, paralyzed by this discovery.

Time faded. Maybe it was minutes or hours. Weightless, Abby was lifted onto the paramedics' stretcher. Lily gripped Abby's hand tightly as the paramedics began to wheel her down the hallway.

"I'm here, Abs. I'm here."

The black hole was claiming her. Abby realized what a piece of shit she was for not being stronger. Even as she tumbled into the abyss, she could hear Lily's voice.

"I'm sorry, Abby. I'm so sorry."

Wait . . . Why was Lily apologizing? She wanted to ask, but Abby was plummeting at rapid speed, the darkness pulling her down, down, down.

Abby could still remember one of the earliest search parties. Lily had been missing for only a few days, but hundreds of people had gathered in the center of town, gathered together in the rain. Teenagers. Middle-school children. Parents. Interspersed were cops and FBI agents, busy scanning the crowd, searching for answers.

As the rescue dogs barked, the crowd headed out in all directions, flyers in hand, flashlights lighting the way. Other volunteers handed out coffees. Then there were the Jesus freaks, with their prayer cards. Abby was grabbing a coffee before she headed back out, when a frizzy-haired woman thrust one of the cards at her.

"Prayer will bring Lily back to us. God will hear your prayers," the woman had said.

"Fuck you," Abby had replied, smacking the card from the woman's hand. "Fuck. You."

"Abigail, what's wrong?" Mr. Hanson had appeared by her side. He'd offered a rushed *I'm sorry* to the woman and ushered Abby away.

"She's going on and on about God. I mean, God didn't take Lily, he sure as shit isn't going to bring her back."

"I know, Abby. I know."

"I don't care about God. I just...I want her back. I want my sister back."

Mr. Hanson had hugged her. She'd let him hug her!

"I do too, Abigail. But it's early days. Don't give up hope. You can't give up."

She'd wanted to believe what he was saying, needed to believe him.

"You think that's true? That we'll still find her?"

"I have no doubts about it. Come on. We'll keep searching together."

All those weeks Mr. Hanson had joined her family on search parties, trudging through forests, wading along the banks of rivers and marshes, and even searching the nearby Amish land, hoping to find some sign of Lily. Mr. Hanson had even organized grief-counseling sessions after school for the entire student body.

Sometimes he'd stop by her house and sit on the porch with her father, smoking cigars, quoting Faulkner as platitudes. And that fucker...he'd even sponsored student council fund-raisers for that goddamn memorial Abby had to pass every day for two years. Endless days she'd spent trudging through the halls, feeling lost without her other half, always seeing Lily's happy face staring back at her. But she'd been grateful to Mr. Hanson. Grateful that he'd never treated her as if she was crazy. Grateful that he'd always shown her such kindness. He'd stop by her locker every so often.

"We're all here for you, Abby," Mr. Hanson had told her. "I know you miss Lily, but she loved you very much. You have to know that." When everyone else had moved on, hearing it from someone like Mr. Hanson kept her going.

Lily's voice was growing more and more distant.

"Abby, listen to me, he's going to jail and I'm here. Don't leave me, Abby. I'm right here," Lily said, her voice cracking.

Abby tried to hold on. She tried to keep it together but she was teetering closer and closer to the edge of that damn black hole. The black hole she willingly jumped into, numbing herself with booze and pills and sex. The black hole the doctors spent years trying to free her from, offering various "coping tools." The black hole Wes and the baby were trying to lure her out of.

It was Mr. Hanson's voice, so calm and clear and compassionate, that she couldn't bear now. "Lily was a fighter, wasn't she? Do you think she'd want you to quit?" Mr. Hanson had said when he visited her in the hospital after her suicide attempt. He'd always talked about Lily as if he knew her. As if he understood their bond.

All the while, he was keeping her. Keeping Lily. Killing Abby from the inside out. Murdering her sweet, kind father. Turning her mother into some weak, needy, desperate woman. Destroying any happiness their family might have had, piece by piece. She owed Lily so much more, but this darkness was what Abby knew best. She wanted the black hole to take her. She wanted to escape the truth about Mr. Hanson. Abby was still thrashing about when she felt the merciful prick of the EMT's needle, and then she slowly, gratefully drifted away.

EVE

Eve sat breathless, watching as Rick Hanson, Lancaster's most respected teacher and someone she'd considered a friend, was led out in handcuffs. *It couldn't be*, Eve thought. Maybe Lily had made a mistake. *There was no way. It couldn't be Rick Hanson.*

Rick was the girls' favorite teacher. He was everyone's favorite teacher. She remembered when he'd come to town years ago, all the moms in carpool gossiping about him, wondering if a man who looked like that could possibly be a decent teacher. Eve liked him instantly; his enthusiasm for his students' success was apparent. After Lily was taken, he'd been so supportive, always checking in on them, stopping by the hospital after one of Abby's episodes, delivering homework and well wishes. There had to be some mistake. But then, as if on cue, Sky sat up, her entire body vibrating as she clawed at the window.

"Daddy Rick, come back. Daddy!" Sky wailed and wailed, and all Eve could do was stare out the window, watching as they escorted him to the police cruiser. It was Rick Hanson. He was the man who'd abducted her daughter. This man. Their family friend. He was the one.

Eve tried to calm Sky, but the child's screams continued. The realization washed over Eve in waves. Her daughter had been raped and impregnated by this monster. Sky was still wailing, and Eve tried in vain to soothe her. "It'll be okay, Sky. It's going to be okay. Mommy will be here soon. It's okay, sweetheart."

If Rick could hear or see Sky, he didn't acknowledge her. He moved forward, head held high, no guilt or recrimination on his stoic features. Even when they put him in the squad car, Eve was amazed at how he carried himself—the ease and confidence of a man who'd been wronged.

Seeing this sweet, delicate child in such pain was horrible, but Eve was grateful for the buffer Sky provided. No matter what Eve wanted to do to Rick Hanson, what punishments she wanted to inflict—and the list was endless—she had a more important task: keeping her granddaughter safe. But she understood Sky's pain. Understood the desperation and longing to be near your parent... or your child. It didn't matter that Sky's father was a monster. Her love for him was real. In that moment, the pinching ache in Eve's neck coursed through her entire body. She fought to keep the pain away, to focus on the present moment the way the doctors advised. The pain always showed up when she was stressed. *Stop thinking about yourself. Focus on this right here.*

The squad car carrying Rick Hanson pulled away, and Lily burst out of the school, ignoring the onlookers as she raced over to Eve. Lily swung open the police car door and plucked a hysterical Sky from Eve's arms, holding the little girl tightly, hugging and kissing her.

"Don't worry, Chicken. There's no trouble. Not anymore."

"I saw Daddy Rick but he didn't see me. Is he mad at us?"

"No. We're fine. Daddy Rick has to go away for a while, but you and I are going to be okay. We're always okay, aren't we?"

Sky sobbed into her mother's shoulder, whimpering for Rick, but this time Lily didn't calm her. She held on, letting Sky weep as Lily turned her attention to Eve. Lily was gesturing to the EMTs who were wheeling Abby out.

"I don't know what happened to Abby...but she lost it."

Eve gazed at her other damaged child and shook her head, not quite sure how to tell Lily what Abby had endured, not sure if it was fair to let her know how hard it had been.

"Abby gets this way sometimes. Since you...since you were taken, she's...she's struggled."

Lily didn't comment. Instead, she pulled Eve toward the ambulance where emergency personnel were loading

Abby into the back. They'd given Abby sedatives and she was groggy, whispering, "Mr. Hanson. It was Mr. Hanson."

Eve grabbed Abby's hand.

"Abby, you're okay. It's Mom. I'm here. Lily and I are both here."

"I shouldn't have done this. I didn't think. I'm so very sorry," Lily whispered.

Eve took in Lily's guilt-ridden expression.

"Don't you dare apologize," Eve said. As far as she was concerned, Lily got a lifelong free pass. Besides, Lily could never have known about Abby's breakdowns, that they happened with such frequency they had become the norm. "It's done, Lil. That's all that matters. Now we can get you both help."

Eve could tell that Lily was finally starting to falter. Pale and trembling, the adrenaline had likely worn off and she was unsteady on her feet. Eve gestured to the EMT and she took Lily's hand and helped her into the ambulance. Lily motioned for Eve to follow.

"You're coming, right?" she said to Eve.

But the EMT shook her head.

"Sorry, Mrs. Riser, but I'm afraid there's not room for all of you."

"I want you with us. Please, Mom," Lily begged, her eyes welling with tears. Eve knew this was a safety issue; they couldn't have too many passengers, but she hated telling Lily no.

"Eve, I'll drive. We'll be right behind you, Lily," Tommy said, gesturing toward his nearby cruiser.

Lily stared at Sky and Abby, exhaustion and worry winning out.

"You promise?"

Eve nodded. "We're right behind you."

With Sky still in her arms, Lily reached out and hugged Eve, and then she sank down onto the gurney and let the EMT close the ambulance doors.

Eve found herself separated from her girls once again. She wanted to bang on the doors, to insist that she go with them, but instead she let Tommy usher her toward his patrol car. As they hurried along, Eve realized how many people were watching them. Dozens and dozens of students were taking pictures, filming them with their phones. She wanted to scream. What was wrong with them? Why would anyone want to document *this*? Eve couldn't fight the tidal wave of shame washing over her. She'd always been a private person, always kept to herself. Even after Lily went missing, Dave was the one who did all the press conferences. Now, people were going to ask endless questions—probing questions—about Lily and her sex life and all the things Rick had done to her. All Eve wanted to do was get away from this place, away from all these prying eyes and lenses. As they climbed into the car and pulled out of the parking lot, sirens and lights flashing, the ambulance leading the way, Tommy shook his head in disbelief.

"It's a miracle, Evie. It's a goddamn miracle."

A heavy silence lingered, both of them trying to process what they'd witnessed. Eve finally spoke.

"I don't understand. I'll never..."

"Been a cop for twenty-eight years, and I've never seen anything like this. Goddamn it, Eve, this is proof that evil is real. It's not Scripture. It's living and breathing and walking around among us; I'll tell you that right now."

A thought struck Eve as she listened to him. What if the driver of that ambulance was involved? A friend of Rick Hanson's, maybe. Eve knew it was irrational, but they'd trusted Rick Hanson. Maybe there were more people involved. Why did she always have to follow the rules? Why hadn't she insisted on going with her girls? The thought of losing them again was too much to bear.

"Stay close to the ambulance. Don't let it out of your sight," Eve ordered Tommy, her voice filled with desperation. He gave her a startled look but obeyed, stepping on the gas. Eve didn't care if he thought she was crazy. Maybe she was, but she'd do anything to keep from losing her family again.

"Just get me to my girls, Tommy. Do whatever it takes to get me to my girls."

LILY

Broken collarbone. Sprained wrists. Two broken ankles. Broken jaw. Six healed rib fractures. Cigarette burns. Ligament scars. Vaginal tearing and extensive trauma. Anemia. Vitamin D deficiency. Visual impairments. The list went on and on and on.

The worst injuries Rick inflicted were in the beginning when Lily still believed she could fight her way out. He'd broken her collarbone and both ankles when she'd tried to escape. He'd been holding her captive for six months, and Lily had decided she had to do something. And she thought she had a chance. She'd seen the light peeking out from the upstairs for almost forty-eight hours. But it was a trap. Lily had barely stepped foot outside the basement when Rick kicked her down the stairs. That beating nearly cost Lily her life. It was also the last time, until today, that Lily ever considered running.

Her other injuries were from the "games" they'd played, when Rick got "carried away." He'd always apologize, bathing her, gently setting her wounds in splints, bandaging them with the intimate care of a physician, and promising he'd be more careful next time, promising that once she went along with his demands, he wouldn't have to be so rough (a promise he never kept).

Lily had forced herself to forget each wound that was inflicted, especially once she had Sky. But now she could see that her body was a road map of Rick's insanity, each scar and impairment revealing his depraved proclivities. Her body was officially evidence.

Cataloging that evidence was an entire fleet of medical personnel. Dr. Lashlee, an attractive resident in her early thirties with a genuine smile and an easy manner, kept Lily calm. Even when she began trembling uncontrollably as they asked her to undress, or when she sobbed through the pelvic exam, Dr. Lashlee's voice remained measured, her words reassuring. The old-school RN, Carol, a wrinkled woman with smoker's lines and tired eyes, held Lily's hand, letting go only to jot notes in her chart. In the corner, a female detective took photos and made notations into a tape recorder.

Another doctor arrived shortly after the exam began, a statuesque Middle Eastern woman in starched khakis and a silk shirt, who introduced herself as Dr. Amari.

"I'm chief of psychiatry here at Lancaster General. I know you were asking about Abby. I was with her and she's stable now. If you don't mind, I'd like to spend some time with you and Sky."

Lily shrugged. "That's fine," she said.

"If this examination becomes too invasive, please speak up. We want to make you as comfortable as possible."

Lily wanted to tell this woman—this clueless woman— that nothing they could do to her could possibly be too invasive, but she refrained. It was easier to simply block out what was going on now in this warm, well-lit room, with everyone acting so polite and accommodating.

Lily had initially resisted the physical exam. Sky was terrified, and Lily was so tired and overwhelmed by everything that had unfolded. Plus she didn't want to leave Abby. But Abby was still in a drug-induced haze, and Sheriff Rogers made it clear that Lily's work wasn't done.

"We have to nail this son of a bitch to the wall. That means documenting your injuries, running DNA tests, and getting your statement on the record. We can't screw this up."

Her doubts about Sheriff Rogers vanished instantly. They shared a mutual goal: Rick's complete and total destruction. She reluctantly agreed to the exam. But first she'd had to deal with her mother. Lily knew the truth would come out, but she hoped that she could spare Mom the trauma as long as possible.

"Please, go with Abby. Sky and I will be fine here."

Mom resisted, but Lily insisted.

"Please. I need to know Abby's not alone."

After a few more minutes of negotiation, Mom had

caved, heading off to see Abby while the nurses whisked Lily into a room and went to work. Drawing blood, taking X-rays and photographs, and on and on and on. Lily's exam was exceptionally arduous, but it was nowhere near as painful as watching Sky's exam.

Sky wailed the minute the doctors' hands touched her tiny frame, and she never stopped crying. She was horrified by their alien touch, not to mention the bright lights, the noise, and the cold metal instruments. Lily knew how she felt, and she'd experienced life outside that cold, dark basement. She could only imagine how overwhelming this amount of stimulus was for a child who, until today, had spent her entire life in isolation.

"No, Mommy! Make them stop. I wanna go home. Take me home, Mommy."

Lily's purpose over the last six years was keeping her child safe. But she accepted that she was powerless right now. This exam had to be done. There was no medical care in Rick's world. No vaccinations. No annual checkups. The only preventive measures Lily had for keeping Sky well were daily prayers. But this was the real world now, a world where children needed medical attention. Not only that, but Lily wanted confirmation that Sky was healthy—or as healthy as a child raised in captivity could possibly be. She endured Sky's wails and pleas to stop, knowing this was in her best interests.

"It's okay. It'll all be over soon. Be Mommy's brave little girl."

When the doctors finished with the poking and prodding, Lily and Sky were relocated to a private room in the back wing of the hospital. VIPs, her mother always called patients who stayed there. Police officers were promptly stationed at the entrance. "A security precaution," one of the nurses said reassuringly when Lily inquired about it. She figured it was better safe than sorry where Rick was concerned.

The nurses delivered warm bowls of vegetable soup and toast. Sky was starving and she devoured the food, her tears finally beginning to subside. After they ate, Lily curled up in bed with Sky, the two of them wrapped in warm blankets, and Sky finally drifted off to sleep.

An IV dripped fluid into both their arms, medications to treat their dehydration, lack of vitamin D, and all the other nutrients they'd been denied. Lily was dozing when Mom and Sheriff Rogers returned. She sat up, careful not to wake Sky.

"How's Abby?" Lily asked her mom.

"She's asking about you. She's worried you're mad at her."

"That's crazy. I'm not... Why would I be mad at her?"

Lily didn't understand. She found Dr. Amari lingering at the entrance of the room. Lily surveyed the empty spare bed in the room and then looked at the doctor.

"Dr. Amari, is there any way Abby can stay in here with me? We both need... we need to be together."

"If I consent to that, it's important that you both rest."

"Absolutely. You have my word."

"I'll make the arrangements with the nurses. And, Sheriff, I know you have questions, but if you can keep this visit short, I would appreciate it."

"I won't be long," he said. Dr. Amari left, leaving Lily alone with Mom and Sheriff Rogers. He cleared his throat, shifting from side to side.

"Lily, your statement can wait until the morning, but it's important that we find the location where Rick held you and Sky. We've asked Hanson, but he's not talking. If you can remember any details at all...?"

Lily recalled the route—her route to freedom—in vivid detail. Each step, each twist and turn, was seared into her brain.

"There's a cabin off Highway 12. It doubles as his office. He tells his wife he goes to write. He kept us underground...in a basement. There's a door in the back of the cabin that leads downstairs. His wife probably knows where the cabin is located, but if you have a pen, I can draw you a map."

Sheriff Rogers pulled out his notebook and a pen from his front jacket pocket. Lily's hand shook as she carefully drew the map. She handed it back to him.

"Has Rick...? Did he say anything?"

"Not a word. But don't worry. He's not going anywhere. You and Sky are safe now. You have my word. Get some rest, and I'll see you first thing tomorrow."

"Thank you again."

Sheriff Rogers gazed at Lily, clutching his hat in his hands.

"We worked like hell to find you all those years ago. I'm sorry we failed you, but I'm so damn glad you're here. That you're alive. Today is one helluva good day."

Lily gave him a big smile.

"It's better than that, Sheriff. It's spectacular."

Lily heard her mom half sob, half laugh, no doubt remembering her girls and their game. Startled, Sheriff Rogers moved closer to Mom.

"Eve, are you okay? Did I say something?"

She shook her head, squeezing his hand.

"It's okay. We're okay now."

It seemed like he wanted to say something else, but he just tipped his hat and headed out. Eve wiped away her tears, hovering over Lily.

"I really need to get it together, don't I?"

"You're fine, Mom. But can you check and see when they're moving Abby?"

Mom relented, apparently sensing Lily's concern.

"Okay. But if you need anything, you'll have the nurses text me?" Mom said, still nervously hovering at the door.

"I promise," Lily said, hugging her mother again. Lily knew she would never tire of these hugs. From here on out, she'd mentally record each and every hug and kiss, every single moment of kindness she experienced.

Lily watched her mother disappear down the hall and she realized for the first time since they'd escaped from Rick, she was alone. Only this time it was different. It was so different. Rick was locked up. There was a guard stationed outside her room. She was wearing clean, comfortable clothes. She had food in her belly. Her daughter was safe. She had her life back. It was almost too much to comprehend.

Overwhelmed by her thoughts, Lily leaned back against the pillows. Her eyes slowly fluttered closed. Images of Rick in shackles, lying awake in a dark, dank room with other inmates screaming obscenities consumed her. She imagined the inmates tormenting him the way he'd tormented her.

"You stupid piece of shit."

"You worthless maggot."

"You're no one. No one at all."

She doubted that the criminals in the county jail could ever match his depravity. As Lily closed her eyes, she felt a wave of sadness wash over her, so profound she couldn't quite explain it. The emotion was fleeting, almost as if she'd dreamt it. Lily forced the feeling away, letting sleep claim her. Rick was gone and she was free. That's what she wanted. All she'd ever wanted.

RICK

Lying on the cold metal cot, his hands cuffed so tightly he was losing circulation, Rick continued replaying the day's events over and over again, trying to reconcile where he'd gone wrong, how this had happened.

At first when he'd spotted Lily outside his classroom, wearing that ridiculously oversized sweatshirt, her blond hair in a messy braid, he thought it had to be the other one. It couldn't be his Lily. His baby doll would never break the rules. She'd never violate his trust.

But then she made eye contact and he knew it was Lily. That was *his* girl, standing in the middle of the hallway, surrounded by police, staring at him with an expression he hadn't seen in years—one of total defiance. He couldn't believe her insolence, but there wasn't time to react. The cops descended upon him, shouting and yelling, bending his arms back, cuffing him as they read him his rights.

A feverish hysteria grew in his classroom, the kids' excitement building and their iPhone cameras flashing.

He noticed students filming videos, which he knew they'd probably already uploaded to various websites, hashtagging and geotagging, sharing them on YouTube channels and Instagram profiles. Within moments, he'd known his undoing would be transmitted to the masses. But all he kept thinking was, *How?* How could she have deceived him? After all the training, all those hours and days and weeks he'd spent teaching her what she needed to know, making her love him the same way he loved her, she'd done *this*. Trapped him in public like some pathetic animal, humiliated in front of the world. This betrayal was unbearable. He loved her—truly loved her—and she'd done this to him.

From the first day he saw her, her freshman year, he'd been drawn to her fresh face and sun-kissed blond hair. Her dimples and open smile nearly did him in every time she walked into his classroom. He'd been teaching for almost fifteen years, and his instincts and understanding of his students were exceptional. He could spot the class clowns, the rejects, and the sluts (though it didn't take a Rhodes scholar to recognize them). He'd had occasional dalliances with students, but he chose carefully. He'd let the girls break things off, pretending to be heartbroken when all along he'd been pulling their strings. They meant nothing. Casual distractions, easing his boredom until he was free to indulge in what he really wanted—a girl of his own to do with as he wished.

He knew that Lily wasn't the type to engage in an affair with an older married man, much less her teacher. But that knowledge, that innate goodness, only made him want her more. Watching her in class, so inquisitive and bright-eyed, challenging him and her classmates, he'd longed for her to be his. He saw Lily's kindness, the way she always made time for the outcasts and loners, in spite of her popularity. He'd study her long, tanned, toned legs, sometimes heading to the stadium to observe track practice, hoping to catch another glimpse of her and all her beauty on display. The more he watched her, the more he wanted her. He'd have to control his rage, seething when he'd spot her in the halls draped all over her worthless jock boyfriend. The way she'd look at that kid drove him crazy. Rick deserved to be the one she stared at longingly.

He'd urged Lily to join the school paper, and they'd spent countless hours together, working on stories. Hearing her bubbly, infectious laugh, getting to know and love her almost made up for having to listen to her prattle on about that idiot boyfriend.

"Wes this" and "Wes that" and "Isn't he amazing?" Rick would nod, pretending to care. It drove him insane. He'd wanted his name to be the one she spoke of with lust and longing in her eyes. As the year came to an end, he made the decision that she was the one. She had to be his.

He knew Lily's twin sister as well. Abby was in his

other English honors class, but there was something about her, a harshness, an underlying edge to her personality he found unappealing. Besides, he wasn't selfish. Lily was more than enough.

Rick realized that taking her would be a challenge. There was the possibility that the right moment might never present itself. But that didn't mean he shouldn't be prepared. "Luck is preparation meets opportunity," was one of Missy's bullshit catch phrases, but Rick figured it couldn't hurt. What if he got lucky? He'd spent months working on the cabin. The construction of Lily's new home, all the shopping he needed to do, convincing Missy that his writing space was sacred, and it was best that she not visit and interrupt his work. The preparations took months of planning and thousands of dollars to orchestrate. But he'd done it all for Lily. And now here he was. She had made him into a fool.

He hadn't reacted when they arrested him. That's what they were expecting. Some sort of freak-out or emotional tell that would prove his guilt with a capital G. He knew that defying expectations would play in his favor.

In a measured tone, he'd ordered his students to sit down. "Guys, get back to work. I'll be back in class soon, and I expect you to have read the last three chapters."

They didn't listen. He knew they wouldn't; they were teenagers after all, total shits who loved a circus, but it was important that he appear unfazed by all of this.

That was easier said than done when the heavy one came at him, hitting, kicking, and biting. Abby was disgusting—a whale of a woman—and looking at Lily, he realized what a smart choice he'd made. His Lily would never let herself go like that.

But the more Abby hit him, the more excited he became. Her actions reminded him of Lily's in the beginning, during her training. When the cops pulled the beast off him, Rick wondered if he'd chosen the wrong sister. Maybe that one wouldn't have betrayed him. How was he to know? He'd given Lily a wonderful life. He had given her a child, one of the hardest decisions he'd ever made. He'd spent the entire seven months thinking about what he was going to do with it. Drown it. Drop it at a fire station. Bury it in the woods. In the end, he realized this baby was a part of him, his seed, his creation. And they'd built a life together. In fact, he almost liked the child. She was a mini Lily, and he'd enjoyed watching her grow up. But that didn't matter now. Like Brutus turned on Caesar, Lily had betrayed him.

He sighed inwardly. Too late for regrets. He had to be smart. Strategy was an important part of any plan. He'd known the risks all along, and he'd figure something out. Yes, he'd been caught. But if Lily thought she had the upper hand, she was a fool. Rick saw two guards approaching his cell, both of them wearing black leather gloves and stoic expressions. He recognized the look in their eyes. They wanted him to suffer.

Bring it, Rick thought, needing to feel something, needing some kind of distraction. As the officers came at him, readying their assault, Rick couldn't help but laugh. There wasn't anything they could do that would hurt more than what Lily had done. His heart was already broken. That stupid bitch had torn it in two.

ABBY

"Get these fucking things off me," Abby demanded as she fought against the arm restraints that bound her to the hospital gurney. "I'm not going to hurt anyone. I want to see Lily. I need to see my fucking sister."

The nurses ignored her. She knew the staff was used to crazy people yelling at them and that she wasn't helping her cause. But she wanted to be with Lily and they wouldn't listen. Why wouldn't they listen? Abby saw Dr. Amari approaching, and she forced herself to lower her voice, to maintain some semblance of calm.

"Dr. Amari, tell them I'm okay. I'll be okay."

Dr. Amari sighed as she leaned over Abby, her hand gently resting on her restrained arms.

"You're not okay, though, are you?"

Abby knew how this bullshit worked. No matter what she said, the doctors always found a way to twist her words. If Abby said she were fine, Dr. Amari would reference Abby's freak-out at the school. If Abby expressed how angry she was, they'd keep her in the crazy ward and she'd never get back to Lily.

So Abby remained quiet. Dr. Amari gently unhooked the restraints and sank down beside Abby on the bed.

"What happened, Abby? You've been making such good progress."

Dr. Amari had to know what had happened at the high school. She was a woman who never saw her patients without having all the answers. But if Abby wanted to see Lily, she had no choice but to play along.

"It was Mr. Hanson who took Lily! Our English teacher kidnapped her. All these years…all these fucking years. When I saw him today, when I realized what happened, I…I lost it. But I'm okay now. I'll be okay."

"You understand that I have an obligation to keep you and your baby safe?"

"I'm not going to hurt it."

"*It?*"

Abby closed her eyes and took a deep breath. Damn it. She hated shrinks, hated how they analyzed every goddamn word.

"I'm not going to hurt the baby. I'm not going to hurt anyone."

Dr. Amari slowly stood up.

"That's good to hear. I've spoken with Lily and I'm willing to transfer you to her room so you can spend the night together. But you have to take care of yourself and your baby."

"Yes. Please. I'll do whatever you want if I can just see Lily. Please..."

"I'll put in the orders now. But, Abby, listen to me, I know how happy you are. You and Lily deserve time to reconnect. But I'm going to encourage you both to begin counseling immediately. It will be a difficult adjustment period for everyone."

"Absolutely. As soon as Lily's settled, we'll make an appointment."

Apparently satisfied with Abby's response, Dr. Amari headed off to make the arrangements.

Relieved, Abby leaned back and closed her eyes. No way that was ever going to happen. Hell would freeze over before Abby would see another shrink. The only reason she'd needed one in the first place was because Lily was gone. Now that her sister was home, Abby was going to get her life back on track.

She was still thinking about all the things she was going to do with Lily, all of the things she wanted to tell her, when she heard a voice at the door.

"Abby?"

She saw Wes lingering in the doorway. Abby sat up, touching her stomach involuntarily, feeling her entire body clench.

"What are you doing here?"

She thought she'd made herself clear in the squad car today. Crystal fucking clear. Wes ignored Abby's raised voice.

"I had to make sure that everything...that you and Lily were both all right. That the baby was all right."

He'd moved over and sat beside her, grabbing her hands in his. She'd always been comforted by his touch. The first night after Lily was gone, he'd wrapped his arms around her, his six-foot-four frame towering over her. She'd relied on him for so much. But that was before Lily came back. Now she couldn't worry about him or what he wanted. Abby had never kept anything from her sister. But this...Lily had loved Wes. She'd loved him more than anything. Every single second of Lily's life before she vanished had been about Wes and their relationship. It had driven Abby crazy.

"Wes and I are going to the movies."

"We have to go see Wes's grandmother."

"Wes and I aren't sure what we're doing for spring break."

Abby used to tease Lily. "We-we-we all the way home." It wouldn't make sense to Lily that she and Wes had gotten together. Lily would never understand. How could she?

"Listen to what I'm saying, Wes. Give me...give us some space."

He pulled his hand away but his gaze never left hers.

"I know you think everything is about you, Abby. But it's not. I loved Lily...She was my first love."

Abby stared at him, unblinking. He'd never once talked about his feelings for Lily since they'd gotten together, and now he was saying this, making it about him. She tried not to let it bother her, listening as he continued.

"I was concerned about you and Lily and our baby. Now that I know everyone is safe, I'll leave. But Lily needs to know about us. I'm not saying that you have to tell her today, but she's going to find out. It will be better if it comes from you."

He stood up and leaned down to kiss her good-bye. She let him. *Give him what he wants and he'll obey.* As he headed out, Abby knew she was being unfair but there was nothing she could do. She had to get rid of him. Maybe a restraining order? Abby was still contemplating her options when Carol, a fellow nurse, arrived to transport her to Lily's room. Abby wanted to walk but Carol wasn't having it.

"I'm not going to break the rules, even for you. Hop in. Your chariot awaits." Abby obliged. Carol wheeled Abby down the halls, chatting excitedly about the blessing they'd all been given. Abby ignored her prattling, still thinking about what to do with Wes.

At the entrance to Lily's room, Abby stood, watching her sister sleep, breathing in and out, a slow, steady rhythm. As if she sensed Abby's arrival, Lily's eyes fluttered open. Beside her, Sky slept on, exhausted after their ordeal.

"I didn't mean to wake you," Abby said.

"You didn't. I was only resting my eyes."

Abby turned to Carol. "You can beat it now."

Carol didn't budge. Abby fought to keep her temper in check.

"Seriously, Carol, there are sick people in this hospital. Go do some real work."

Carol gave in, offering Abby an affectionate pat on her shoulder.

"Get some rest, Abby. And, Lily, welcome home."

In spite of herself, Abby was grateful for Carol's friendship. Every one of the nurses she worked with here had kept her going. First as a patient and later when she was hired as an LVN. They'd kept her accountable and given her a purpose.

Carol left and Abby sat motionless in the wheelchair, trying to think of what to say or do. Lily made the decision for her, lifting up the covers and patting the bed for Abby to join. Abby wanted nothing more than to crawl in beside her sister, but instead she stared down at her enormous belly.

"No way there's room for me. I'm a total cow."

"Stop saying that."

"It's true."

"Abby, you're not a cow. You're stunning."

Abby was hideous. But hearing Lily say otherwise, she almost believed her. She moved over to the bed and climbed in. It was a tight squeeze, but they made it work. Sky lay tucked in on Lily's other side and didn't even stir. Once Abby was settled, Lily gently laid her head on Abby's shoulder.

The room was still; the only sound was the *beep beep beep* of their BP monitor. It was so warm and peaceful. Abby's chest grew tight. She closed her eyes. She did her breathing exercises but it didn't work. A sob escaped, and Abby cried again. For Lily's lost years. For her suffering.

Lily gently rubbed Abby's back, the way she did when they were kids.

"What happened to Dad?" Lily finally said.

Abby cringed. They'd said it was a clogged valve, but Abby knew better. Some hearts keep beating when they're broken; others just give out. Abby let out a long sigh.

"He had a heart attack."

"When?"

"A few months after...after you were taken."

Lily obviously wanted more details. Abby reluctantly continued.

"Dad was so strong when we lost you. He took charge in a way I'd never seen. He kept Mom and me fed, kept us from losing our minds. He wouldn't let us say anything negative. He said we couldn't give up hope. That we had to believe in you, believe that you'd come back. He did all these interviews. Organized the search parties. And then one day he went to work, and Anna heard a crash in the office. She found him sprawled out on the floor. They tried to operate, but his heart...he didn't have the fight in him."

Abby still mourned her father every single day, and now Lily would too. A miserable silence passed, and then Lily spoke.

"And that man, the man I saw today at Mom's. Who is he?"

Abby didn't know what to say. She didn't have a clue. Mom wasn't exactly a lady of virtue since Dad died. But Abby was in no place to judge.

"He's no one important."

"Is she dating him?"

"It's all a little complicated."

Abby cringed. What a stupid thing to say. As if Lily didn't know how complicated it was. But Lily didn't seem to notice.

"How was it? After I was gone?"

Abby wondered what she should say. That life sucked? That everything went to hell?

"I want to know, Abby. I need to know what it was like."

"It was terrible, Lilypad. So terrible."

Abby realized a moment too late that she was rubbing the vine-like tattoos that covered her wrists, her drunken attempt to cover up the trail of scars. Lily reached out, running her hands over the uneven lines, lines that even years later marked the sadness that had once engulfed Abby.

"Jesus Christ, Abby, what did you do?"

Abby jerked her hands away.

"It's done now, Lil. It's all in the past. Let's not dwell on it."

"I don't want to hurt you, Abs. I shouldn't have done

that at the school today. I should have told them who he was."

Abby sat up. "Are you kidding?" Abby said. "Seeing that look on his face was worth the ambulance ride. And don't forget, I got in a few good shots too."

Abby and Lily locked eyes. They both started to laugh, giggles at first, then louder and louder, until they were in hysterics, holding their stomachs until the laughter finally subsided. Abby spoke first.

"I missed you so much, Lil. So fucking much."

Lily didn't answer, still holding on to Abby's hand, studying it with unabashed interest. "You're not married?"

Abby's joy evaporated, replaced by soul-crushing fear. She shook her head.

"Marriage is for old people, Lil," she said, trying to keep the subject light.

"But you're having a baby?"

"It's a long story."

"I want to hear it. All of it. There's so much I've missed, Abby. I want to know all about your life. About everything."

"We have time. We have all the time in the world. But Dr. Amari made me promise that we'd both get some rest."

Abby's heart was still racing as she attempted to shut down this conversation. She began to ease herself out of the bed. But Lily held on to her.

"Stay here. Sleep with me tonight."

Abby didn't need convincing. She slowly eased herself back down, pulling the covers up to her chin.

"Good night, Lilypad."

"Good night, Abby."

Lily clutched Abby's hand. Lily's breathing grew steady and then she slowly drifted off. But Abby knew that tonight sleep would elude her. Lily hadn't asked about Wes, but she would. And then what? What was she going to do? Abby stared up at the ceiling, thinking about tomorrow and how she was going to fix this situation. She'd stay awake all night if she had to. She wasn't going to let anyone come between her and her sister. Not again. Not fucking again.

EVE

Once her girls were settled, Eve met with Dr. Amari. She'd wanted to discuss a treatment plan. They'd both worked at this hospital for over twelve years. Dr. Amari was candid, warning Eve that things wouldn't be easy.

"You'll have to take the girls' lead, Eve. This is something they're going to have to do. But you'll play an important part in helping them recover."

Eve promised she'd do whatever it took to repair her family. She'd been headed back to Lily's room when she'd spotted Wes sitting in the waiting area, head in his hands, looking sadder than she could ever remember, and that was saying a lot.

Eve rubbed her neck, feeling that familiar pain, the ache that started when things in her life spiraled out of control. She'd done yoga, visited tons of chiropractors, tried acupuncture, but none of it worked. Finally, one of the many therapists she'd seen had given her "tough love."

"Stress has to go somewhere, Eve. It's a living organism

inside you. Until you exorcise all those demons, none of it will go away," he'd said.

Eve stopped seeing the therapist that day. Why pay a hundred and fifty dollars an hour to listen to someone drone on and on about how Eve had the power to fix her own life? If she'd had that kind of power, she'd have fixed it already. But boy, did she have power now. Eve was already thinking about the lawsuit she was going to file against the school. That was a given. She'd sue the school, the school district. Hell, she was thinking about suing the city of Lancaster. All of them were going to pay for failing to protect her baby. But that was for later. Right now she needed to make sure Wes was okay. As much as she wanted to ease his worries, Eve knew that the more he pushed Abby, the worse he'd make things. He looked up when he saw her, his eyes bloodshot from exhaustion and worry.

"Did you see Abby? I mean, it's crazy. She's freaking out. She's convinced herself that Lily will hate her if she finds out about us."

"You know how Abby is," Eve began.

"Fucking crazy?" he said. Frustrated, Wes stopped himself. "I didn't mean that. But we're having a kid together. That has to count for something."

"Abby needs some time. They both do."

Wes was pissed. She could see that, but he fought to control it. Eve had always admired that trait, one she'd witnessed over and over again throughout the years.

She knew it was a defense mechanism, a way to protect himself. Wes was a good kid in spite of the shitty hand he'd been dealt. His mother died when he was in middle school, and he'd been raised by his father. Joe wasn't a mean drunk, but he wasn't equipped to be a single dad. He was basically worthless when it came to raising his kid or holding down a job. Eve knew that was part of the reason Wes had spent so much time at their house, a place with a semblance of order and normalcy. She often thought that Lily was Wes's salvation, that she'd helped fill the void in his life. At first it bothered her that Lily and Wes had been so serious. "They're too young," she'd tell Dave. But Wes was such a good kid she couldn't really object.

After Lily's disappearance, Wes was still there. Eve had watched Abby transform into someone she didn't quite recognize. One day Abby was getting busted for shoplifting paint and ditching school. The next, she was catatonic, refusing to leave her bedroom or speak to anyone. Abby had been angry with Eve for so many things. Dave's death. Eve's terrible decisions when it came to men—and there'd been many. Wes was Abby's savior, pulling her from the brink time and time again.

When Abby and Wes had started dating—or whatever they called it these days—Eve was grateful, willingly relinquishing responsibility. A twin should never be alone. They come into this world with a partner. If Wes was willing to fill Lily's void, Eve wasn't going to stop him. She'd let it continue and then right before high school graduation, Wes arrived at the hospital and knocked on Eve's office door. They'd gone for coffee in the commissary, sat at the same table she and Dave had eaten countless meals at—Dave the handsome ER doctor, Eve the paper-pushing hospital director. Wes was nervous, playing with an empty sugar packet as he stared down at the table.

"I got into Penn. Full ride," he'd said.

Eve beamed like a proud mother. "That's amazing, Wesley. Congratulations."

But Wes wasn't celebrating. In fact, he appeared tormented by this opportunity.

"I'm not sure I should go. I mean, Abby's staying here, and I...I don't know."

His thoughtfulness touched Eve. But she also felt ashamed. She'd failed him. This kind, sweet boy had done his part. It wasn't his responsibility to keep Abby from falling apart. That was Eve's job.

"Stop it, Wes. I know how hard you've worked for this. How much you've accomplished in spite of your circumstances."

"I know. It's just Abby..."

"She will be fine. I know you love her, but listen to me. You cannot give up your future for her. You deserve this. You're going to do this. You hear me, don't you?"

He'd left, seeming tormented by the weight of his decision. Eve had been certain that he would stay, that his sense of obligation would be too much, but he'd headed off to college that fall. Abby had faltered at first, but eventually she got her act together. She'd returned to school and finished her LVN degree. She'd started seeing a therapist. But the cracks were still there. The binge drinking. The pills. The casual sexual encounters. The hospitalizations.

When Wes returned, when they'd seen him at the TGI Friday's, Eve knew instantly that there was unfinished business between the two of them. She hadn't been thrilled about the pregnancy. They were still young, and Abby's sobriety was precarious. Still, there was a small part of Eve that hoped the baby gave Abby a reason to get her act together. But it wasn't working out that way.

Wes cleared his throat, waiting for Eve to tell him what to do.

"Eve, I'm as happy as anyone that Lily's back. But Abby can't shut me out."

Eve knew that's exactly what Abby would do if it meant protecting Lily from the truth. But she wasn't going to tell him that.

"Give her a day or two. We'll figure all of this out."

"All right. I'll wait. For now. But I can't just sit around and do nothing. There has to be something you need?" Wes asked.

That's what she admired about Wes. He didn't dwell. He was all forward motion.

Eve had a million tasks looming ahead, but the most pressing was picking up the rest of their family from the airport.

"My parents and Dave's mother are coming in tomorrow at noon. Could you pick them up from the airport?"

"It's done. Text me the flight information. Anything you need, Eve, I'll do it."

"You're a good man, Wes."

He'd never been great at accepting compliments, so he simply ignored her.

"Do me a favor and tell Abby that I love her."

Eve was certain this was the last thing Abby wanted to hear right now, but she owed Wes some peace of mind.

"I will. Hang in there, sweetie," she said.

He left, leaving Eve alone in the deserted lobby. She collapsed into one of the hard-backed chairs. She wanted to see the girls, but she needed a minute. The next thing Eve knew, someone was shaking her. She looked up to see Tommy staring down at her. She smoothed her hair, knowing she was probably a complete and total disaster. Tommy didn't seem to notice. He shuffled his feet, hat in hand. She recognized the tense expression on his face.

"What's wrong?"

"I wanted you to hear it from me. They've sent in the FBI to oversee the case. They're not real happy with how things went down today at the school. I tried telling them I had no choice, that we played things Lily's way, but there's a chance I'll be benched."

"That's crap. You know that's crap." Eve could barely contain her anger. Tommy had been there all these years, tirelessly working on the case, and now the FBI wanted to swoop in. "This is your case. I'll fight. I'll put up a fight."

He held up his hands. "You need someone impartial. I hate the guy, and they probably know that. I'll still be involved, I just won't be calling the shots."

Eve went to shake his hand, but she somehow found herself wrapped up in his arms. He hugged her tightly, and she breathed in the masculine smell of cologne and sweat. She held on for longer than she should have, and he finally pulled away. There was something else he wasn't telling her.

"What is it? What's wrong?" Eve asked. "I can handle it. Just tell me."

"There are half a dozen videos online of Rick's arrest and Abby's meltdown so far. It's officially gone viral. Excuse my French, but it's a goddamn shit show. You need to be prepared."

Eve grabbed the chair to steady herself.

"I can't deal with that, Tommy. Neither can the girls."

"I know. I'll do everything in my power to keep you shielded from it."

She saw the kindness in his eyes, the kindness she'd

seen that first day when he'd stood in her kitchen and swore that he'd find her child.

"I've got to meet the feds at Hanson's cabin, but if you need anything, Evie, you still have my number."

"Of course."

They stared at each other, their silence saying more than words ever could. He finally left and Eve was alone again. Profoundly alone. She kept thinking about what would happen with Lily and Sky. How would they all navigate the Wes and Abby situation? Rationally, Eve knew that tomorrow would bring on more challenges than she'd ever imagined. But right now, Eve was going to focus on all of her blessings. She'd been reunited with Abby, Lily, and Sky. She had a granddaughter. The rest of it was meaningless. Her life, her girls' lives were going to be perfect from here on out. It had to be.

LILY

Where is he? Where is Rick? That was Lily's first thought when she opened her eyes at dawn. She frantically scanned the room for him, the way she always did when she woke up. She'd learned to wake early in order to prepare for any shift in Rick's mood or temperament. Maybe she'd never stop feeling this way, this sliver of terror she'd confront at dawn before her real life could begin.

Sky lay curled up in Lily's arms. They'd had a full house last night. Abby lay snoring on one side, Sky on the other, and her mother sleeping on the other hospital bed. Only Mom was gone now. All that remained on top of the bed were the folded blankets and a stack of pillows. Lily glanced around nervously until she spotted a piece of paper on the hospital's bedside table.

"'Went to get a few things for my girls. Be back soon. Love, Mom.'" Lily read the message aloud, clutching the note in her hand, running her fingers along the familiar cursive scrawl. *Love, Mom.*

Lily's eyes filled with tears. She couldn't bear the thought of losing her mother or sister again. She had to fight to keep the bad images from worming their way in. She stretched, her muscles aching from yesterday's run, and she slowly eased herself out of the bed, careful not to wake Sky or Abby. Quietly, she made her way over to the window.

Lily had been so consumed with keeping Sky safe, with making sure that Rick was caught, that she hadn't had time to really take everything in. But now, in the early-morning hours, Lily stood watching the sun as it began to make its way over the horizon. Lily had missed thousands of sunrises, and now here she was, gazing at the glorious start of a brand-new day. Bursts of golden yellow, burnt orange, and splashes of red all mingling together—a sunrise so picturesque that it couldn't possibly be real. Below her, the city was coming to life. Nurses huddled together outside sucking on their cigarettes. Worried family members paced back and forth, talking on their cell phones. But not a single one of them seemed to notice the unimaginable beauty unfolding around them.

Pay attention, Lily thought. All of this could be taken from them in an instant, and no one cared. *That's not true*, Lily told herself. *I care.* There was nothing she cared about more than this sunrise, and then it struck her. This wasn't a onetime thing. Lily would see the sun rise again and again. She had a lifetime of sunrises ahead of her.

Lily pressed her forehead against the cool pane of glass and imagined sunbathing in the backyard until her skin turned golden brown. In the spring, she would lace up her sneakers, and with the scorching sun beating down on her back, she would run until her lungs ached. There were so many possibilities now. She could do all those things and more. She was free.

Lily would have stood there forever, but the nurses arrived to take more blood. Abby woke up, more than a little groggy. When her gaze met Lily's, her face broke into a huge grin.

"Thank God it wasn't a dream," Abby said.

"I know. That's exactly what I was thinking."

They shared another smile, and then Carol appeared.

"Carol, I told you to get lost."

"Since when are you my boss? I picked up an extra shift, smarty-pants. Now, are you coming with me to get a clean bill of health, or do I need to call for reinforcements?"

Abby sighed, turning to Lily. "The vultures need to poke and prod me and make sure I don't belong in the loony bin. Will you be okay?"

"I'll manage. But hurry back."

"You know I will."

Abby slowly made her way out of bed as Dr. Amari arrived, carrying a giant white teddy bear, a lopsided purple bow tied around its neck. Abby motioned for Lily to help her into the waiting wheelchair. As Lily stepped closer, Abby spoke in a whisper, obviously not wanting Dr. Amari or Carol to hear.

"Watch out. That woman wants to interrogate you. To make sure you're not crazy."

"And if I am?"

"You'll be in good company," Abby said, contorting her face.

Lily laughed loudly, and the sound surprised her yet again. After all she'd endured, how was it possible that laughter could come this easily?

"I won't be long. Isn't that right, Carol?" Abby asked again as if to reassure them both.

"Trust me, Lily, your sister will chew those docs a new one if they try to dillydally. We'll be back before you know it."

They left and now it was just Lily and Dr. Amari. Sky, thumb in her mouth, was still sleeping peacefully.

"They need to draw some more blood," Dr. Amari said, gesturing to the teddy bear she'd brought as a bargaining chip. Lily wasn't sure if it was the surprise of waking up in a new location, or the prospect of more tests, but the instant Lily woke her, Sky began to wail. Luckily for Lily, Dr. Amari came prepared. "I thought Sky might like this."

Sky surveyed the bear's bright eyes and lopsided smile. A grin slowly spread across Sky's face as she pulled the bear close to her.

"Mommy, can I keep this one?" Sky asked hopefully.

"Of course, Chicken."

Lily smiled at Dr. Amari. It seemed even a child raised in captivity wasn't immune to bribery.

"What do you say, Sky?"

Sky appeared to be thinking hard, her brow wrinkling. She finally stared right at Dr. Amari.

"Thank you very much."

Dr. Amari smiled, and Lily knew without a doubt that she had raised her child well, in spite of Rick. As Sky clutched the bear, the nurses went to work, poking them both. Staring at the stuffed animal, Lily realized Sky could have anything she wanted now. Rick didn't believe in spending money on frivolities. His money had to stretch—something he'd told her over and over again when she requested anything that wasn't on his approved list. There were no limits now. Lily was in charge of their destiny. There were so many things she wanted. Music. Movies. Clothing. Her own clothes and underwear. She imagined what it might be like to buy whatever she wanted. She was both excited and overwhelmed at the prospect.

After breakfast, eggs and toast, simple, basic things since they weren't used to rich foods, Lily and Sky both dozed off. Lily woke to her mother returning, loaded down with bags from the local Walmart, bags filled with jeans, T-shirts, underwear, and brand-new sneakers.

"I'm sorry I left, but I wanted to get you and Sky a few things."

Lily smiled with gratitude. It was like her mother had read her mind. Lily ushered Sky into the bathroom and dressed her in a pair of jeans and a bright pink fuzzy sweater that Sky vowed never to take off.

Lily dressed herself, loving the bagginess of the black V-neck sweater that hung over her small frame, and the comfort of the dark blue jeans. Lily threw her hair up in a bun and headed back to the room with her family.

Abby had returned by then as well. She also wore fresh clothes—a gray maternity dress and leggings with knee boots. She'd combed her hair, and her lips were stained with pink gloss. Lily thought she'd never seen her sister look so confident and strong. Her full, round cheeks glowed, and her eyes shined brightly. Yesterday, Lily had been struck by Abby's weight gain, but today, her sister reminded her of a Botticelli painting. All glorious curves and round edges.

Abby took out her iPhone and started snapping photos of Lily and Sky. Mom requested a group photo, so they called Carol in. Everyone gathered around looking at Abby's phone, inspecting the photos, which continued to get sillier and sillier. Lily couldn't believe how small and compact the phone was.

"We'll get you one, Lily," Eve offered up. The thought made Lily uncomfortable. Who in the world was she going to call?

Sky was fascinated by the phone too. She couldn't stop staring at it, touching its buttons, looking at herself on the camera screen. She kept on posing and smiling and saying cheese. Lily was almost able to forget where she was, until Sheriff Rogers arrived.

"Morning. Sorry to interrupt."

Eve jumped up quickly. "It's okay, Sheriff. Come on in."

Sheriff Rogers entered and gave everyone a courteous nod hello. "Lily, Eve, and Abby, I'd like to introduce Agent Janice Stevens from the FBI and her colleague Dr. Lynda Zaretsky. Agent Stevens has been nice enough to take over this investigation."

Lily realized the sheriff wasn't in charge anymore, and she turned her attention to the two women. Agent Stevens was tiny, immaculate in her appearance, her black hair tied in a severe bun. Dr. Zaretsky was at least five ten, statuesque with an athlete's build.

"Lily, we appreciate you speaking with us today," Agent Stevens said. "The doctors have said that you're ready to be discharged, but it's important that we get your statement on the record before too much time passes. Would that be okay?"

"Yes, of course. I want to make sure you know what Rick did. That everyone knows…"

"They will, Lily. The hospital has been kind enough to let us use one of their conference rooms for our interview. We'd like to record the proceedings for evidence. Would that be okay? Do we have your permission to record it?"

"Sure. I mean, yes, you have my permission," Lily said, feeling awkward and uncertain.

"Good. My colleague Dr. Zaretsky will be conducting the interview. She's a forensic psychologist and consultant with the Federal Bureau of Investigation."

"It's nice to meet you, Lily. Is there anything you need before we head downstairs?"

Lily took a moment to consider this. She kept imagining others she'd encounter: doctors, policemen, a kindly janitor lurking in the shadows, waiting to steal her away just like Rick. Lily wanted to run again, to take Sky and go someplace no one else could find them. But then she remembered Rick's warning, "You've made a big mistake," and she had to prove him wrong. This was her chance. The world needed to know who Rick Hanson was. No matter how difficult it was, Lily had to tell them.

"I'm ready."

Her throat grew tight when she realized that Sky couldn't hear what she had to say. Sky knew that Rick sometimes made Lily cry, but she always blamed herself, always said she'd been naughty. It was all the other things Sky didn't know about Rick and who he was. Things she'd hoped her child would never know about.

"Sky, Mommy needs you to be a big girl and stay here with your grandma Eve. Can you do that?"

Lily tried to convince herself that Sky was okay, that she wasn't affected by all the changes that had happened in the last twenty-four hours. But something in that moment triggered Sky and she lost it, her terror on full display.

"No! No! No! Don't leave me. Please, Mommy. Don't leave me," she screamed out. Sky clung to Lily, and Lily realized that for the first time ever, Sky had disobeyed her. But Lily couldn't expect Sky to function in the real world as she had in confinement. She stared at her weeping daughter, feeling lost, as if she was failing as a parent in the most public way possible. Mom appeared and sat down beside them on the bed. She spoke to Sky in a soft, soothing voice.

"Sky, listen to me. We'll go downstairs with your mom. We'll sit right outside and you can watch her through the windows. If you get scared, all we have to do is knock and she'll come right outside."

Lily was transported back to her own childhood. This was the mother Lily remembered. The powerful, commanding presence that made the bogeymen disappear. Sky was considering this proposal but she wasn't sold yet. Eve continued.

"And while we wait, you and I can take more pictures of you and your friend bear. What do you say? Can we do that?"

Sky frowned, still unsure. Lily offered her daughter an encouraging squeeze. "I don't want to leave you either, but I have a very important job to do. I need you to be Mommy's brave little girl."

Sky bit her lip, her tiny brow furrowing so deeply she appeared much older than her six years. She leaned into Lily. "If you get scared, Mommy, I'll be right outside."

Lily's heart burst. She longed to pull Sky back into her arms. Instead, she allowed Eve to pick Sky up. Lily mouthed *thank you* to her mother, and they all made their way downstairs, a somber parade of people.

Outside the conference room, someone had already set up a row of chairs. Eve promptly settled on one of them, pulling Sky onto her lap. Lily hovered nearby, staring inside the room at several male FBI agents setting up their video equipment. Dr. Zaretsky and Agent Stevens joined the other agents, a briefing clearly taking place. Lily's stomach churned, but she forced herself to remain calm. *Clear your mind*, she reminded herself. *Control your breathing. This is just a temporary state.*

"We're ready for you, Lily," Agent Stevens said, returning to where Lily was waiting.

Lily reached for Abby's hand and pulled her forward.

"I'm afraid we don't allow family members in these interviews. This is very sensitive subject matter and it can be...it can be difficult, " Dr. Zaretsky said gently.

"She's coming with me," Lily said, her tone surprisingly defiant. She stopped to look at Abby. "Unless you don't think you can? After yesterday..."

"No. I'm fine. I want to be there for you, Lil, but I don't want to ruin anything. I'll just wait here." Lily turned back to the agent.

"Then I want Abby with me."

The agent was calm but firm.

"Lily, we understand where you're coming from, but..."

"I said I want Abby with me. Or you don't get your interview."

Lily stared at them, a sense of pride welling up inside. With Rick, she'd never talked back, never considered defying him, especially once Sky was born. But she wasn't going to let anyone tell her what she could do. *This is the new Lily*, she told herself. *Remember this when anyone tries to break you.*

"I see. Can you give us a moment?"

"Of course." Lily watched as Agent Stevens and Dr. Zaretsky conferred privately. Lily knew they would give in. They had to. Catching Rick was too important. She hated being difficult, but Lily simply couldn't stand to have anyone else telling her what to do. Dr. Zaretsky returned moments later. "If you're ready, let's get started," she said, and gestured for both girls to follow her.

Still holding Abby's hand, Lily entered the conference room filled with floor-to-ceiling windows and a giant open space. It was twice the size of Lily's former home, but Lily couldn't think about that now. It would be dangerous to constantly compare her two different lives.

As Lily settled into one of the hard-backed chairs, the other agents slipped out of the room. Agent Stevens settled into another chair nearby while Dr. Zaretsky closed the door. Lily had to fight the urge to make sure it wasn't locked, make sure that she could leave anytime she wanted.

"Lily, we cannot express how sorry we are for what you and your daughter have endured. But we are so glad you are here and that you escaped. We want to make sure the person responsible for your abduction is punished," Agent Stevens said sympathetically.

"We've located Rick Hanson's cabin, and we're collecting evidence, but we need your statement. Making this case stick means we have to act fast. We can take breaks if you need to, but—"

"I'm ready. I've been ready."

Dr. Zaretsky took over.

"I'm a child and adolescent forensic interviewer, or a CAFI for short. I consult with the FBI on cases in which children were abused or kidnapped. I have a background in social work and a private practice in upstate New York where I work with victims of abuse. Do you have any questions about my role in your case?"

"So your job is to interview people like me, to hear our stories about what people like Rick do?"

"Yes."

"And are there a lot of people out there like me? People who've been through what I've been through?"

Lily could see Dr. Zaretsky's wheels turning, trying to assess the right amount of information to share.

"There are a lot of sick people out there. But there are also a lot of very brave children and young women like yourself."

The answer was appropriately sympathetic. *What a terrible job*, Lily thought. *Listening to people recount their most degrading experiences day after day.*

"My job is to listen and to make sure that the courts and the lawyers have your testimony on record. If at any time you need to take a break or you have to stop, all you have to do is say the word. Got it?"

"Got it."

"If you were to start from the beginning, to think about Rick Hanson and how it all began, what do you first remember?"

Lily thought back to ninth grade.

"Rick was my English teacher freshman year. He was one of those teachers that made even the most boring subjects fun. Like if he were talking about Chaucer, which is just weird, you know, he'd make it fun. And he'd always compliment me, 'Wow, Lily, blue really is your color, isn't it?' Or, 'With a smile like that, who needs the sun?' He'd rave about my book reports, always telling me that I was one of his smartest students."

"And you liked it when he said those things?"

Lily's cheeks flushed, remembering how much she'd enjoyed his attention.

"Before I started dating Wes—" She paused,

realizing that no one here besides Abby knew anything about Wes. "Before I started dating my boyfriend Wes, I used to imagine what it might be like to date Mr. Hanson, to hold his hand and have him tell me I was pretty. I mean, that was before I had a boyfriend. It was a silly crush, a distraction from school." Those fantasies made Lily sick now, but it wasn't like she considered Rick as an option. "All the girls had crushes on him. We'd wear lots of makeup to his class and we'd fight to sit in front. He was cute, I guess, if you like that type."

Dr. Zaretsky interjected, "When you say 'that type,' Lily, what exactly do you mean?"

Lily was searching for the right words, when Abby spoke up.

"Mr. Hanson was like a movie star. Magnetic and confident," Abby said. "He had this charisma. People said he resembled a young George Clooney without the salt-and-pepper hair. He was cool. He acted like one of us, always dressed really well: the only teacher who wore designer jeans and rock concert T-shirts. He'd talk about getting drunk and partying with his wife and their friends on the weekends. It was like he was one of us."

Dr. Zaretsky's attention was still focused on Lily. "So, Lily, Rick Hanson never gave you a reason about why he targeted you specifically?" Dr. Zaretsky asked.

Abby leaned forward, wanting to hear the answer as much as anyone else.

"No. I don't know why he chose me. I wish I did."

"I made it easy for him, that's why he took you," Abby said.

Lily raised a questioning brow. "Abby, what are you talking about?" Lily asked.

"I left you that day at school. I should never have left you." Lily was still confused. Abby continued. "If I hadn't been mad about that stupid sweater—"

"What?"

"It was my fault, Lil."

"Stop it, Abby. Stop."

"But if I hadn't—"

"He decided way before that. Months, maybe even a year before. He said he'd always wanted a teenage girl. Someone he could mold."

"What was the distinction, Lily? Why pick a high school girl?" Dr. Zaretsky probed, leaning forward, her eyes filled with compassion.

"I hadn't been ruined by the world yet. I was pure. Untouched. That's what he said later. His wife wore yoga pants. She didn't shave her legs. She got annoyed if he stayed out too late or had one too many beers at the Rotary Club barbecue. She talked back. When she was having her period, she didn't want to have sex. Her weight fluctuated, and she didn't listen to him when he told her how she should dress or style her hair. And I was all his. A girl who would never say no. I was the girl who obeyed his every request. I was his perfect, obedient baby doll."

This terrible truth hung in the air. Dr. Zaretsky looked at her notepad again. Lily wondered if there was anything on it, or if the woman kept it there to buy her time when things got too uncomfortable.

"Do you know how long it was from the time he decided to take you until he actually acted on his desires?" Dr. Zaretsky said after a few moments.

"He'd said he bought the property when I was a freshman, right after he decided that we were meant to be together. He spent months leading up to when he took me, shopping every weekend, buying furniture at swap meets, painting, putting up wallpaper. Once that was done, he went to thrift stores, bought clothes he liked, vintage dresses, evening gowns, day dresses, sexy lingerie, an entire wardrobe just for me."

Lily paused, searching for water. She spotted the nearby pitcher and poured herself a large glass. She gulped it down, grateful for a break.

"He installed soundproofing so no one could hear my cries for help. He installed locks. When I arrived, the room had bare essentials. A bed. Blankets and pillows. A hot plate. Anything else I wanted or needed he used as bargaining tools. Books, music, and food were rewards during what he called 'training sessions.' Good behavior earned rewards. Bad behavior resulted in varying degrees of punishments."

"Can you tell us what kind of punishments?" Dr. Zaretsky asked.

"Jesus, use your imagination," Abby said.

"I realize this is incredibly difficult to discuss, but we need details. They are crucial in building a solid case."

Abby was twisting her hands back and forth nervously. Lily reached out and stilled them.

"Broken bones. Rape. Starvation. More beatings. The abuse varied, depending on his mood, or, as he liked to say, 'the severity of the infraction.'"

Lily could do this. She was strong enough to do this. She thought back to the fight she'd gotten into with Abby and the voice mail she'd left for her mother. After she'd hung up, she'd figured her mom would show up, annoyed and ready with the standard "Why can't you girls get along?" lecture. At a little before six o'clock, she'd seen Mr. Hanson, his leather backpack slung over his shoulder. He'd approached her in the quad, looking concerned.

"Lily, it's getting late. You okay?" he'd asked.

Lily had sighed and gestured to her crutches. Without her sprained ankle, she'd have just jogged home, always eager to improve her time. But that day she was stuck at school, at the mercy of her parents to come get her or Abby to feel guilty and return to pick her up.

"They should really make these things motorized. It'd be much more effective."

"Where's Abby?"

"We had a fight, and my mom isn't answering her cell. But I left her a message. She should be here soon."

141

He'd glanced at the deserted parking lot. Lily realized later that he'd been weighing his options. Calculating the risks.

"I could give you a lift. You're over in Crested Glen, right? It's on my way."

Lily was instantly relieved. Midterms were a few weeks away, and she had a long night of studying ahead of her. And she'd loved Mr. Hanson. Everyone did. She'd stood up and followed him to the faculty parking lot. She'd never once noticed the crisp fall air or the last glimmer of the sun before it sank into the horizon.

"I should have taken it all in, but why would I? Who notices seasons when you're sixteen and absorbed with the truly important things like dating and track meets and pop quizzes? There was always another season, another sunset or full moon or snowfall right around the corner. But if I'd known that was my last taste of fall, I'd have savored every second, inhaled the smell of burning leaves in the distance, studied the pine needles that covered the grounds. Instead, I grabbed my crutches and blindly followed him."

Everyone waited to hear what she'd say next.

Lily had thought about that moment endlessly. Replayed it over and over. What if she'd said no thanks? Or what if Mom or Dad had pulled into the parking lot just then? What if she had told Abby she'd find the sweater instead of letting the fight spiral out of control? What if someone had seen her getting into Mr.

Hanson's car and said hello? Maybe he would have dropped her off and wished her a good night.

"I climbed into his Mercedes and commented on how awesome his stereo system was. Foreigner's 'Juke Box Hero' was on the radio. I'd never heard of them, which he thought was hysterical. He said I needed serious schooling when it came to music. I joked that he should teach a class. When the song ended, he switched off the radio. We talked about the upcoming winter break. My sprain would be healed by then and I was excited about our annual trip to Whistler. I was so busy talking that when he passed our subdivision, I was sure it was an accident. I told him he'd missed my turn, but he didn't react. He started talking about how pretty I was, how well I carried myself, that I was different from the other girls. Warning bells were ringing in my ears. And I thought that was crazy because this was Mr. Hanson." Lily's voice trembled.

"We can take a break," Dr. Zaretsky said.

Lily didn't stop. She couldn't. She had to get this out. "I told him he could turn around at the next stop sign. But he didn't react. It was like he wasn't even listening. 'I'm a firm believer in luck. And today is our lucky day.'"

She'd been trying to wrap her brain around what was happening. Mom and Dad had gone on and on about strangers, about the differences between good and bad people. She'd watched *Dateline* and *Law and Order* with Abby, shows that turned real-life tragedy into packaged entertainment. Lily wasn't naïve. She knew what could happen when you trusted the wrong person. But this was Mr. Hanson, for God's sake.

"I remember how Rick smiled. But it wasn't a real smile. Something about it said, 'You have every right to fear me.' It felt like he was silent for ages, and then he spoke. 'Lily, I realize this might not make sense at first, but after we've been together awhile, you'll understand. I don't expect you to love me right away, but one day, you will.' When he said that, I thought I was going crazy. My heart was racing. Blood pounded in my ears, and my vision turned spotty. I realized there was something very wrong with Mr. Hanson. Something dark and twisted. I knew I had to get away. I pulled at the door handle, but it was locked. I clawed at it, begging him to stop the car. I grabbed my phone but he was one step ahead of me. He smashed it against the dashboard. By then, I knew I was in serious trouble. I was crying. He pulled the car over to the side of the road, and I begged him to let me go. He kept whispering for me to be quiet, ordering me to be a good girl. But I couldn't stop crying. And then he back-handed me across the face."

Lily remembered the force of that first blow. "I'd never been hit before. Blood poured from my nose onto my cream blouse. I remember thinking that it was ruined and how I'd used two months of babysitting money to pay for it. It was so stupid. I was still crying but Rick stared at me. Unaffected. No sympathy. There was never any sympathy. His face was like granite. Perfectly carved. Emotionless. And then he laid out his rules. Crying was forbidden. Running was forbidden. Leaving was forbidden. 'I will never kill you, Lily,' he'd said. 'I love you too much for that. But if you break my rules, you will pay.'"

Lily took a quick breath but kept going. "I knew he was serious the minute he said he loved me. The minute he dragged me into his sick and twisted dungeon, I knew with all my heart he meant what he said. When I woke up, I didn't know where I was. The basement was so dark and cold. He said this was our new home. He'd handcuffed me to the bed, completely naked. He told me I would be reborn. That my *training* would begin. I spent months cuffed to that bed. He didn't unchain me until he decided I'd made appropriate progress. Until I agreed with him, convinced him that we were meant to be together. Six months chained to that bed. Six months!"

Lily could feel Abby trembling beside her and she wished she'd listened to Agent Stevens when she'd said no family was allowed. But it was too late now. Lily wasn't thirsty, but she gulped water down, needing a moment to gather her thoughts. The training, what really went on in the training, she could never discuss with anyone. She wasn't sure she could even put into words what she'd endured. Her only escape from his demands, from the brutality he inflicted upon her, was remembering the people she loved. No matter what Rick did, he could not steal her memories.

When he came for her, Lily retreated to the past, replaying her spectacular moments like they were her favorite films. Her eighth birthday when Abby shook her awake, the two of them rushing downstairs to find chocolate chip pancakes on the table and brand-new matching pink bicycles in the driveway. The summer night before seventh grade, lying on the grass with Abby, the two of them singing off-key to the *Wicked* soundtrack—"Defying Gravity" their favorite—as they traded who would sing Glinda and Elphaba, and chronicling their celebrity crushes. The homecoming dance, her gold dress and matching shoes causing a sensation among all her friends, and seeing Wes's face light up as he spun her around the dance floor. As time went on, the things Rick did to her were not things she cataloged; they were opportunities to return to her family. Rick had destroyed her future, but Lily controlled her past. But she knew she had to tell them something, that they couldn't build a case on the memories that had helped Lily survive. She took a deep breath.

"Rick liked inflicting pain. He liked knowing that you were in pain, but his power was making you endure that pain without complaint. Pretending that you enjoyed and could withstand whatever he dreamt up. Days passed. Weeks. Months. I'd etch a mark on the floorboard with my nails, tracking how long I was trapped there in that godforsaken room. I covered it with books so he wouldn't see, but every day I looked at those marks, charting how long he'd kept me locked away. And my family kept me going. Mom...Dad." Lily's voice cracked when she spoke of her father, but she ignored it.

"I thought about Abby and my boyfriend, Wes. Some days I imagined that Wes was going to burst through the door and beat up Mr. Hanson and carry me out of that hole, like a superhero. I kept praying that Wes would be the one to save me."

Lily blinked back her tears. Wes had been the perfect boyfriend. The gentle way he'd held her, his tender, passionate kisses, nothing demanding or sinister in his embrace. He was everything Rick wasn't, and when Lily wasn't thinking about Abby or her parents, her thoughts always turned to Wes. He'd given her something pure and innocent to focus on when things were darkest.

But she hadn't asked about him. She didn't want to know what Wes was doing now. It was easier to pretend that he was just a figment of her imagination than to imagine that he'd moved on without her. But when Lily glanced over at Abby, she realized that something was wrong. Her sister was trembling uncontrollably and clutching her stomach. Lily had a devastating thought.

"Wes isn't...He's not...?" Lily tried to speak. "He's alive? Rick, he didn't..."

What if he was dead? What if Rick had punished him because he loved Lily too?

"Abby, is Wes okay?"

"Yes. Wes is alive, Lil. He's...fine..."

Relief coursed through Lily's body. Maybe she'd see him again. Maybe he'd drop everything and tell her how much he'd missed her.

Lily, you're the one. I've been waiting for you all this time.

She realized that everyone was staring at her, and she forced herself to ignore those silly schoolgirl thoughts.

"Once I realized I was never getting away, that no one was coming to rescue me, that I would never see my parents or Wes or Abby, I decided that I would make Rick angry enough to kill me. I wanted him to beat me to death. Or strangle me. I knew he was capable of it. Other days, I thought about killing myself, but it was like he could read my mind. He made it clear that if I were gone, he would need a replacement. He reminded me each day, every moment we spent together, that he was lucky. I had a spare and he would take her if I were gone."

Abby let out a gasp, startling everyone in the room. Lily clutched Abby's hands.

"No...oh my God, Lily. No."

"He already had me, Abs. I couldn't stand the thought of him taking you too. I couldn't stand it."

Abby stood up, clutching her stomach.

"I'm sorry. I can't do this...I'm so sorry, Lil."

Abby burst out of the room, running past Sky and Mom, who looked startled. "We can stop now. If you want..." Dr. Zaretsky said. Lily wanted to make sure Abby was okay, but she had to finish this.

"I'll check on her when we're done. Please, let's keep going."

Dr. Zaretsky resumed her questioning. "When did you realize that you were pregnant?"

"Two years, three months, and twenty-four days from the first day he took me. I realized my body was changing, and I was sure when Rick figured it out, he'd kill the baby. I kept hoping the thing inside me would die before he discovered the truth. I couldn't imagine that he would ever be okay sharing me with someone, even an innocent child. I was so convinced that he would kill my baby that I started thinking of ways to kill it first. And then a few days later, she kicked. I knew she was a girl in that instant. And I loved her more than I'd ever loved anyone or anything. That love made me strong. It made me want to fight to survive. I knew if he hurt this child, I would fight him. I would fight him until he had to kill me. When my baby came along, she was all that mattered."

"And when Rick discovered you were pregnant, how did he react to the news?" Dr. Zaretsky asked gently.

"I'd braced myself, expected him to lose it. I've never been so scared in my life. But when I told him, he smiled the smile that left all the girls giddy and had the teachers and moms gossiping about whether or not his marriage was happy. He kissed me, and then he kissed my belly. 'Don't you see, Baby Doll?' he'd said. 'I told you we were meant to be together. This proves it.'"

"And he never hurt you during the pregnancy? He never assaulted you or tried to harm the fetus?" Dr. Zaretsky asked.

"No. Not once. The abuse...the rapes continued after Sky was born, but our lives during my pregnancy almost passed for normal. He treated me like a princess, buying baby books and new clothes and an occasional toy. He kept suggesting names, but I already knew what I'd call her. It was what I'd missed most locked inside that room. When she was born, she became my Sky. My entire world."

"Lily, did he ever hurt Sky? Was there ever any abuse? Physical or...?"

"No. Never. He never touched her. I wouldn't let him. He didn't..."

She needed them to know she had protected her daughter, that she had done Rick's bidding to ensure Sky's safety.

"Whenever Rick wanted 'alone time,' I'd put Sky to bed. It was a closet. It was small and tiny but separate. That lock on the closet door wasn't his idea. That lock was for me. It was my salvation. She never tried to open it, never came out when I told her that Daddy and Mommy needed grown-up time. I know it sounds strange, that he wouldn't force himself on me, that he didn't do things to me with her there, but in some strange way, he respected his relationship with Sky. I don't think those feelings would have lasted. I'm almost certain of it. But in his own way, Rick loved her and treated her like any other doting father would treat his daughter."

"But he still abused you physically and sexually while Sky was locked in that closet?" Dr. Zaretsky said, her expression not betraying what a horrible question she was asking.

"I kept her safe. You have to believe me when I tell you that."

"Lily, we know you're a good mother. We're not questioning that. But we need to know if Sky had any awareness about what was going on. Did she ever question what was happening? Did she hear you crying or calling out for help?"

"No, okay! No! After a while, you learn…you learn not to cry or scream. But he would have come for her. Not right away, but in a few years, when her body began to change, when she got breasts and hips, when she began to look like the younger, prettier version of me. I could tell he was losing interest. My body was changing. My face. I wasn't a child anymore. And I was so scared, because it didn't matter what he did to me. I had accepted that my body wasn't my own. But Sky…the thought of him hurting her that way would have ruined me. And then yesterday he finally screwed up. He finally screwed up."

"Why do you think, after all these years, he left that lock undone?" Dr. Zaretsky asked.

"I don't know. He always thought he was smarter than the entire world. That he had fooled everyone. He was so proud of the fact that he lived this double life. That he could have me and Missy and the respect of the entire community. And I think he never thought I'd disobey him. He spent so long training me, he couldn't imagine that I would ever go against him. But he was wrong."

Lily exhaled, hoping she was done, hoping she'd told them enough. But the questions continued for several more hours. They'd wanted more details about exactly what Rick did to her, so many details. Horrible, endless questions about their life together, about the cabin, about Rick's life with his wife, whether Lily thought she knew. The answer was no; God, she hoped it was no. When they were done, Lily leaned back in her chair. She couldn't remember a time when she'd been more exhausted.

"We may have more questions later, but we're done for today. You're a very brave woman to have survived what you've survived. I feel honored to have met you. You're a real hero."

Lily blinked, feeling uncomfortable with those words. If anyone had seen how pathetic she'd been at times in that cabin, how weak she was, no one would have called her a hero.

Dr. Zaretsky and Agent Stevens both shook her hand.

"If I have any more questions, I hope we can contact you," Agent Stevens said.

"Whatever you need."

"I'm going to brief your family, let them know that we're done. And then we'll figure out the best way to get you out of here without the press seeing you," Agent Stevens said as she headed for the door, Dr. Zaretsky trailing her.

"Thank you."

They'd almost reached the exit when Lily called after them.

"How is he? Rick, I mean, how...?"

Lily saw Agent Stevens stop. She made eye contact with Dr. Zaretsky and Lily realized how she sounded. Her voice laced with concern, an intimate tone, the way a wife might inquire about a husband. Disgusted, Lily back-pedaled, wanting them to understand what she was asking.

"What I meant was, did Rick say anything about what he did to us? Did he confess?"

"He's not saying a word. They've set a bail hearing for later this afternoon," Agent Stevens said.

Lily's whole body tensed. "Bail? He's going to get bail?"

"There's no way that's going to happen. Hanson's not going anywhere. But he's still entitled to due process. Just trust us when we say that justice is on your side, Lily. You have to believe that."

Lily prayed that was the truth. Agent Stevens and

Dr. Zaretsky both slipped out, leaving Lily all alone. She could see Mom talking to the agent, Sky dozing in her lap. Lily sat there, digesting everything she'd just told them, wanting nothing more than to leave this place. The door opened and Dr. Amari slipped inside. Abby still hadn't returned, and Lily was worried.

"My sister . . . is she okay?"

"Abby's fine, Lily. She just needed some fresh air but she's eager to see you."

Lily stood up.

"I'm ready."

"Wait, Lily, there's something we need to discuss."

Lily knew that there was something wrong, but she couldn't possibly guess what. Rick was locked away; Abby was fine; Sky and her mother were right outside. Lily sank back down into the chair, gripping her hands tightly, trying to imagine what could have this woman looking so disturbed.

"I want you to know that we're all here to help you through this. Whatever you need, whatever you decide, there are alternatives."

Lily was trying to be strong.

"Please just tell me what's going on so I can get out of here."

Dr. Amari sighed deeply.

"We did all the standard tests, blood work, urine samples, and it's confirmed. I'm so sorry to have to tell you this, Lily, but you're pregnant."

ABBY

Abby felt like a piece of shit, but she wasn't capable of hearing any more about Mr. Hanson, about all Lily had endured. She wasn't proud of it, but Abby had rushed outside, gasping for breath. She'd been cornered by Dr. Amari, who steered her away from the reporters who were gathering and had continued on and on with her psychobabble. She'd finally given Abby a few moments alone and now she felt stronger, like she was finally ready to see Lily again.

When Abby made her way back to the conference room, she could see that the FBI agents had completed their interview. But now Abby could see through the windows that Dr. Amari and Lily were deeply engrossed in conversation. She didn't know what they were discussing, but the minute Lily stepped out of the room, Abby sensed that something had shifted in her sister. It wasn't anything she said. She came out of the room, Dr. Amari trailing behind her, and smiled as she scooped up Sky.

"Chicken, you were so good. Now what do you say we blow this pop stand?" Lily asked.

"Yes. Can we go home?"

Lily glanced at Mom and Abby, ignoring Sky's question.

"What do you say? Can we go home now?"

Before they were discharged, Lily and Sky had a final exam with Dr. Lashlee, the general practitioner who had treated them both last night in the ER. She ran through a litany of medical issues due to their malnutrition and prolonged lack of sunlight and vitamin D. Dr. Lashlee gave Lily and Sky sunglasses to protect their eyesight from the harsh UV rays. She also urged them to visit a dentist and ophthalmologist to see what additional damage had been done. Then she signed the discharge papers, and Lily and Sky were finally free.

Hospital rules stated that a patient must be taken out of the building in a wheelchair. Carol wheeled Lily, with Sky curled up on her lap. Mom wheeled Abby out (she'd fought that battle and lost) while Sheriff Rogers led them toward the hospital's employee entrance, which would shield them from the media frenzy that had descended outside.

Something was gnawing at Abby, something that was telling her things weren't quite right. And then it hit her. *Wes.* Lily knew about Wes. That was the only explanation.

Abby was convinced that her mother had opened her

trap, but Mom was too busy trying to buckle Sky into the car seat the hospital had provided. Abby watched as Lily climbed into the backseat beside Sky, her expression revealing nothing. Once Lily and Sky were buckled up in the back, Sheriff Rogers motioned to Mom.

"I'll lead the way. Stay close to me and we'll do everything we can to keep you away from the circus."

Abby tried to ignore the moony-eyed gaze her mother gave the sheriff. She didn't have time for the *Days of Mom's Lives*. Instead she climbed into the front seat, glancing back at Lily and Sky. Her mother navigated the SUV onto the highway, carefully following Sheriff Rogers. Mom prattled on to Lily about new construction and the town's massive expansion project. As if Lily gave two shits about any of that. Sky and Lily were busy staring out at the passing landscape, like aliens on their first visit to Earth. Sky was fascinated by the Amish horses and buggies, peppering Lily with a flurry of questions. Lily answered, but Abby could sense the muted quality in her delivery.

Ten minutes later, their SUV slowly turned into the subdivision and onto their street, and for an instant, Abby forgot about Lily's sudden mood shift. She was too overwhelmed by what she was seeing. It was fucking incredible. There were hundreds of people standing in their yards, in her neighbors' yards, and hundreds more spilling onto the streets. Townspeople of all ages waved signs of support: WELCOME HOME, LILY. GOD ANSWERS PRAYERS. TWIN POWERS ACTIVATE.

"Holy shit. Can you believe this, Lil?" Abby asked.

Lily appeared shell-shocked, her eyes drawn to the massive crowd.

"They can't be here for me. They can't..."

"Of course they are, Lil."

Lily scanned the crowd, and Abby knew she was searching for familiar faces. Maybe even Wes?

"Is that Mrs. Marshall? And the Bakers?"

Abby nodded as they passed Mrs. Marshall, who was waving, tears streaming down as she clutched Mr. Marshall's arm. The kindly elderly couple used to invite them over every Sunday, always armed with their homemade oatmeal spice cookies and teaching the girls "Chopsticks" on their baby grand.

The SUV inched its way through the crowd, several uniformed cops directing them into the driveway as dozens of other officers strained to keep well-wishers back. Abby was scanning the crowd when she saw him. *What the fuck?* There was Wes standing on the sidewalk, one of hundreds in the throng of people. Abby couldn't believe this. Why would he do this to her? Why would he put her in this position? How goddamn selfish could you get?

"It's amazing, isn't it, Abs?" Mom said.

Abby did her best to keep her breathing under control, hoping no one would notice anything was wrong.

She couldn't stop staring at Wes, wondering if Lily would recognize him. He had filled out since high school, but he still kept his hair neatly shorn and was always stylish. Abby shook her head. She couldn't let things go down like this. Even if Lily already knew about them, about the baby, she needed to explain everything. She had to buy time. She turned to Mom, keeping her voice low.

"This is too much. We should go. We can get a hotel room. Get away from everything," Abby said.

To Abby's relief, Mom agreed.

"You're right. I'll drop you both off and get you set-tled, and then I'll come back and pick up Mother and Daddy and Meme. There's a Holiday Inn over on—"

"No." Lily spoke up, leaning forward, gripping the armrest. "I want to stay here."

"Lily, you'll have to walk through all these people. Their questions. The cameras," Mom said.

"I don't care. I've waited so long...too long, to get back here." Lily's voice cracked. Abby thought about arguing with her sister, persuading her to go somewhere else tonight, but she relented. *Stay away*, she silently urged Wes. *Don't screw this up.*

"Mom, just park. We'll protect her from the cameras," Abby said.

Mom shut off the car and climbed out, pushing her way to the passenger side. Abby slipped out of her down coat and climbed out of the car. The crowd roared their welcome, reporters shouting questions as they surged forward. There were so many cameras flashing, Abby was blinking back stars. Dozens of people surrounded them, cell phones raised high, filming the homecoming. Abby realized that everything they did from this moment on would be documented. Chronicled and then dissected for the world to see.

Lily lifted Sky out of the car seat and Abby carefully draped her coat over Sky's face, wanting to block her niece from the media's prying eyes. They headed up the driveway, flanked by Sheriff Rogers and several other officers, who were trying to clear the path. The reporters were relentless, pushing, prodding, and trying to get a reaction.

"How did you get away?"

"What's it like being home?"

"Is Rick Hanson the father of your child?"

Abby wanted to scream at them, spit on them, but she stayed focused, moving at a fast clip, holding on to Lily and Sky, Mom trailing behind. They were on the porch now. Only a few more steps and they could shut out these people, escape their prying eyes and hateful questions. But at the top of the steps, Lily gasped. Abby wasn't sure what had happened until she saw Sky running down the steps of the porch into the crowd.

Lily froze, no doubt caught off guard by Sky's impulsive action. All the reporters and the cameras turned to follow Sky, who kept running. Abby tried to chase after the child, but she was so heavy, her movements slow and clumsy. She found herself swallowed up by the crowd. She struggled to break free when people began to move aside. Abby saw Wes carrying Sky up the driveway. The little girl was wailing, kicking, and screaming. "I wanna go home. I want my daddy!" She pummeled Wes with her tiny fists.

Abby could see Wes's lips moving, no doubt trying to soothe the child. But Sky continued to wail like an animal caught in a trap. The danger resolved, the camera flashes resumed, the screams and shouts grew to an ear-shattering volume, and the mob surged forward, grateful for a new moment to capture.

Abby barely followed what happened next. In a daze, she saw Lily's grateful expression as Wes placed Sky in her arms. Lily didn't seem to notice or recognize him. She just raced into the house, protecting Sky, cradling the child. A moment later, Abby felt Wes's arm around her waist, ushering her inside, Eve whispering for Abby to stay calm.

Abby stood in the foyer, the frenzied crowd outside still audible. Her grandparents nervously hovered in the kitchen. Lily was still trying to console Sky, who was screaming, "I wanna go home. I want Daddy Rick." Each scream pierced Abby's heart: tiny, little pricks over and over again. Mom sank down beside Lily.

"This was too much for her. We should get Sky back to the hospital. I'll call Dr. Amari."

Lily adamantly shook her head. "No! No doctors.

She'll be fine. I just need a few minutes to calm her down. I know I can calm her down."

The wails continued, and no one else moved or spoke. Mom stood, clutching her neck as if it might fall right off her shoulders. Wes hovered near the door, and Abby willed him to turn around and walk out. But he didn't. He was staring at Lily as if she were an endangered bird and he was the savior tasked with rescuing her. Lily still hadn't noticed him. She was too busy rubbing Sky's back and soothing her with calm words, her voice soft and melodic.

"You're going to love it here, Chicken. We're going to be so happy. You trust Mommy, don't you? This is where I grew up and where you'll live now. We're going to be so happy. I promise you that."

Lily kept whispering the same thing over and over until it took on a chant-like quality. Abby wanted to believe Lily's words more than anything.

Before long, just like Lily had promised, Sky grew calmer, her body relaxing. Her eyes began to flutter closed, and she drifted off. Lily's gaze traveled the room. Abby held her breath, wondering what Lily would say when she saw Wes, but Lily was focused on her grandparents, nervously huddled in the kitchen. Lily gently settled Sky onto the sofa, then rushed over to them and they enveloped her.

Grandma and Grandpa Forster were solid midwestern people, never shy about expressing their affection. They covered Lily with kisses and hugs, their voices booming as they told her how much they'd missed her. There was no hesitation on their part, no reluctance. They didn't consider that Lily might not be ready for this much affection. Abby worried that it would upset Lily, that it would be too much, but Lily soaked up their adoration.

After their well wishes, Lily broke away and turned to Meme, their paternal grandmother. When they were little, Dad wanted them to call his mother Mee-maw, but neither one of them could say it properly, and *Meme* had stuck.

Time hadn't been kind to Meme. She'd suffered a double loss—first Lily and then her son in a three-month span. She had never been the same, her heart shattered beyond repair. Bent over, clutching her walker, her portable oxygen tank resting on the seat, her face lit up, reminding Lily of the ballroom dancing photos she'd seen when Meme was young. Lily towered over the older woman, and had to bend down to gently wipe the tears from Meme's wrinkled face.

"I missed you, sweet girl. I missed you so much."

"It's okay, Meme. It's okay. Don't cry. I'm right here. I missed you too..."

"Davey is looking down on you, Lily. My boy is smiling so darn hard right now, and he's wrapping those big, strong arms around you. Around both his girls."

Abby didn't believe in any of that higher-power God bullshit. But just this once, she hoped Meme was right.

Maybe her father was out there somewhere, witnessing this reunion. Lily finally turned around, her gaze landing on Wes, who was still hovering in the doorway. Lily pushed her long blond hair out of her eyes and moved to him. In that instant, Abby knew that Lily hadn't forgotten Wes. If anything, Lily's feelings, like her life, had remained frozen in time.

"Wes, I can't believe it's you. That you're here. I . . . I never thought I'd see you again."

Abby was consumed with regret as she watched Wes move to hug Lily. She flinched almost imperceptibly. Abby wasn't sure if anyone else noticed, but she wondered if Lily was preparing for a blow to the head or a punch to the gut—the kind of punishments Rick doled out. But Lily must have sensed that Wes would never harm her, because she let him hold on to her. Abby saw how perfectly they fit together. She couldn't help but wonder if Wes noticed how slim and lovely Lily was, how good she looked in spite of everything she'd endured.

Abby sank down onto the sofa. Why hadn't she thought about this moment all those years ago when she'd begged Wes to kiss her? When she'd slept with him over and over again? Why hadn't she believed more in Lily? She'd told everyone she met that her sister wasn't dead, and yet she'd still taken what Lily loved most.

Wes finally pulled away from Lily. He nervously cleared his throat. "Lily, we have to tell you something."

Lily stepped back. No one moved. Abby jumped up

from the sofa, eyeing her mother. *Please. Make him stop*, she pleaded silently. Thankfully, Mom stepped forward.

"Wes, now is not the time."

"Abby, we can't do this. Lily needs the truth."

Abby wanted to murder him. She literally couldn't believe he was doing this.

"Wes, please. We'll talk later. When things have calmed down."

Lily glanced back and forth between Wes and Abby. "Talk about what? Abby, what's going on?"

Abby opened her mouth, but no words came out. Wes reached for Abby's hand.

"We're together, Lily. Abby and I are together..."

Abby jerked away from his touch. "He's wrong. We're not together. We were..."

Wes's anger got the best of him, and he forgot about Lily for a split second.

"Jesus Christ, Abby, we're having a goddamn baby. How is that not together?"

Abby watched Lily as hurt, disbelief, and then heartbroken resignation danced across her face.

"Lil, I can explain. I can..."

Lily took a step back, eyeing Abby's swollen belly, then Wes's face, and back again as if trying to put all the pieces together. Abby was crying now.

"Please, Lily, you have to know..."

Stone-faced, Lily moved over to the sofa and picked up Sky. "It doesn't matter. Really, it doesn't," she said.

Abby wanted to tell Lily exactly what happened, but Lily turned her back on Abby and Wes as she addressed the rest of her family.

"I'm not feeling well and Sky's exhausted. I think we both need some rest."

She moved toward the stairs.

"Say we're okay, Lily. Please. I need to know we're okay," Abby whispered as Lily passed her. But Lily didn't say a word as she headed up the stairs.

Abby heard her grandparents and Mom moving around, dissecting what had occurred, but she wasn't listening. She was staring at Wes.

"Abby, I'm sorry, I only came by to check on you, I never meant for it to happen like this. But now Lily knows and we can all move forward. She'll understand. We'll make her understand."

She let Wes wrap his arms around her, let him feel her warmth, breathe in her scent. She hugged him tightly, pressing her body against his, the baby, his baby, pressed against his stomach. She wanted him to feel powerful and strong, like the big man he thought he was.

She leaned in so that only he could hear her. "I will never forgive you. If you come near Lily or me again, you will never see your baby. You hear me, Wes? Stay the fuck away."

RICK

"Yo, Hanson, you piece of shit, you've got a visitor."

Rick sat up from his cot, eyeing the middle-aged, dopey-faced guard with disdain. Rick knew this guard. Fred something. He'd taught Fred's two unremarkable sons, a couple of refrigerator-sized boys who thought they were hot shit because they could tackle other meatheads on a football field. He'd met Fred at Parents' Night and he'd thought he was a prick then, acting like he knew literature when he'd probably never even cracked open a book.

Today, though, Rick saw hatred in the man's eyes. It didn't bother him. There were lots of people like Fred, people afraid of taking risks. They ignored their baser desires, content to live ordinary, unfulfilled lives. Some people were destined to follow the rules; others were outliers, people who eschewed society's moral conventions and went for what they wanted. Rick knew that Lily's accusations would leave him a pariah in the eyes of many, but he was certain he'd have his supporters too. All misunderstood men did. Rick wasn't interested in Fred though.

His attention was focused on the female guard, a trainee, he'd realized, who was in charge of fastening his handcuffs and ankle cuffs. She was a piggish-looking woman with a massive forehead, a weak chin, and a squat body that her polyester uniform only seemed to accentuate. Her bleach-blond hair was long and frizzy, and she was in serious need of professional styling. She was the kind of woman that a man would have to be blackout drunk to take to bed. Rick didn't know her name yet. But she had basically saved his life. If she hadn't stopped his beating, if she hadn't intervened, warned the two men that their jobs were in jeopardy, Rick would have ended up in the ICU or maybe even a body bag. He hoped at some point to get a moment alone with her to thank her, but for now he was focused on his first visitor, his wife Missy. As Fred and the fat-assed guard led him toward the visiting room, Rick was curious to see how this would play out.

Finding a wife had always been a priority. His appetite, his sexual desires were not the norm. He'd been with plenty of girls in high school and none of them even scratched the surface of what he wanted. He was smart enough to know that he needed to be careful. If he was going to indulge—and he most certainly intended to do so—he needed to organize his life in a way that made that possible. Marriage was important.

People trusted a married man. They viewed them as stable. The wedding band itself symbolized responsibility and commitment. It was the perfect disguise. After a brief stint in the army, he'd enrolled in college, using the GI bill to pay his way through school. He enjoyed plenty of the vapid coeds on campus, but as graduation neared, he'd realized it was time to start planning for the future. There were specific requirements for his bride-to-be. She needed to be attractive, but not so much that she would draw the attention of other men. She needed to be sexy enough for them to have an ordinary, active sex life. She needed to be book smart but not intuitive or perceptive or jealous by nature. She needed to have traditional views on marriage and family, and solid religious values.

He was lucky that even in this day and age, large public universities were still breeding grounds for girls with those specific traits. He thought the search for his future wife would be difficult. He'd had to take an elective and there was a psychology and human behavior course that he thought would be an easy A. He'd walked in and Missy instantly caught his eye. She was put together, well dressed, had a moneyed look about her. But it was her eagerness, like an untrained puppy, that really got his attention. Missy always sat in the front row, bombarding the professor with overly simplistic questions or complicating her own answers when called upon. It was clear she'd spent too much time watching

Criminal Minds and *Law and Order*, determined to show her intelligence to the world. Her innocence and lack of intellect made her perfectly suited for his needs.

He'd bided his time, asking fellow classmates about her, observing her at frat parties. Upon further inspection, he saw that she had perfected the art of flirting, knowing how to make a guy feel special with a look or a well-placed touch. She could hold her alcohol—never appeared sloppy or out of control. She'd volunteered with campus ministry and was studying early childhood education. The best part: She was from North Carolina, old money. Her parents were eager to see their only daughter get what she wanted. He couldn't have designed a better future wife if he'd tried ordering her from a catalog. There had been several other candidates, but the other girls were far too eager to spread their legs for any frat bro in sight. From what he'd observed, Missy was genuinely a good girl. If he had to be legally committed to one woman, he could do worse. Once he'd decided she was the one, he'd made his move, approaching her at the student union building. Missy sat alone, her oversized sweater falling off her shoulder as she nibbled on the tip of her pen. Her eyes lit up when he approached. He'd grinned and casually leaned against the table where she was studying.

"Missy, right? I just wanted to say your assessments on attachment theory were really insightful."

Missy was beyond flattered. Her eyes lit up and she'd launched into an impassioned speech about attachment theory and its effect on relationships. Rick patiently waited until she'd run out of breath and a rational argument. He leaned in closer and brushed the hair out of her eyes. He saw the excited glimmer, a look he'd seen with dozens of conquests. He'd known then and there that she was his. If he'd asked her to come back to his dorm, she would have gone willingly. But she wasn't some one-night stand. She was his future wife. He'd wanted to do things right. He'd asked if she was hungry, and they headed over to the Porch, the campus favorite, tucking into a corner booth and talking for hours about her family, about classes, about their future.

He was an English major and an aspiring novelist, but upon graduation he hoped to teach high school. Missy said her parents had been pressuring her to go to law school, but she also wanted to work with children. He'd walked her back to her sorority house and kissed her tenderly. A month later, he told her that he loved her, and eight months after that they were married. She was attractive enough, and the sex was adequate, but mostly, they worked because Missy's trusting nature allowed him to lead a specific kind of life.

Fred and the frumpy nameless guard led Rick down several long corridors and into the secure visiting area. A row of glass windows separated inmates from visitors, a phone connecting the two. He was surrounded by guards, and so was Missy. She didn't notice him at first. She was sitting, staring into space, grief clouding her features. In almost fifteen years of marriage, he'd never seen her leave the house without a full face of makeup, but today she'd made an exception. Her eyes were red-ringed, her cheeks were swollen, and she was wearing a tracksuit, of all things. Rick was beyond disappointed in her.

Missy looked up and saw him. Her hand fluttered to her mouth in that overly dramatic Southern manner she'd never lost. He knew the bruises made him appear monstrous, but he gave a half smile, thankful they hadn't knocked out any teeth. He slowly took a seat, wincing for dramatic effect as he picked up the phone. On the other side of the glass, Missy clutched the receiver, her words spilling out.

"The FBI raided our house. Men with guns came in and they took everything. Computers. My personal files. My cell phone. They ransacked the place. And there are reporters, Rick. So many reporters camped outside on our lawn and more keep coming. Mother and Daddy arrived this morning, but we can't get them to leave. It's all so awful. The things they're saying... what they're saying you did," she said, her voice low, her words running together.

Rick knew Missy wasn't going to listen to his denials, and it wasn't worth his time to try. The minute the DNA tests came back, he'd be sunk. But he needed Missy's help right now. There was only one course of action.

"I'm guilty, Missy. I admit it. I am guilty of wrongdoing."

She stared at him, her eyes widening. *Bingo.* He knew instantly that this was the right play. She had expected him to deny it completely. She expected him to make all sorts of excuses, but he'd hold on to her with honesty, at least for now.

"But I'm not guilty of what they're saying. That girl came on to me. She seduced me. Yes, I admit it, I had an affair. She told me that she wanted me, that she loved me. She said we belonged together."

He let his voice trail off, heard the crack in it.

"You had a child with her," Missy said, her voice thick with hurt and betrayal.

"She tricked me into getting her pregnant. This was all part of her plan. That's why I need your help, Miss. I need a good lawyer. Someone who can make everyone see that I'm not a bad man. That I'm a great husband and teacher and this isn't all my fault. They have to know that there's something not right about that girl. Will you help me, Miss?"

Missy shook her head as if she might be able to shake away everything that had happened. "Mother and Daddy want me to file for a divorce. They say it's the only way to avoid more scandal. The only way I won't look like a total fool."

Rick tried to control his expression. God, he hated her parents. Self-entitled pricks who pampered Missy until she was barely able to care for herself.

"Don't do that. Please. I've made some horrible

mistakes, but you strayed in our marriage too. And I forgave you."

"You're not serious. That meant nothing. You were gone all the time, and I was...It was one night, and I told you all about it. But this...this can't compare. The things you're accused of doing. They're despicable."

Shit. He'd gone too far on that one. He backpedaled. "You're right. I'm making excuses. I love you. Since I saw you that first day on campus, I've loved you."

He saw how much she wanted to believe him, to believe in the life they'd built. He went in for the kill. "I still want everything we dreamt of. I still want us to have children. Missy, I know we could have that life, but I can't do it without you."

He saw her wavering.

"I can prove to you that the girl isn't entirely innocent in all of this. I have proof. I can show you, but you have to stand by me, you have to see me through this."

She stared at him, her eyes brimming with tears. "I have to go."

Rick reared back, shocked by her response. "Missy, wait! Please!"

But she hung up the phone and made her way out. He banged on the window.

"Missy. Don't abandon me. Missy! Missy, please... don't leave me, Missy. I need you."

He pounded on the window until she was gone, the guards dragging him back toward his cell. Rick couldn't believe that bitch wouldn't listen to him, that she wasn't going to help him. He really should have killed her. He shook with annoyance, already forgetting Missy and her dim-witted ways. *Come on, Rick. Be smart*, he told himself. All he needed to do was regroup and figure out a plan. Everything would be just fine ...

EVE

Eve couldn't quite grasp how quickly her joy, her relief at Lily's return, had turned to despair. It wasn't Lily's reaction to the news about Wes that concerned Eve. It was her lack of one. Lily's expression never changed, but her eyes flickered with pain. Before Eve could say a word, before anyone could explain, Lily had rushed upstairs. There was a time when she would have followed Lily. She would have made certain that everything was okay, but something stopped Eve. As difficult as it was to accept, Lily didn't want her right now. She wanted space, and Eve was going to respect her wishes. She also had Abby to think about. Since Wes had left, Abby hadn't moved from the sofa, her expression one of pure concentration as if she were trying to solve a mathematical problem that had no answer. Eve could feel the tension creeping up her shoulders.

"She's going to be okay, Evie. You all are," her mother said, gently patting her shoulder. Her father had a different opinion.

"Phone the doctor, Eve. Tell her that Lily's in trouble. This is all too much too soon. She'll be better off at the hospital."

"Daddy, stop it. You heard what Lily said. Let's give her some time."

"Eve, I think—"

"Daddy, this isn't a discussion."

His face grew red. The older her parents got, the more sensitive they were. Not to mention her father, a CEO of a medical supply company for thirty-six years, was a man used to getting his way. He mumbled angrily under his breath. "Well, maybe we shouldn't be here."

Eve wasn't going to do this. Not now. "Maybe you shouldn't be."

"Now, you listen here, young lady, we came all this way to help..."

"I didn't ask you to."

She hadn't. In fact, she'd told them not to come. She knew they would all need time to figure out what had happened, to reconnect with just the three of them, but her father never took no for an answer.

"I'm not going to let you ignore warning signs while your daughters fall apart," he said.

Eve felt her anger bubbling up. "You think I'm going to let them fall apart? I'm not letting anything fall apart. But this is my house. My family. I'm going to handle this my way. And if that's not acceptable to you, maybe you should just go home."

"So, you're kicking us out?" her father asked, his eyes squinting with anger.

"I'm asking you to respect where we're at."

There was a moment of silence, and then her father stormed out of the room in a huff. Dave's mom moved over to Eve, clutching her arm.

"Don't mind him. You're right. We shouldn't have come, but I had to see our girl again. I'll come back once you've been able to deal with all of this. And listen, I know you're tempted to give everything you have to the girls, but take care of yourself too."

Eve held on tightly to Meme. "You do the same."

Meme turned and headed upstairs. Eve braced herself for a confrontation with her mother, but she surprised Eve.

"Our girls are together. They're safe and you're all together. That's what matters. I'll handle your father. The old goat just hates it when he's not in control," she said.

Eve could hear her father on the phone with his travel agent, demanding a flight out first thing in the morning. Normally, Eve was the peacemaker. She hated when her father was upset, and she'd do anything to fix things. But tonight, she didn't care about his feelings. She was exhausted. She sank onto the sofa beside Abby, knowing they needed to talk about Wes and how she'd treated him.

The TV was on, Abby staring vacantly at it, when a

picture of Lily and Abby at sixteen appeared on the screen. They were doing a story on Lily's homecoming. Eve couldn't believe it. She went to reach for the remote.

"Turn that off."

But Abby refused, cranking up the volume instead.

Lily's image was now magnified on the giant HDTV. That damn photo from the memorial Rick Hanson had helped organize. And then the image cut to Lily today as she reached out to grab Sky from Wes. Eve couldn't help but think that Lily appeared simultaneously like a wounded bird and a powerful warrior. As the camera focused on the over-coiffed reporter, Eve realized that he was standing right outside her house, an expression of extreme concern on his face.

"While friends and family rallied around the Risers today, members of accused kidnapper Rick Hanson's family are standing by his side."

The image changed, and Rick Hanson's wife Missy appeared onscreen. She stood in front of the Lancaster County Jail, surrounded by a sea of reporters. Delicate and weary, in a tasteful but expensive navy dress and pearls, she gave off a respectable vibe, like the wife of a politician. Eve knew that Missy Hanson was a first-grade teacher, exceptionally pretty with long dark hair and a hint of a Southern accent. She'd dropped off a tuna fish casserole after Lily vanished, and sent a card once a year to let Eve know they were thinking about her family and praying for answers. What was she doing on the TV? Eve leaned in, holding her breath as she listened to Missy speak.

"My husband is not evil. I know that would make all of this easier. He made terrible choices but I do believe that there are questions that remain unanswered about the girl he allegedly abducted. In fact, I have evidence that shows there may be a very different side to this story."

Eve lost her breath as Missy held up a photo. The camera zoomed in on a selfie. God, Eve hated that word. It was so pedestrian. But it was clear that's what it was. It was probably a year or two old. Lily's arm was outstretched, grinning as Sky and Rick leaned in. They all wore matching party hats, and cheesy grins. From all appearances, they seemed like an ordinary happy-go-lucky family, not Rick's captives. Eve was so sickened by the picture she had to look away. Abby sat, clutching her belly, staring unblinkingly at the screen.

"I know some of you may have a hard time understanding why I am here, but I took a vow to stand by my husband through sickness and health, and I will honor that vow. I hope you will wait to pass judgment until all the details of the case are revealed. Thank you."

Eve reached out for Abby, knowing that this would rock her daughter to the core.

"It's okay, Abs. No one's going to believe that story. No one," Eve said.

But Abby was up on her feet. She grabbed Eve's keys and raced to the door. Eve tried to block her path.

"Abby, wait... calm down."

Abby whirled around.

"I'm going for a drive. Leave me alone. Just leave me the fuck alone."

Abby burst out of the house, reporters screaming out questions, camera flashes exploding, nearly blinding Eve from the doorway. Eve let her go, hoping she'd cool off. She'd called Wes, knowing he might see the news, hoping maybe he might be able to find Abby and calm her down.

She needed to go to bed, but Eve wandered the house, unable to relax. She cleaned the kitchen from top to bottom, but she couldn't stay in this house for another second. Abby had taken Eve's keys, which was why she found herself calling a cab. She gave him an address around the corner and made her way out through the backyard gate. Eve told herself that she was just going to the Belvedere, her local haunt, that she could drink enough to blot out her worry. But somehow Eve found herself standing outside the Lancaster Police Department. Eve had always hated coming back there, hated the memories dredged up by doing so, but she had to see Tommy and make sure nothing would come of that photo or Missy Hanson's ridiculous claims.

Eve approached the desk, and saw Charlie, the desk clerk. He'd been here since that first night when she'd been questioned, but he never once treated her like a criminal. His kindness was something she hadn't forgotten. He beamed when he saw her, reached out to shake her hand.

"Mrs. Riser, I can't tell you how happy I was, how happy we all were to hear that Lily's okay."

"Thanks, Charlie. We're overjoyed...beyond..."

Charlie's smile faded. "Is something wrong?"

Eve's brave facade was slowly crumbling but she couldn't fall apart now.

"I was wondering if Sheriff Rogers was in. I had a few questions."

"Yes, ma'am. I can take you to him..."

"There's no need. I know the way."

Eve hurried away from his probing gaze. She reached Tommy's office and saw him through the window, hunched over a stack of paperwork, his hat off, a cup of coffee by his side. For a moment, Eve wondered if she should just turn around and go. But it was too late. Tommy glanced up and looked stunned to see her there. He jumped up to open the door.

"Evie, come in. Come in. Are you okay? I mean, I'm sure you're not...I just wasn't expecting you. What brings you here so late?"

"I needed... I needed..." She exhaled and sank into a chair.

He stopped and stared at Eve, realizing why she had come here.

"Look, Rick Hanson is crazy if he thinks those photos can explain away what we found in that hell-hole..." Tommy trailed off, realizing he'd said too much.

Eve knew that she'd been a coward this morning. She had agreed to look after Sky because she didn't have the guts to listen to Lily's confession. But Eve realized if she was going to see Lily and Sky through this, if she was going to go up against Hanson, she couldn't live in ignorance.

"I want to know what happened to my daughter. I need to know."

Pained, Tommy rubbed his face, his hazel eyes rimmed with red, bags drooping beneath them.

"Eve, that's not a good idea. There are things in her statement that a mother should never hear. Trust me when I tell you this."

"Tommy, please..."

"I'd be going against protocol. Again."

"But for me... for me, you'd break protocol?" It was an awful thing to ask, she knew that, and yet Eve didn't care.

Tommy sighed, weighing his options, the responsibilities bestowed upon him. He slowly stood and moved over to close the blinds to his office, blocking out any prying eyes. He reached across the desk, and slid a file folder over to Eve.

"This is the FBI's preliminary report, along with a

catalog of the evidence we collected at the scene. I can give you some privacy, if you'd like."

He went to leave and Eve reached out to stop him. She let her hand linger on his.

"Please. Don't go." Tommy didn't say a word. He moved his hand away and settled back behind his desk. He sat quietly while Eve read the sixty-page report, a detailed account of her child's sexual and physical abuse at the hands of a man she'd considered a family friend. She stopped several times, wondering if she'd made a mistake, wondering how she'd ever get these images out of her mind. When Eve finally closed the report, she thought she might actually throw up. How could someone do this, not just to her daughter, but to another human being? How could she live in a world where there were people capable of doing this? She looked up at Tommy, tears falling in a steady stream.

"Is he here?" she asked him. Eve couldn't even say his name.

"He is. Got the shit beat out of him today, so he's in protective custody."

"Who beat him up?"

Tommy didn't answer, which was answer enough. Eve wanted to shake the officers' hands, thought about offering to make them a home-cooked meal so she could hear every sordid detail of how he'd suffered.

"How bad was it?"

"Not bad enough."

"Nothing will ever be enough. You know that, right?" Eve asked.

"I know, Evie. Trust me, I know."

Eve slowly pushed the report back to him and stood up. "Thank you."

"You need a ride? I can have one of the guys take you."

The images, the things she'd read were battling for space in her brain, making it difficult to think. She opened her mouth to accept his offer, but instead of words, a sob escaped. Tommy wrapped his arms around her and she leaned into him, weeping again for Lily. She cried for Abby and Dave and her parents, and for all the people Rick Hanson had casually destroyed.

"I'm right here, Evie. I've got you. You'll be okay. I'm right here."

Always so kind and decent, she thought, and she knew she was messing with Tommy's life again. He'd made his choice all those years before, and she wasn't it. And yet Eve had still come here; she'd still wanted to see him. She was like one of those runaway roller coasters they showed on the news. Nails and bolts flying off the framing, hurtling into disaster. She was his disaster but she couldn't seem to stop herself. The noise and bustle of the police station faded away. She didn't know how long he held her. She wanted to stay—she would have but her family needed her, and he was not hers. Eve pulled away and grabbed her purse.

"Will you be okay?" Tommy asked.

"I hope so." Eve's hand was on the doorknob when he pulled her back into his arms, his heart racing as fast as hers.

"What are we going to do, Evie?" he asked.

Eve stared back at him. "I have no idea."

ABBY

Abby was analyzing the situation, trying to decide her plan of attack. She had been parked outside Missy Hanson's home, watching the reporters who had gathered here, an even larger horde than the one camped outside Mom's house. It was bad enough that Lily hated her and Wes had ruined everything. But now this...

Abby still couldn't believe the shit she'd seen on the TV. *Allegedly abducted? Allegedly abducted. A different side to this story. Missy is standing by him?* What was wrong with this dumb bitch? Anyone who looked at those photos had to see Lily's terrorized expression, her hopelessness. How could people possibly believe that Lily cared about Rick Hanson? But what if they did? What if Mr. Hanson used this to...No, Abby couldn't let that happen. That's why she was here. She had to speak to his wife; she had to make her understand.

His home wasn't hard to find. Everyone at school knew where the Hansons lived. Located in the richest subdivision, the stately mansion was a gift from Missy

Hanson's parents. Her dowry, he'd joked during their Jane Austen module. Abby jumped out of the car and marched up the steps, making her way through the media gauntlet. She ignored their questions as the press surrounded her like rabid dogs, frenzied at the prospect of a new angle on this sensational story. Abby pounded on the door until Missy appeared, looking flustered.

"You can't be here. You can't. Go away or I'll call the cops."

"Let me in, or I swear to God, I'll make a scene. Let's see how they react when a pregnant woman collapses on your front porch."

Missy's patrician features appeared to be wilting under the pressure of recent events. She surveyed the mob, then slowly opened the door and Abby slipped inside. This was where her sister's tormentor had lived. The decor consisted of muted earth tones, high-end furnishings, and expensive artwork. Missy's parents, her mother in pearls and pastels, her father in a button-down, were flawless. *Like stepping into a Brooks Brothers catalog*, Abby thought. They were sitting at the dining table, but when he saw her, Missy's father stood up.

"Miss, what's going on?"

Missy's mother stood too, wringing her hands nervously. "Edward, this isn't right. She can't be here."

Missy plastered on a tight smile.

"Mother and Daddy, we're just going to have a quick chat. I'll be back in a moment." Head held high, Missy led Abby into the study and closed the door behind them.

"Tell me what you want," Missy said, getting straight to the point.

"Missy . . . God, what a stupid name. But listen, Missy, your stupidity offends me. It offends me and annoys me, and it ends today."

Missy tossed her head, her eyes flashing. "I'm not going to be insulted in my own home. My father was right. You should go."

Missy moved to leave the study. Abby grabbed Missy's arm and held it tightly.

"Every time I close my eyes, I see my sister begging Lancaster's favorite English teacher for her freedom. I see Lily's desperation and loneliness and terror as he rapes and beats her over and over again. You can go on the news. You can go on every talk show with that fake-ass photo, but none of that changes what he did to her. None of that makes Mr. Hanson a nice guy. Mr. Hanson likes to torture little girls. He likes to destroy families and feast on that misery."

"You're wrong—"

"Are you really stupid enough to finish that sentence? I'm not wrong. If you knew what he did, if you heard what he did . . ." Abby's voice cracked. She kept squeezing Missy's arm, taking pleasure in hearing her whimper. "Are you seriously trying to tell me you never once saw a glimpse of the monster that ruined my sister? Not once?"

Missy hesitated. Abby wanted to destroy this woman; she wanted her to pay for what she'd said on the steps of the jail.

"Monsters don't breathe fire, Missy. The monster in this town is a real man who teaches high school English. A man who's kept a sex slave locked in his basement for years, and his wife was too dumb to know about it."

"Stop it. Please, stop it."

Missy had begun to cry, snot streaming from her nose. Abby loved watching this woman crack. She fed off Missy's distress like carrion after a road kill.

"Admit it, you stupid bitch. Admit you knew something was off. You did, didn't you? Didn't you, Missy?"

"Yes... I mean, I didn't know for sure but... but he was gone so much. I knew he wasn't writing a book. And I saw websites. Things he wanted to do. But I thought..."

"That as long as he still put on his V-neck sweater and came home smelling of cologne and chalk dust and told you about his day at work, as long as you still had barbecues with the neighbors and missionary sex once a week, you could forget about what you saw."

"I'm so so..."

"Don't. Don't waste your breath on useless apologies. 'Sorry' is a word. An empty, meaningless word. And what he did, what *you* let him do, can never be erased by a word."

Missy was sobbing uncontrollably now. Her father appeared in the doorway, his face an angry red mask.

"You need to leave."

Abby moved closer to Missy, her voice a whisper. "If you go on TV again and call my sister a liar, I will kill you."

Missy broke down. Abby ignored Missy's father's shouts and threats and headed out of the house.

By the time she climbed back into her mother's car, Abby was grinning. Lily might not be speaking to her. She might not know how much Abby cared. But Abby was going to do whatever it took to make sure these people never fucked with her sister again.

LILY

"Tears are for the weak." That's what Rick always preached. Before Rick took her, Lily was a crier. She cried at anything. Country music. Hallmark movies. A YouTube kitten video.

"My little softie," her father had teased her. But Lily didn't cry over the news about Wes and Abby. The news had stunned her. Wes. Her Wes. Her first love. The boy who—with one look—had made her feel as if the entire world had fallen away.

Lily couldn't stop thinking about Abby's giant belly, her sad eyes and heavy features, the scars lining her wrists. How had all of this happened? How was it possible that her sister had fallen for Wes or vice versa? They'd disliked each other with an intensity that bordered on irrational. Abby kept going on and on about how cliché it was that Lily was dating a jock.

"His only marketable skill is hitting a ball over a net. And he barely talks, like he's some kind of superhero.

He thinks it makes him deep and brooding when it really just makes him an asshole."

Wes thought Abby was a stuck-up bitch and hated that she was always a third wheel. They'd both driven Lily crazy with their stupid bickering, constantly forcing her to take sides. And now they were together. They were having a baby together.

Lily had wanted to scream at Wes, to ask him why he hadn't waited for her. But that wasn't fair. No one, not Abby, not Wes, not even Lily herself could have imagined that she would return home. She knew all of this rationally, and yet the pain was searing.

She'd been lying in bed for hours. Sky was fast asleep but Lily couldn't stop her mind from spinning. She'd never allowed herself to wallow in self-pity, to ask *why me*. There wasn't mental energy to waste dwelling on something she couldn't control. But now that's all she could think about. Why did she get Rick, and Abby got Wes's love and devotion, and his baby? Why did Abby get a nice, kind man? *Because I'm not worthy, that's why*, Lily thought.

Abby got to have Wes's baby, and Lily got Rick's. The thought made her ill, thinking back to those nights Rick would whisper his fantasies as he violated her over and over again. And here she was, pregnant with another child. Rick's child.

"How far along am I?" she'd asked Dr. Amari at the hospital after she'd delivered the news.

"It's early. Only six weeks. You can still terminate."

"You mean kill it?"

"I'm saying there are options, Lily, if you want to discuss them."

But Lily didn't want to discuss anything. She didn't want anything else that would bind her to Rick. And yet, when she thought about the baby, her baby, Sky's sibling, she was paralyzed. This was her child too. Its life was in her hands. If she were still living down in that hole with Sky, she'd have fought like hell to protect it, the same way she'd protected Sky. But things were different down there. Down there, Sky had nothing to do with Rick. Her daughter was a gift, sent from above, a sign that hope could still live on, even in the darkest of places. She didn't know how she'd feel about this child. What if it were a boy? A sweet, young boy, who grew into a handsome young man who followed in his father's footsteps? What if he were evil? What was she supposed to do with a child like that? Lily closed her eyes. They'd been together. Abby and Wes.

Together.

Lily was sickened. One of her biggest regrets was not giving Wes her virginity. Rick stole that from her too. She always wondered what it might have been like, to wake in Wes's arms, to experience everything she'd read in her mother's romance novels or seen on TV. Those tender moments, sweet, romantic kisses, the mutual respect as you discovered each other's bodies.

Those things didn't exist once she became Rick's property. They couldn't exist.

Lily knew she'd never sleep now. She slowly crawled out of bed and gave Sky a tender kiss. She grabbed a sweatshirt and wrapped a blanket around her shoulders. Dr. Lashlee had said she'd feel cold until she put on some weight, and she was right. Lily couldn't stop shivering.

She made her way downstairs, enjoying the comfortable silence. In the kitchen, she beelined for the refrigerator, swinging open the heavy doors. An endless array of options greeted her. Casseroles and lasagna. Chocolate pie. Brownies. Milk and beer. Chardonnay and vodka. Whatever you were craving, it was there for the taking.

In the cabin, Lily and Sky ate whatever Rick delivered. He controlled Lily's weight religiously. "No fatties allowed," was Rick's mantra, which meant treats were nonexistent. She grabbed a piece of fudge from one of the platters and devoured it, savoring the rich, decadent taste. She would have kept eating, but something outside caught her eye. Lily froze. Someone was sitting on the back porch swing, rocking back and forth. She almost screamed, called out for help, but the figure turned. Lily saw his profile. It was Wes. What was he doing out there?

She thought about rushing back upstairs. Locking herself in her room again and cuddling up with Sky. But her curiosity, her desire to know more about him, got the best of her. Lily slid open the sliding glass door just as Wes looked up from the swing, a cigarette in his hand. She felt disappointed by him. The Wes she'd known would never smoke. He'd been vigilant in his training, refusing to do anything that might poison his body. When he saw her, he leapt to his feet, stubbing out the cigarette as if he sensed she might judge him.

"Lily, I didn't mean to scare you."

"No, it's okay. I . . . What are you doing out here?"

"Abby took off after your argument, so your mom asked me to look for her . . ."

"Is Abby okay?" Lily asked. No matter how hurt she was feeling, she couldn't stand the thought of something happening to her sister.

"She came back here about an hour ago, but she's pretty pissed at me. I kept telling myself I should go home but I just couldn't seem to leave. I didn't realize how late it was. I should go."

He gave Lily a quick nod and headed for the back gate. She'd been watching him, analyzing what he looked like now. He was cute, but not as cute as Lily remembered. It was almost as if he hadn't grown into his matinee-idol good looks. His nose was a bit too big for his face, his hair was a little too short, and he had a thick, heavy stubble. But his eyes hadn't changed at all. Deep gray and piercing. God, she'd missed those eyes.

"Wait, don't go," Lily called out.

Wes spun around, startled by her plea. Lily hadn't

considered what she'd say next, so she simply waved. She moved over to the swing where he'd been sitting, and sat down, shivering slightly. Wes shrugged out of his heavy down jacket and handed it to her. Lily wrapped it around her shoulders, his woodsy smell and spicy aftershave overwhelming her senses. Wes hovered a few feet away, still waiting for Lily to speak. She'd grown used to silences, always waiting for Rick to talk, never wanting to speak out of turn. At this very moment, Lily wondered what Wes was thinking about her. She knew that her skin, hair, and teeth had been damaged by her ordeal. She was scrawny, no longer toned or tan from her endurance training. His opinion shouldn't matter, but she still wanted him to think she was beautiful.

"It didn't happen overnight, Abby and I..." he said.

Lily offered up a slight smile. "So that's it? No awkward silences. No 'how've you been?' Or 'how 'bout them Phillies?'"

Wes looked uncertain.

"I'm joking, Wes. I still know how to joke."

He smiled and she was transported to sophomore year and that sweet boy leaning against her locker, grinning as he waited to walk her to class. But Lily wasn't going to let people treat her like she was made of glass, tiptoeing around her. Not anymore. She was going to reclaim every remnant of who she'd been.

"I'm sorry about how I reacted earlier. I...I guess I

never thought about what would happen if we…if Sky and I got out. I spent so much time surviving, so much time thinking about the past, I never considered what was happening out here. And I love…I loved you so much."

He winced and Lily realized how stupid she sounded.

"I'm not making this better, am I?"

"I loved you too, Lily. I still—"

"Don't. Please."

"No, I have to explain, because you can't be mad at Abby. It would kill her if you were mad at her. I have to make you understand what happened between us." He apparently forgot about her judgment, or maybe his nerves got the best of him. Wes reached into his pocket, pulled out a cigarette, and lit it, taking a long drag before he spoke.

"You know Abby drove me crazy. We never thought about each other like that…romantically. All we wanted was to find you. We were obsessed. Consumed. Every day we were putting up flyers, joining the search parties, scouring the forests and woods for hours on end. And then they called off the searches and your dad died, and…Abby was wrecked. By the start of senior year, people didn't want to be sad anymore. I tried to be the Superjock and do all those things I used to love, but without you cheering me on, I couldn't seem to care. I quit the team, and somehow Abby and I started hanging out after school. Everyone treated us like we were made of glass, but we could tease each other and listen to music and talk about you. And then one day, we were watching a movie at my house and talking about that time you hit that parked school bus—"

"And that it was a giant yellow school bus…"

Wes smiled. "How do you miss a school bus?"

"How many times do I have to say that it was in my blind spot?"

He laughed and then caught himself, as if the moment was too solemn for jokes. He continued.

"I don't even know who kissed who. We both freaked out. Didn't talk for days, but by then she wasn't your sister anymore. She was my best friend. She wasn't you, Lily. I wasn't replacing you. Abby was never like you. Never as lighthearted or easygoing, but she did everything with this intensity that made her hard to ignore. Most importantly, she understood how losing you changed me."

"So you've been together ever since?"

"No. I got into Penn. I didn't want to leave her, but we both decided we needed to see what life was like when we weren't both missing you or punishing ourselves for not being able to save you, or for not being the one who disappeared. And then…" He trailed off.

"Then what?"

"I finished school and came back here to take care of my dad, and somehow, we fell back into old patterns."

"So that's all it is now? Old patterns?"

He evaded the question, but Lily realized he never said he loved Abby. He hadn't said it once.

"Abby never stopped believing that you were alive. You have to know that. Anything you want, she'll do it, Lil. She'll leave me. She'll give up our baby if you ask her to."

"That's crazy. I would never ask that. And she'd never do something like that."

"You don't know her. Not now. You don't know what losing you did, what you coming back means to her."

Lily didn't answer. What else could she say? *Leave her. Be with me. We'll raise Rick's children together. We'll have the life we were meant to have.* It was almost impossible, being this close and knowing he'd moved on. If this were Rick, he'd want her to lash out at Wes and Abby. Get even for their betrayal.

He would say, *Make 'em suffer, Baby Doll. They deserve to suffer.*

After all, Wes hadn't simply chosen another woman to love; he'd chosen her twin sister. If she used Rick's logic, it would make sense that she'd want to destroy them both. But Lily was grateful that Rick hadn't completely ruined her. She was still capable of her own thoughts and actions. Wes seemed to understand that Lily had heard enough.

"Good night, Lily. I'm so sorry for what you've been through. But I'm glad you're home. You have to know that."

He disappeared into the darkness. Lily sat on the porch swing, still wearing Wes's coat, inhaling his scent.

She realized what she had to do. She couldn't keep this baby. That was clear now. She was going to call Dr. Amari and set up an appointment. Once she'd taken care of that, she was going to prove to herself that Rick was wrong. She was capable of being loved by someone good and kind. She knew she was. Lily knew what she had to do—she had to make Wes love her. Whatever it took, she would make that happen.

ABBY

The alien invader was kicking up a fucking storm. That's what first jolted Abby out of bed. But it was the smell of coffee and bacon that made her grab her robe and hurry out of the room. She needed to make sure Lily wasn't freaking out about the photos. She made her way down the hall, expecting to find Lily and Sky in their room, but the door was wide open, the bed neatly made. Driven by anxiety, Abby picked up the pace, worried something had happened.

Abby rushed into the kitchen and stopped short. Lily was wearing their father's faded "Kiss the Cook" apron and manning the griddle. Eve was cutting strawberries, while Sky stood on a stool beside her grandmother, watching with fascination. It was as if Abby had entered the twilight zone. She wondered if she'd slept for several days or even weeks, or if somehow the events of last night hadn't occurred.

Eve saw Abby first and smiled reassuringly. "Are you

hungry? Lily wanted to make us all breakfast before your grandparents left for the airport."

"I'm starving. What can I do?"

A genuine smile spread across Lily's face. She waved Abby over.

"You can butter the toast. Eggs are almost done."

Abby took a place beside her sister. "Lily, we need to talk."

"No need. I was so overwhelmed yesterday I wasn't thinking clearly. But I can't focus on the past. It's always been about you and me, Abs. We're good. No matter what."

Abby couldn't believe her ears. Lily wasn't mad. Her sister didn't hate her. Normally Abby hated displays of affection, but this morning she threw herself at Lily, wrapping her arms around her. "I love you so much, Lilypad. You have to know that."

"I do, Abs. I love you too. More than you'll ever know."

Abby stood there, trying to read Lily's expression. It was completely genuine. She had no reason to doubt her sister's intentions, and relief flooded her. Lily squeezed Abby's arm.

"C'mon, let's eat before everything gets cold."

"Breakfast is served," Lily called out as she made her way into the dining room to her grandparents' applause. Sky followed giddily.

Abby cornered Mom.

"Does she know about the photos?"

"Not yet. I meant to tell her, but she's in such a good mood."

"Let's wait."

"Abby..."

"Just a little bit longer. Let's not give him the power to ruin this day."

"Okay," Eve conceded.

She grabbed the jam and butter off the counter and joined the others. Abby couldn't remember the last time her mother had agreed with her, but she'd take this win.

The family ate in the formal dining room. They hadn't eaten at that table in years, but today everyone dug into heaping plates of eggs, bacon, toast and pancakes, and fresh berries. Abby almost couldn't believe it. A family breakfast. *Her* family.

As they ate, they reminisced, regaling Sky with stories about her mother and aunt as children, double trouble. The realities of what happened to Lily lingered in the silences, but for today, everyone was willing to pretend this was an ordinary breakfast on an extraordinary day.

As the meal began to wind down and their grandparents headed off to pack, Sky happily joining them, Lily stared expectantly across the table at Abby and Mom. "I was thinking Sky and I could get haircuts and some new clothes."

"Once all of the reporters lose interest, we will absolutely—" Mom began.

A flash of annoyance crossed Lily's face. "No. Today. I want to go today."

Abby couldn't imagine why Lily would want to venture outside. Maybe in a few weeks, or months, once the madness died down. But now . . .

"Lily, it's a mess out there. Your face is all over the news," Abby said gently.

"Maybe if we wait a few days—?"

"I don't want to wait. I . . ." Lily played with the long braid of hair she had draped over her shoulder, a look on her face. A memory, perhaps?

"He wouldn't let me change my hair. Or wear anything that he didn't approve of. I . . . I want to feel like myself again and I can't. Not like this. Not looking the way he wanted me to look."

Shit. Every time Lily mentioned Mr. Hanson, Abby fought to control her rage. She had to help Lily forget about him. Abby took out her phone and scrolled through her contacts.

"Remember Trisha?" she asked her sister.

"Trisha Campbell, from the track team?" Lily asked.

"She's a hairstylist now at City Styles in the Park City mall. I'll call her. See if she can't get you in."

Lily beamed. "That's perfect. We could get our hair cut and then go shopping."

"I'll drop Mother and Daddy and Meme off at the airport, and I'll come back for you girls. It'll give you some time to get ready, okay?" Mom said, already springing into action.

By midday, when Mom returned, they were fully prepared to dodge the press. Lily's face was concealed by a ski hat and sunglasses; Sky wore a hooded sweatshirt, a blanket covering her car seat. Once they were on the road, everyone removed their disguises, and Lily resumed her role as tour guide, pointing out more sights for Sky to see.

They arrived at the Park City mall, and no one seemed to give them a second glance. The overly painted clerks at the makeup counters chatted with each other. Elderly mall walkers made their rounds, never glancing in Abby and Lily's direction. Mom carried Sky, pointing out the store displays, while Lily and Abby walked arm in arm, a few feet behind them. Abby never came to the mall after Lily was gone. This place was filled with far too many reminders of her sister. There was the Forever 21 and Claire's, where they'd stocked up on school clothes and trendy accessories that rarely lasted a season. There was the food court where they'd devoured french fries and pizza, dissecting Lily's relationship with Wes and Abby's latest crush. And now here they were, walking past all these stores like it was just another day.

They made their way up to City Styles, a brightly lit salon in the center of the mall. The instant they walked in though, their anonymity vanished. It seemed as if everyone was watching them, watching Lily. Abby wanted to bolt, but Lily ignored the attention.

Trisha headed over. Still tiny, barely five feet tall, she was adorable as ever with her bright brown eyes and a streak of purple in her jet-black hair. She'd been the fastest girl on the track team in more ways than one, but she was also the girl you could count on to make you laugh. Today she wasn't cracking jokes. In fact, Abby had never seen Trisha look so serious.

"Oh my God, I can't believe it's you, Lily. When Abby called this morning, I kept thinking and thinking about what to say, and I'm lost. I just don't know."

"How about hello?" Lily said.

Trisha grinned. "Right. Hello. Is it okay if I hug you?"

"That would be great, Trish."

Lily held out her arms, and Trisha had to tiptoe to hug her. She sniffled but didn't cry. Lily pulled away and gestured to Sky.

"Trisha, this is my daughter."

"Oh my God. What an angel you are. It's a pleasure to meet you, young lady. How old are you? Wait, let me guess. I'd say twenty-one."

Sky giggled and Abby smiled at Lily. Trisha hadn't changed at all.

"No. I'm six."

"Wow! Six? I can't believe it. You're a stunner. Now tell me, Sky, are you ready for a makeover?"

Sky didn't seem to understand.

Lily reached out to stroke her daughter's long dark locks.

"Trisha's job is to make people look pretty. What do you think about cutting your hair? Making it a little shorter?"

Sky shook her head. "No! I don't want to cut it."

"Okay, maybe one inch. Like this much?" Lily held up her finger. "And they'll put curls in it too. You'll look like a fairy princess."

"Like Snow White?"

Abby chimed in. "Prettier than Snow White. You'll be Princess Sky."

A smile slowly danced across Sky's face, lighting up her eyes. Trisha motioned to a chair where Paige, another stylist, was waiting. She wrapped a cape around Sky's shoulders and lifted her up, settling her into a booster chair.

Next to Sky was Trisha's station. She motioned for Lily to take a seat. Trisha gently combed out Lily's long blond locks. "So, what are we thinking?"

Lily stared at her reflection. "I want it gone. All of it."

Abby heard the edge in Lily's voice. Trisha must have, as well, but she kept her expression neutral.

"So we'll cut it short. And what about the color?"

"Yes to both. I want to change everything."

"We could go darker blond."

"I want that." Lily pointed to Abby's hair.

Abby lifted her hand self-consciously and touched her short red bob.

"You want the same haircut? As *me*?"

"Unless you care? I love the red. And it might be nice to look alike again."

Abby smiled. "We'll have to fatten you up for that to happen."

"Abby..."

"I'm kidding, Lil. You'll look like a movie star with short hair. It'll show off your cheekbones." Abby turned to Mom. "Don't you think so?"

Mom smiled. "You'll look like a million bucks."

Lily gave Trisha the thumbs-up. "You heard them, Trisha. Make me a star."

Trisha went to work on Lily. Sky sat beside her mother, mesmerized by her image in the mirror, watching as Paige trimmed her hair. When she began to blow-dry Sky's long tresses, the loud whirring initially frightened her, but Sky began to giggle as the hot air tickled her neck. Red dye covered Lily's wet hair as Trisha chattered on about their high school classmates. Abby's phone buzzed. The text from Wes was written in all caps.

VERY IMPORTANT. CALL ME ASAP.

She hit ignore and switched off her phone. No way she was going to talk to him after what he'd done. She leaned in to Mom. "If Wes calls, don't answer. I mean it."

"Seriously, Abby? Stop acting like a child. He's concerned."

"We're having a nice day. He'll just screw it up."

"He's not the enemy here."

"That's one opinion."

"I heard what you said. You can't threaten him about the baby, Abby. It's his child too."

"I'll take relationship advice from you when you tell me who you were entertaining when Lily came back."

Her mom grew quiet, a deep blush washing across her face, but she switched her phone off. Abby felt victorious. Mom hadn't exactly been Mother Teresa since Lily was taken. She knew her mother had started screwing Sheriff Rogers after Lily disappeared. Abby had come home early from searching for Lily and she'd heard them kissing. She'd gone over to Wes's before she was forced to hear anything else. She was pissed about it at first, and considered telling her dad, but then he died, and none of it mattered. She didn't really care what Mom did. She just wanted her to drop the Wes business.

An hour later, when Trisha turned Lily around, Abby gaped, amazed at how a hairstyle could transform someone. Lily was breathtaking. The deep shade of red offset her pale skin, making her appear ethereal and lovely instead of gaunt and washed out. The bob was cut in a way that softened Lily's features and highlighted them all at the same time. Her eyes were deep pools of green that almost sparkled when she smiled. She was so pretty and so thin. A surge of irrational jealousy coursed through Abby. Like so many teenage girls, they'd both been obsessed with their weight in high school. But when you have an identical twin, it's magnified tenfold. Abby fought the rush of envy, reminding herself this was a special moment.

Lily was staring at her image as if she was seeing herself for the first time.

"What do you think, Abby?"

"I think you're the most radiant person I've ever seen." Abby leaned in and wrapped her arms around her sister. They stayed like that, Lily staring at her reflection, Abby's arms draped around her neck. They weren't identical yet, but the resemblance was still uncanny. Anyone could tell that they were twins. Trisha grabbed her iPhone.

"I've got to get a picture of you two."

They posed but before Trisha could take the picture, Abby pulled away.

"Wait...that's not my good side."

Lily burst out laughing. This was their thing growing up. Abby always complained about her good side, and taking pictures always took forever. But she allowed Abby to readjust, and Trisha snapped a series of photos.

Sky's makeover was complete as well, her dark ringlets pulled up high into a ponytail, a pink bow topping it off.

"What do you think, Chicken? How do we look?"

"We're so pretty, Mommy."

"Yes, we are."

Abby clapped her hands.

"Who's ready for some shopping?"

Lily picked up Sky and twirled her around.

"Princess Sky and I are ready to go."

After hugging Trisha good-bye, they left the salon. Lily led them to Macy's and JCPenney and GapKids. Mom took out her Amex and bought an entire wardrobe for Lily and Sky. Who knew shopping could be so fulfilling? Abby sat outside the dressing room and watched as Lily modeled an endless array of jeans and T-shirts, sweaters and boots. Sky paraded around in her new clothes, giggling as she watched Lily strike a pose. The smile on Lily's face was infectious. Once they'd spent a small fortune and were loaded down with bags, they headed out. They were on their way back to the house when Lily announced, "It's chips and salsa time."

Mom smiled and made a U-turn at the next light. "Lily's wish is my command."

They dined at El Rodeo, Lily and Abby's favorite Mexican restaurant, the four of them tucking into a back booth. The doctors had warned Lily to be mindful about her diet, to ease herself into different foods, but Lily wanted real food; she wanted her favorite things she'd been denied. They ordered a feast, Lily letting Sky sample bits of everything, from the homemade tortillas to the cheesy enchiladas to sizzling fajitas. The meal was filled with laughter and great food. Abby thought they'd avoided being recognized until the owner appeared, promising that their entire meal was on the house. He clutched Lily's hand tightly. "Your courage, young lady, is remarkable. Anytime you want to eat at my restaurant, it's on the house."

"Thank you so much," Lily said gratefully.

He walked away. Lily dug into a heaping bowl of guacamole, giggling as she stuffed her mouth. "You think he knows what he's getting himself into?" she asked.

Abby laughed. "Not even close. Poor man's going to go bankrupt."

It was a perfect evening until they heard Sky, her voice shaky and excited.

"Mommy, that's us! We're on the TV! That's you and me and Daddy Rick!"

Abby spotted the television in the corner. That photo of Lily, Rick, and Sky was plastered on the screen, a news story that continued to dominate headlines. Why did every goddamn restaurant have to have a TV? It was a fucking Mexican restaurant! Lily grew perfectly still. She didn't make eye contact with Abby or Mom. Instead she focused her attention on Sky.

"Mommy, why are we on TV?"

"It's hard to explain, Chicken. Basically, Daddy Rick did something that made people upset and now he has to go away for a while."

"Is he mad at us?"

"Not at all. I talked to him and he said he misses his best girl."

"Will I get to see him soon?"

"It may be a while, but he loves you so very much."

Sky took this in, nodding as if she understood. Abby wanted to throw the table and scream at Sky that this man wasn't worthy of her love, of anyone's love, but she remained quiet, in awe of her sister's strength once again.

Lily finally glanced up at Mom and Abby, as if waiting for their judgment. Mom made eye contact with Abby, and for once they were instantly on the same page.

"Sky, will you walk to the front with me?" Eve asked. "I'm pretty sure there's some candy up there."

Sky seemed to sense Lily's distress. "Mommy, do you mind if I go with Grandma?"

"Not at all, Chicken. Aunt Abby and I will be right behind you."

Sky took Mom's hand, glancing back at Lily, who kept a smile on her face until they rounded the corner. Lily's breathing was heavy, her complexion ghostly pale. She avoided Abby's gaze, staring down at the bloodred tablecloth.

"Why do you call Sky 'Chicken'?"

Lily was clearly not expecting this question. She looked up from the paper napkin she was currently ripping to shreds.

"There was a fairy tale I used to read to Sky, the story of Chicken Little. Every time I read 'the sky is falling,' she'd laugh hysterically. She loved hearing her name in a book. She'd repeat it over and over. I always thought it was so ironic. I'd call her my Chicken Little. Before long it just became Chicken."

Lily's breathing had slowed. Abby's plan to calm Lily

down had done the trick. Abby guessed she'd learned something from all those damn therapists after all.

"He made me take that photo. He was ready for this. He knew that he'd use it one day. He knew!"

"No one's going to believe him. No one."

"Are you sure?" Lily asked, her question hanging in the air. Abby wanted to say yes. But she couldn't. There was no way to predict what other people might think. Abby wished now that she could do more, that she'd done so much more to Missy.

By the time they left the restaurant, the sun was beginning to set. The mood had changed. Fucking Rick Hanson ruining things once again. Abby's back was killing her, the alien invader clearly not happy either. Lily's eyes drooped as she cuddled up next to Sky, who was already fast asleep. Mom drove in silence, caught up in her own thoughts.

They arrived back at the house, now familiar, if not still annoying with the reporters that were camped out for what to Abby seemed like the long haul. Only now they were employing new tactics, calling Lily a cock tease, asking if she was in love with Rick Hanson, doing whatever they could to get a reaction out of her.

"Ignore them, Lily," Abby said, as they hurried inside. But the minute she stepped into the living room, she froze. Sitting on the sofa was Wes, and across from him was Sheriff Rogers. "How'd you get in here?" Abby said, glaring at Wes.

He sighed. "Eve gave me a key."

Abby was going to have a serious discussion with her mother later.

"I thought I made it clear that I didn't want to see you," she said to Wes, ignoring the sheriff. "I told you I didn't want to see you or speak with you."

"Abby, can you not pick a fight right now?" Mom asked, her voice tinged with exhaustion and annoyance.

Lily zeroed in on Sheriff Rogers.

"Is this about that photo? Rick's photo?"

Her question startled him. "That photo . . . it's bullshit! Just Hanson grasping at straws."

"Then what's going on, Tommy?" Eve asked. His expression was filled with regret.

"I'm afraid I need to take Abby down to the station."

Lily gasped and carefully readjusted Sky in her arms. "Why? What's wrong?" she asked, keeping her voice low.

"Missy Hanson filed harassment charges. I'm sure it's a misunderstanding, but I still need you to come with me, Abby," Sheriff Rogers said gently.

Mom stepped forward, eyes flashing. "Tommy, you've got to be kidding. Abby hasn't harassed anyone. That's crazy. When in God's name could she have possibly—?"

Mom realized there was merit to this claim, and her eyes flashed with anger.

"Jesus Christ, Abby, what were you thinking?"

Abby heard her mother's underlying question loud and clear. *Why do you mess up everything?* Abby didn't bother answering. Who cared what Mom thought? All Abby could think about was that bitch Missy Hanson. What a stupid bitch. Abby turned to find Lily staring at her.

"Abby, what did you do?" Lily asked.

"She called you a liar, Lilypad," Abby said, wanting Lily to understand. "She was on TV, telling the world that what Rick did was all your fault. That you wanted it. She was showing that photo…"

Sheriff Rogers held up his hand. "Not another word, Abby. Please. Don't say one more word."

Anguished, Lily moved over to Sheriff Rogers and clutched his arm.

"You can't let this happen. This is what he does. This is how he controls things. The way he manipulates people." Lily's voice was growing louder.

Sheriff Rogers patted Lily's arm, and Abby realized he was probably used to handling hysterical women.

"It's okay, Lily," Sheriff Rogers said. "I'll be right there with Abby. We'll get her processed, pay the bail, and she'll be home before you know it. Hanson can't do anything to you. You're safe now."

Wes addressed Abby as Sheriff Rogers took her arm. "I've already called a lawyer. He's going to meet us at the station."

Abby barely registered Wes's statement. She was

watching Lily, who was on the verge, tears streaming down her face.

Abby fought not to show how ashamed she was. She locked eyes with Lily. "Don't worry about me. I won't let that fucker hurt either of us."

Sheriff Rogers led Abby to the front door. She glanced back and saw Lily watching them go, Wes by her side. He grabbed Lily's hand, leaning in close to whisper something in her ear. What was he doing? She wanted to yell at him to get lost, but right now she had to focus on Missy Hanson. Abby was going to do whatever it took to make Missy sorry for ruining her and Lily's perfect day. God, that bitch would be sorry.

LILY

Wes drove, hands gripping the wheel, eyes on the road as he steered his pickup toward the county jail. Lily sat beside him in the truck, trying to remain calm, trying to remind herself that Abby had done this for her, because she loved Lily.

There was no question that Lily would do anything for Abby. She loved her sister enough to leave her daughter behind. She'd left Sky and climbed into Wes's truck to accompany him to the police station, entrusting her mom with Sky. She'd been distraught leaving Sky behind, but Lily had no choice. Not if she wanted to make sure Abby was all right. She also hoped her sacrifices would lessen the blow when she and Wes were together.

Only they'd been driving for ten minutes and Wes hadn't glanced at her once. In fact, it was almost as if she wasn't even there.

Look at me, Lily wanted to scream. *I'm the one you want. It's me!* She was prettier than Abby, thinner...Lily had counted on her new hairstyle and new clothes to transform her into someone desirable, a woman that men would want, a woman *Wes* should want. But he hadn't even noticed.

Lily knew it was dishonest. She should have told Abby that she still had feelings for Wes. There'd been plenty of time for them to have that discussion. Lily wasn't doing anything wrong. Wes had been her first love. Abby had to understand that. Once she and Wes were back together, and Abby saw how happy they were, she would have to forgive Lily. How could she not?

Wes nervously tapped his fingers on the steering wheel as he eyed the pack of cigarettes in the truck's console.

"If you want to smoke, go ahead. It doesn't bother me," she said.

"Really? It drives Abby crazy. Even if I just have one here and there, she acts like it's the end of the world."

"Smoke all you want," Lily said, promising herself that once they were together she would never impose rules and regulations on him. They'd both be free to do whatever they wanted. She'd be the perfect girlfriend.

Wes gave her a brief smile, grabbed the pack of Marlboros, and quickly lit one. He drew in a heavy drag, and then blew out the smoke. "She's always doing this. Not thinking before she acts. She's so damn reckless."

"She did it because of me."

Wes shook his head emphatically. "She does dumb shit like this all the time."

He reached out and grabbed Lily's hand, squeezing it. His tender touch transported her back to that innocent girl, riding shotgun with the boy she loved. When Wes put his hand back on the wheel, Lily experienced a profound sense of emptiness.

"Abby's so damn emotional and headstrong. She drives me crazy." Lily fought the rush of annoyance that he was still talking about Abby. She reached out and gently touched Wes's hand.

"She'll be okay," Lily said.

She needed to remind him of how he'd felt when they were together. He needed to remember. He smiled and this time he didn't let go. She knew it. He did care. She knew it wasn't a grand gesture, but she'd take things slow, build back up to where they were before. Right now this was enough. She loved Abby. She'd do anything for her sister. But as far as Wes was concerned, all bets were off.

ABBY

Abby held her breath, trying to stay calm as she paced around the holding cell they'd placed her in. How could she have been so stupid? This was the last thing Lily needed. This was the last thing any of them needed.

It had been almost five years since she was in any legal trouble, but it appeared nothing here had changed. The metallic, piss-like smell remained, along with the shouting and hopelessness, the endless stream of crazy criminals and the overworked cops who dealt with them. As a teenager Abby had done everything she could to punish her mother, to punish the world for Lily's disappearance. She could still recall Mom's disappointed face staring back at her each time she was called down to the police department, checkbook in hand, ready to bail her out of trouble. She remembered the lectures and the threats, which did nothing to deter her. But she'd gotten her shit together. Abby didn't belong here. Missy Hanson was the one they should be locking up. She fought not to yell out or cause a scene.

Be good, she told herself. *Don't get into any more trouble.*

Abby was fingerprinted and her mug shot was taken. She met the lawyer that Wes had hired, Dan or Doug something. He'd been quick to say this was some kind of Hail Mary stunt and that Missy Hanson was simply trying to earn sympathy. But Abby had made the threats against Missy Hanson, and she'd done so in front of witnesses. The charges were harassment and trespassing, both misdemeanors, but Abby was determined to fight it.

She couldn't believe she'd been dumb enough to think Missy would leave them alone. You don't spend your life with a man capable of the things Mr. Hanson had done without being twisted yourself.

By the time Lily and Wes showed up, all Abby had to do was post bail. Wes insisted on paying, and for once, Abby didn't argue. Her morning sickness had been endless, and they'd cut her shifts at the hospital. She'd need every penny once the alien invader arrived.

Abby also had to agree to stay at least five hundred feet from Missy Hanson and her family—a bitter pill to swallow, but Abby agreed. For now, at least.

She was free to go. Wes led the girls outside, trying to protect them from the reporters who had multiplied like roaches, swarming around them, screaming out questions.

"Did you really threaten Missy Hanson?"

"What did you say to her?"

"Lily, are you going to kill Rick Hanson's baby?"

one reporter shouted, loud enough to drown out the rest, her voice crystal clear, the weight of her question hanging heavy in the stillness that followed.

At first, Abby was confused. Why the hell would Lily kill Sky? But Lily stood motionless. The reporters, sensing they'd hit on something even more salacious, inched forward. The same reporter followed up with another question, despite Lily's silence.

"You're pregnant with Rick Hanson's child, aren't you? Are you going to abort the baby?"

No one spoke. Abby couldn't believe what she'd heard. Lily was pregnant? With Rick's baby? Another baby? She'd never said a word. Abby surveyed the sea of curious faces, and her anger soared. Why did they have to humiliate her sister? Why were they putting Lily on trial? Why not Rick? They needed to get to Wes's truck. Now. She had to get Lily away from here. Wes was trying to open the door, shoving reporters out of his way.

"Stop it. Stop with your questions. Leave us alone," Abby shouted.

One of the reporters pushed his way through. Abby stumbled, gasping as she tried to protect herself. She turned, seeking out the perpetrator.

"What is wrong with you people?"

Things were reaching a fevered frenzy, when Lily seemed to spring back to life. She grabbed Abby and hugged her close, staring at the cameras, her gaze calm and direct.

"You want to know the truth? Yes, I'm pregnant, and yes, it is Rick Hanson's baby. What I do now is my decision and my decision alone. You can ask all the questions you want, but we're done answering them." Lily raised her eyebrows at Abby. Then she turned back to the reporters. "Now, go fuck yourselves."

Despite her shock, Abby had never been more proud of Lily. Seconds later, they were in the truck. Lily sat in the middle, beside Wes. Abby was on the opposite side, near the window. The weight of Lily's secret consumed any remaining space in the pickup.

As they drove, Wes darted glances at both girls, wanting to say something, but for once he seemed to know when to keep his mouth shut.

"Lily, about the baby—" Abby said.

"I don't want to talk about it."

"But, Lil, you have to figure out—"

"Abby, I'm not discussing it." Lily's tone was clear.

"I won't say another word," Abby said.

Lily's shoulders sagged, as if she'd found a moment of relief, and she went back to watching the road. Wes patted Lily's hand gently. Exhausted, Lily sighed and leaned her head on his shoulder. Abby's stomach dropped again. It was the alien invader and her hormones. It had to be. *Stop being stupid. Lily needs a friend, someone to make her feel safe.* Wes had a knack for that. And it wasn't as if it mattered to Abby. She didn't give two shits about Wes. She didn't care about him at all.

EVE

The girls wouldn't discuss anything that happened at the jail when they returned home. They flat out refused, with Abby leading the charge.

"We're going to bed, Mom. You should do the same," Abby said as she led a dejected Lily upstairs. Eve glanced at Wes, his shoulders hunched, as he shook his head.

"It's bad, Eve. Lily's pregnant with Hanson's kid. Somehow the press found out. They blindsided her with it at the jail. Blindsided us all."

Eve stared back at him. Jesus Christ. No one, it seemed, could catch a break. She poured Wes a scotch and made one for herself. She knew he was anxious, that he wanted reassurances that things were going to be okay, but Eve couldn't promise him that. After downing his drink, Wes reluctantly left. Eve finished the bottle, sitting alone in the dimly lit kitchen.

Eve was consumed by the thought of Lily having another baby. *Rick's baby.* She couldn't believe it. She was like one of those bomb technicians she'd seen in the movies. Just when she thought she'd caught her breath, there was a new device to defuse.

Eve despised Rick Hanson with every single fiber in her body, but she still didn't want Lily to terminate her pregnancy. Lily had been through enough. Eve no longer considered herself a believer. Still, there was the off chance that Lily's soul might be in danger, that she could be punished in spite of all she'd been through. But this wasn't her call. Eve would support Lily no matter what she decided. What Eve really wanted was to stop the outside world from dragging her daughter down. She wanted to get rid of the parasites on her porch; she wanted to protect Sky and her girls. But she was helpless and it was killing her.

She downed the last of the scotch and peered outside. The media seemed to be resting, returning to their crypts or wherever they went so they'd be ready for their continued assault tomorrow. Eve reached for her phone and stared down at the keypad.

Don't do it. Don't do it, she told herself.

She texted him and waited. Endless moments.

Be there in twenty minutes, the response came back.

Fifteen minutes later Eve sat in her car in the parking lot of the Dunkin' Donuts, the heater running. This was a mistake. *Go back to your girls*, she tried to tell herself. *Forget about him*. But then she saw Tommy climbing out of his police cruiser and she abandoned all rational thought. She joined Tommy, the two of them leaning against the hood of her still-warm car. In spite of all the time that passed, being together was familiar, comfortable.

"I heard about Lily and the baby. Are you hanging in there?" he asked.

"By the tiniest of a thread," Eve said.

"You're so damn strong, Evie. You'll get through this. Just like you always have."

"I hope so," she said. "I wanted to thank you for everything."

"It's my job, Eve. I'm just doing my job."

"It's always been more than a job. You know that."

He bristled, his eyes flashing with annoyance.

"So that's the reason you wanted to see me? To say thanks. Eve, it's late and we're exhausted and..."

She leaned over and kissed him. Right in the middle of this empty parking lot, her lips found his, and she sank into him. He continued the kiss, tugging at Eve's clothes. She pulled away first.

"We can't do this."

He stepped back, instantly apologetic. "I understand."

"I meant, not here. There's a motel. Five minutes away."

Was she really doing this? Was she that foolish that she was going to start this up again? But there was no hesitation on his part. He got into his car and she followed him. He paid for the room and they both parked near the back of the motel.

He opened the door and she followed him in. He clicked the lock and then he turned to stare at her. Up close, she realized that she'd been wrong. He'd aged a great deal in the last few years. But then so had she. He rubbed his callused hand against her cheek. Eve's eyes closed and she leaned into his touch. He kissed her again, a kiss that showed no restraint. A kiss that held all the sorrow and anguish they'd experienced in the last few days, in the last eight years. All she could think about was his hot breath against her neck, the feel of her breasts in his hands, her smooth, naked skin pressed against his. He'd walked away from her once. He'd done the right thing. Eve should have remembered that. But tonight, she didn't care about right or wrong. All that mattered right now was the two of them, in this room, in this bed. *To hell with the rest of it*, she thought.

RICK

She'd done it. Missy had actually come through. Not only had she hired one of the best defense attorneys in the country but she'd also gone on the national news and proclaimed her faith in him. Rick still couldn't believe his great fortune. Missy wasn't simply good. She was fantastic. Flanked by reporters, perfectly attired in her navy dress, her fresh-from-the-salon blowout, she appeared young, sweet, and oh so trusting. She'd come back to see him and he'd told her about the photo, told her about the safety deposit box he'd hidden it in. She wasn't giving him a free pass.

"I think you need help, Rick. Psychiatric help. But we've been married fifteen years. I can't just walk away."

So his story about Lily hadn't been entirely believable, but he was starting to have a good feeling about Missy, and his odds of getting out of this place. And then several days passed and Missy showed up, trembling, on edge, glancing around as if she were being followed.

"Missy, what's wrong?"

"I think you're right, Rick. I think those girls are unstable."

Rick leaned back in his seat. This was a promising new development.

"What happened?"

"Abby Riser came to our home. She threatened. She threatened to . . . to kill me."

This was so perfect. He couldn't have planned it better himself.

"I told you. I told you they're not well. But listen to me, none of this is your fault. You're innocent in all of this. You have to protect yourself," he'd told her.

"I don't know what to do. Everyone's going around like they're the Second Coming of Christ. No one will believe you."

"Were there witnesses when she threatened you?"

"My parents. And the news people were still there."

"That's good, Missy. All you have to do is tell the lawyer. Tell him you're worried about your safety and you want a restraining order. That girl isn't stable, and you know it. A lot of people might try to hurt you because of what I did. I can't have that on my conscience."

By the time the visit was over, he'd convinced Missy that she needed to stand up and fight. There was a part of him that wondered what else that bitch Abby had said. He could tell that Missy's doubts about him were growing, but she never pressed him for more information. Rick realized that she wanted to believe him. She wanted all of this to be Lily's fault so that Missy could resume her humdrum life, living in blissful ignorance. He really had chosen well.

Rick was disappointed that he didn't get to see Abby's arrest, that he didn't get to see Lily's face. Regardless, it'd been good news. He'd been upbeat for most of the day. He'd even managed to get a few moments alone with that guard he had his eye on. Her name was Angela, but he didn't know much more. He'd tried asking her a couple of questions, hoping to get a read on her, but she was skittish.

"Better keep your mouth shut," she'd said. "I might not be able to stop them if they go after you again."

Rick had done as he was told, but her response pleased him. She was concerned for his well-being. That said something. He considered it another victory. He was eating dinner, or what passed for dinner in this shithole, when Fred ambled by. Rick braced himself, wondering if these beatings were going to be a nightly ritual. But Fred didn't open the cell; he just leaned languidly against the bars.

"I heard congratulations are in order," he said, a taunting tone to his voice.

Rick stared back at him. There was no doubt in Rick's mind that Fred had been bullied in high school. Picked last for sports teams. Stuffed in the lockers. That's why he cared so much about his own children's success. He was a weakling, and now here he was, wielding the only power he'd ever had. *Quite sad*, Rick thought. *Quite sad*. He considered ignoring him, but he was certain that would result in another beating, and his ribs were so tender it still hurt to exhale.

"Oh, really? What do I have to celebrate?" Rick asked, playing along.

"Heard your demon seed spawned another kid."

Rick's entire body seized up. "Lily's pregnant?"

"Good thing that girl is smart enough to get rid of this one. How does it feel, knowing you're in here, and she's going to murder your kid? Guess it's only fair, 'cuz you stole her childhood." Fred chuckled as he headed back toward the exit. "Have a nice night, dickwad."

Rick turned away, not wanting anyone, especially that prick, to see how angry he was, how much effort it took not to lose his temper completely. He kept thinking about Lily, how much she had deceived him. She had said she was happy. That's why he'd let her keep that child.

And this was how she repaid him. By murdering this baby, his baby! Rick seethed, pacing his tiny cell, cracking his knuckles, his mind racing. He knew what he had to do. His decision was made but it was unfortunate. His decision would put a wrinkle in the plan with Missy, but that was fine. She'd served her purpose. There was no way he could allow Lily to kill his child. He went to the front of his cell and began banging on the bars and shouting.

"Guard. Guard. Hello! Guard! It's an emergency. Guard!"

He kept banging on the bars until Fred reappeared, his face contorted in annoyance.

"What the fuck do you want?" Fred asked.

"I need to speak to whoever's in charge," Rick said.

"Oh, yeah? And what the hell do you have to say?"

"I want to confess," Rick replied. Fred stared back, all teasing and joking gone from his demeanor. He reached through the bars and grabbed Rick by the throat, squeezing tightly.

"You're gonna tell him what you did to the Riser girl?"

Rick paused. He shook his head, reveling in the power he held over this piece-of-shit nobody.

"No. I want to tell him about the others."

EVE

"If you think I'm going to ignore the fact that your hospital leaked my daughter's confidential medical records to the media, you're stupider than I thought. I want whoever is responsible to be held accountable, or I will make it my mission to bankrupt that place," Eve said, clutching the phone tightly.

Stuart, the CEO of Lancaster General, clucked into the phone. Eve hated that clucking. He did it when he was frustrated or disagreed with employees, which was pretty much every second of the day. Eve had known Stuart for years, and her disdain for him had only grown. He was a sycophant who'd fire his own mother if it meant improving the hospital's bottom line. He treated his employees with little to no compassion. She remembered his expression when she'd asked for more time off after Dave's funeral. Abby had been floundering, and Eve wasn't doing much better. The look of annoyance on his face, the long pause before he agreed to let her take one more week but then they'd have to talk about her future at the hospital, had left her furious. She'd wanted nothing more than to tell him to shove his job up his scrawny, bony butt. But with Dave gone and Abby needing constant therapy, Eve had no choice but to continue working there. But now that his staff had screwed up, Eve was going to make him pay for it.

"Am I not being clear, Stuart? Should I speak a little slower?"

"Eve, we think one of the lab techs leaked the results of Lily's blood test. Dr. Amari and I are already looking into it, and the person will be dealt with accordingly. It's unacceptable. I'm sorry."

"Sorry? You think sorry is enough? Do you realize I have abortion protestors on my doorstep? They're holding up dolls that look like aborted fetuses. They're calling us baby killers. After all we've been through."

"Eve, you have to understand—"

"I understand that I'm suing your ass."

Eve hung up, her rage still boiling over. She'd slipped out of the motel this morning before Tommy woke, determined to avoid the awkward morning-after dance. Instead she'd arrived home to find the anti-abortion protestors camped out on her front porch. Some waved signs that read, DEFEND LIFE or I AM THE VOICE FOR THE VOICELESS. Others were crueler with coarse images and accompanying pictures of the devil. She'd immediately forgotten her embarrassment and called Tommy. He'd sent over more officers, but there wasn't a whole lot they could do. The sidewalk and streets were public property, which meant these maniacs were free to gather and unleash their hate on her and her family.

She'd found Abby awake, sitting at the dining table, silently absorbing the crowd's unrelenting hostility. Abby had said nothing about Eve's early-morning arrival, and Eve didn't offer up an explanation. Instead they'd both gone upstairs to check on Lily. She was sitting up in bed, watching Sky sleep. She refused to discuss the baby.

"I'll figure this out. But I need some time."

Eve agreed.

"Let's go somewhere. We'll wait until all of this blows over."

But Lily wasn't budging.

"That's not happening. They won't run me out of my house. We're not going anywhere."

So they'd spent the day in Eve's bedroom, shades drawn, playing board games and watching movies, trying to pretend they weren't prisoners in their own home. By nightfall, everyone had headed off to bed, hoping that tomorrow their lives would return to whatever counted for normal.

It was almost ten o'clock, and Eve decided that a hot shower might ease her aching muscles. She flipped on the hot water, and steam began to fill the room. She stripped down and stepped into the shower, hot water rushing over her body. She was overwhelmed and exhausted and feeling so much older than her fifty-one years. How foolish she'd been to think Lily's return would be the end of all their troubles.

Eve stayed in the shower until the water turned cold. When she got out, she dried off and wrapped herself in her favorite old robe. She surveyed her bedroom. *So empty*, she thought. She could still feel the weight of Tommy on top of her, his arms wrapped around her. Alone in her room, her mind racing, her body ached for him. She grabbed her phone and texted, *Thinking of you and the way you make me feel.*

She waited for a response but the screen remained blank, mocking her weakness. Eve dressed in her old flannel pajamas and sank down onto the bed. She stared at her weathered, tired hands, at the veins and lines that appeared one day as if by magic. She was so damn scared about what the future held. She finally put her phone away and closed her eyes.

Sleep consumed her, a dark, voracious, and winged thing stealing her away from the crushing weight of her failures. But she did not dream. Not tonight. Tonight she fell into an exhausted abyss. She didn't know how long she'd been asleep, but she startled awake, a shadow moving toward her bed.

"Who's there? What is it?"

"It's me, Mom. It's Abby."

Eve's eyes adjusted to the darkness, and she saw Abby, clad in a giant gray T-shirt and sweatpants, clutching her oversized belly.

Eve bolted upright and flipped on the bedside lamp.

"What's wrong? Is it the baby?"

Abby shook her head. "It's Sheriff Rogers. He's downstairs."

Eve's breath caught. Tommy was *here*?

"He's with that woman from the FBI. They want to talk to Lily."

It wasn't about Eve at all. It was Lily. Her poor, sweet Lily.

More bombs. More shrapnel, Eve thought instantly. She stood and grabbed her robe, pulling it tightly around her.

Eve followed Abby down the stairs and found Tommy and Agent Stevens sitting across from an anxious-looking Lily. She was wearing an old Lancaster Day School sweatshirt, her arms wrapped around her legs in a protective pose. Abby stood awkwardly nearby, her hand resting on her protruding belly.

Tommy cleared his throat, his eyes on Eve.

"We're sorry to bother you this early, but time is crucial."

"He sent you here, didn't he?"

Lily's question startled everyone. A chill coursed through Eve's body. Her daughter knew Rick Hanson better than anyone. She knew that he was up to something.

"I'm afraid so," Sheriff Rogers said.

"That motherfucker," Abby said. "What does he want now?"

No one spoke for a long moment. Sheriff Rogers finally broke the silence.

"Rick Hanson confessed tonight to kidnapping and holding Lily captive for the past eight years," Sheriff Rogers said. "He also confessed to fathering her child."

Abby exhaled. "Thank God."

Eve frowned over Lily's lack of emotion.

"Tommy . . . Sheriff, what's going on? You wouldn't be here at this hour if Rick Hanson had simply confessed," Eve said.

"I'm sorry to have to tell you this. You can't begin to imagine how sorry. But Lily wasn't Hanson's only victim." He paused and then began again. "Lily, I'm afraid there are more."

LILY

"How many?" Lily asked.

Agent Stevens cleared her throat. The woman's eye makeup was smudged, her hair disheveled. In the early-morning hours, Lily was glad to see this woman wasn't nearly as composed as she initially appeared, that this job still wormed its way in. Agent Stevens anxiously twirled the pen in her hand, stopping every few seconds to tap her notebook. "He said there are two more girls. Recent victims."

Lily slowly stood up.

"I'll go get dressed."

Abby blocked Lily's path, confusion clouding her face. "Wait, why? What are you doing?"

"He wants to see me, Abby. This is how he's going to make that happen."

"No, that's not true. You can't see him. They can't expect you to do that."

Lily zeroed in on Sheriff Rogers. "I'm right, aren't I? That's why you're here. That's what he wants."

"I'm afraid so. It's completely against procedure. Beyond against it. We told him that he could talk to you on the phone, but he refused. He said that he had to speak with you in person. He said he'd never tell us where the girls are without a meeting."

Lily had been naïve to think Rick wouldn't have something else planned.

"It's wrong for us to come here, but there are girls out there whose lives may be in jeopardy," Agent Stevens said.

"Give me five minutes."

Lily moved toward the stairs, but Abby blocked her path. "Fuck him, Lily. Fuck him and his mind games," Abby said.

"I have to go."

"Maybe he's lying. Maybe there aren't other girls."

"He's not lying, Abby. Not about this."

"You've done enough. He's put you through enough."

"They're teenage girls. Like we were. Young girls with families who love them. With fathers who might still be alive, and sisters and brothers who are waiting for them, and boyfriends...Do you really want me to ignore all of that? To let them die because I'm too afraid?"

Lily's entire body trembled but she wasn't backing down. She had to do this. Abby reached for Lily again, refusing to let her go without a fight.

"He's done enough, Lil. He's done enough."

"I know. And one day, it'll be over, but not tonight. I have to do this, Abs. You know I do."

Lily slipped out of Abby's grasp and headed upstairs, hoping her sister wouldn't follow. She slipped on the baggiest sweatshirt she could find and an old pair of jeans. She grabbed her father's worn Phillies baseball cap from the dresser and stared at herself in the mirror. She was as manly and unfeminine as you could get. He would hate it.

Time seemed to speed up. One minute, Lily was staring at herself in the mirror. The next, she was at the jailhouse in a small, windowless room, waiting for Rick to arrive. Her hands shook uncontrollably, and she fought to still them. Normal jail visitations were in a room with the inmates separated by glass. Rick had demanded a face-to-face meeting. So they used one of the interrogation rooms. But Lily wasn't alone. There were three deputies stationed behind her. Agent Stevens had briefed Lily. She would be escorting Rick in. If at any time Lily felt unsafe or wanted to call the meeting off, she just had to tap her hand and they'd end the meeting immediately.

Lily knew that Abby was watching behind the two-way mirror with Sheriff Rogers and several other FBI agents, and she hoped that knowledge would give her strength. The metal door opened and Rick entered, shackles around his wrists, ankles, and waist. He had been beaten, his face mangled, a mixture of yellow and blue bruises. Lily took a great deal of satisfaction in knowing Rick wasn't invincible. He bruised and bled like everyone else.

He gave her hair and wardrobe a dismissive once-over. *Yes!* Lily thought, sitting up straighter. *I'm not yours anymore.* But she didn't speak. She was going to let him call the shots. It would be better if he thought he was in control.

The guards shoved him into a chair and he re-arranged himself, taking his time, studying her. He finally shook his head, like a disapproving parent. "I hate to say it, but you look like hell." His voice was low and cordial, as if he were chatting with a long-lost friend.

She gestured to his bruises and the orange jumpsuit and forced a smile. "I could say the same thing about you."

He tried to set his hands on the table but his shackles made it impossible. Then he grinned. Lily knew what that curl of his lips meant. If they'd been alone, had he not been shackled, with armed guards inches from him, he would have smacked her in the face. He would have hit her again and again until she'd bled, until she'd begged for forgiveness. But here, he could only smile.

"Touché, Baby Doll."

Lily fought the urge to scream, *I'm not your baby doll. Don't call me that.* Her emotional response would excite him. She had to control her feelings here. She had to deny him his pleasure.

"Tell me where they are, Rick. You know that's why I'm here. Tell me."

He shook his head, obviously disappointed.

"We'll get to that. I've missed you so much, Baby Doll. I wanted to see you."

Lily wished she could bash his already battered face. She cleared her throat. "The girls, Rick. Where are they?"

"How's Sky?" he asked, ignoring her question. He stared at her with that look of sick, false, twisted adoration she'd come to recognize and despise. "I hope you'll tell her Daddy Rick misses her terribly."

"As if you ever cared about her."

"I care about her a great deal. And I love her mother deeply. I always have."

"Why did you do this? To us. To those other girls. Can you tell me why?"

He paused, considering, his brow furrowing.

"My mother was terribly abusive. She was young. Too young when she had me. She used to lock me in a closet when she wasn't doing terrible things to me. She'd let the men and women she brought into our home do terrible things. It was a horrible existence, and it stayed with me. It shaped me. Made me who I am today."

Lily stared at him, shaking her head. "You're lying, Rick. You're putting on a show, and I know it."

He smiled. Lily could tell he was pleased.

"See how well you know me, Baby Doll? Tell me, why does anyone do anything? Because I wanted to. Because I could. I'm sure that doctors and therapists will want to label me, to define me. Borderline personality disorder. Narcissist. Psychopath. They probably all apply. But it wasn't my upbringing. My mother was a decent woman. Smart, competent, devoted. She didn't make a lot of money, but we had more than enough to go around. I wasn't abused. I wasn't bullied. I was popular and well liked. Things came easily to me. School, work, women. The trouble with society is that they need to understand and define everything. But there isn't a reason for what I did other than that I wanted you. I needed *you* to be happy. You needed me too. Maybe you can pretend now that it was all a lie, but I know you were happy too. You can't fake that, no matter what you tell yourself."

Lily's stomach churned; sweat trickled down her back. This man repulsed her. *This* was what he wanted: a forum, a chance to manipulate her yet again.

"The girls, Rick. Tell me about the other girls."

"You were my favorite. I need you to understand that. But there's something about a new girl. They are so exciting in the beginning. So full of life."

"Are you going to tell me, or should I go?"

Annoyance clouded his face. "I have a stipulation before I give up their names."

She nodded her head in agreement. The same way she'd nodded her head thousands of times before. She was so close to getting what she wanted, she would indulge him in his games for now.

"I need you to agree to something before I tell you where they are," Rick said. "And that is my unborn child remains unharmed. You must carry him to term. You agree to that, and I will give you their names."

She stared back at him. *This* was what he wanted. This was why he'd forced her to come here. She sat waiting. Was he going to ask for a lawyer? Demand that she put it in writing? Lily was running through all the angles. What he might be thinking. How this might play out. He sighed.

"Lily, do I have your word?"

She took a deep breath, shaking her head.

"Yes, of course. Rick, you can't possibly think I would hurt my child. You've seen how much I love Sky. She's my world. You know there's no way I could ever give up a baby. Our baby."

He leaned back, studying her, no doubt searching for any tells that she might be lying.

"How do I know you're telling the truth?"

"Do you remember our second anniversary?"

His eyes lit up. He was proud of what he'd done. She could tell that. Rick had tried to trick her. He'd given her photos of Abby. Snapshots of Wes. Recent photos of all of them. She'd stared at their faces, the smiles he'd captured, and then Lily ripped the photos to shreds. It'd been a trick. She knew that. She'd told him that was her past. He was her future, and he could do anything he wanted to her. Rick had obliged.

"Remember what we did that night? I do. And I know I defied you. But you're right. Not all of it was lies."

Lily took a breath and reached out to take his hands in hers. Agent Stevens and the guards moved to stop her but Lily held up her hand. She saw a visceral reaction come from Rick. Her touch still affected him. She knew she was so close to getting the truth.

"No matter how much I want to forget you, I can't. And I'd never hurt your child. You have to believe me. This is your baby doll talking."

Her words were powerful. Lily could see that, could see how much he loved hearing her say the name he'd blessed her with. Satisfied, Rick leaned back, ready to talk. "I needed your assurances. Now if someone is ready, I'll tell you where you can find the others."

Agent Stevens leaned down. "Start talking. Now!"

Rick nodded and began to speak, casually and confidently, as if he were narrating a tour.

"Bree Whitaker is sixteen and Shaina Meyers is fourteen. They're at an old abandoned farmhouse off Highway 12."

He continued talking, but Lily kept replaying their names over and over again in her mind. Bree Whitaker. Shaina Meyers. Bree and Shaina. Sixteen and fourteen. Two more girls whose lives were ruined. Two more families destroyed.

"How did you take them?"

Agent Stevens wasn't expecting Lily's question. She

reached out to stop her, but Rick appeared eager to share his brilliance with the world.

"Bree was a waitress at a diner in Philly. I'd been there a few times. She was pretty, one of those chatty types who doesn't know when to stop talking. She was seriously lacking in knowledge of literary greats, so I'd bring her books. Hemingway and Fitzgerald to start. Dostoevsky as a main course. Told her she was a smart kid and I'd be happy to counsel her if she was considering college. I gave her my number. Said if she ever needed anything, to call me. As luck would have it, she was having trouble with her boyfriend, and she asked if I'd meet her for coffee."

"And the fourteen-year-old?"

"Tsk, tsk, Baby Doll, so judgmental. She's quite mature for her age. She was a runaway I picked up hitchhiking. It was almost too easy. Though, I will say neither one of them had your spirit."

Agent Stevens curled her lip, obviously disgusted. "Come on, Lily. This asshole's told us enough to lock him up for two lifetimes."

Lily started to stand up, but her legs shook and she swayed. Rick reached out to steady her. She jerked back, and Agent Stevens smacked Rick hard across the face. He didn't even wince. He gazed at Lily with wounded eyes.

"Baby Doll, it was good seeing you. Give my regards to your family, especially Abby."

Agent Stevens lifted her arm to strike Rick again, but Lily grabbed the agent's wrist. "It's okay," she said. "I'm okay." She turned to Rick, keeping her voice low and measured. "I lied about the baby, Rick. I am going to kill it. I will murder it without thinking twice. Whatever it takes to make sure that *nothing* else you've created survives, I'll do. I'm going to get rid of this *thing* you put inside me, and I won't shed a tear."

For the briefest of moments, his impassive mask slipped, and his true nature was on display. His face contorted as his gaze landed on the piece of paper in Agent Stevens's hands, the names he'd freely given up. He'd trusted Lily implicitly, and she'd duped him again. Rick lunged forward to grab her, but Agent Stevens was already rushing Lily out of the room as the guards moved to restrain him.

"You lying bitch. You cunt!" His screams followed her down the hall.

Lily knew it was irrational, that he couldn't get her, but she ran toward the end of the corridor, her breath coming out in short bursts. Rick had taught her well. He'd taught her how to lie and deceive, how to be a master manipulator. Each day, he'd taught her how to be a little less human. And now, everything she'd learned from him would be his undoing. After all these years, she'd beaten him. Lily broke down, her body racked with painful sobs.

I win, Rick, she thought. *I win.*

ABBY

Waiting... Abby always despised waiting. Waiting for Lily to come home. Waiting for answers. Waiting to see if Mr. Hanson was full of shit. It didn't help that the alien invader was violently kicking her insides, as if it were absorbing her emotions and responding accordingly. Observing Lily's face in that room, trapped with that monster, had been hellish. The police had disappeared in a mass exodus to search for the girls who were both in fact reported missing. Sheriff Rogers thanked Lily before he headed out.

"You were very brave. Could be a while before we have any news, but I'll let you know when we do."

Abby wanted nothing more than to leave this place, but Lily wasn't going anywhere.

"I'm not leaving until I know that they're safe," Lily said.

And so they waited, hunkered down in the cold, sterile lobby. The remaining cops eyed them curiously. Abby and Lily called it the "twin look"—the double take people made when they passed them by. Abby was pleased that people still noticed they were twins.

But it was seeing Mr. Hanson, seeing who he really was, that Abby couldn't shake. She'd observed Lily from the safety of the two-way mirror, her sister shrinking in his presence. She'd heard Lily talking to Mr. Hanson, talking about anniversaries. Abby wondered how her sister could have survived living with him. Abby would have given up. He would have broken her. She'd been swept up in Lily's story, trying to understand what her sister was doing. But when Lily told Rick that she wasn't keeping the baby, Abby had been shocked. Part of her wanted to cheer Lily for her brilliant deception. The other part of Abby was unsettled by her sister's manipulations.

"Did you see his face when he realized I'd tricked him?" Lily had asked proudly.

"He was floored. He couldn't believe that you'd lie to him," Abby said, trying to keep her concern at bay.

"He used to say he could tell exactly what I was thinking at any given moment. For so long, I believed him. It was as if he could read my every thought. He knew when I was thinking about Daddy, or about running, or about . . . about you. But not tonight. Not tonight."

They sat there, occasionally talking about the past, or about Sky and all the things they'd do when this was over. But as the hours ticked by, Abby knew something was wrong with the other girls. The police should have been back by now. Her phone buzzed. A text from Wes.

I'm on my way.

Shit. Mom was to blame for this. She had to be. She'd probably called Wes in hysterics, knowing he'd ride over on his white horse to save the day.

"Something wrong?" Lily asked.

Abby smoothed Lily's hair, remembering how they used to share a bed as kids, lying side by side when the thunderstorms rolled into town.

"It's Wes. He wants to stop by and check on us."

Lily's body tensed.

"You mean check on *you*?"

Abby stayed silent, hoping Lily would change the subject. She didn't.

"I always imagined Wes would wind up in New York or Boston. He hated this town. I can't believe he'd settle for small-town life."

"His dad got sick, and he came back. Said he wanted to be closer to family."

"Or closer to you?" Lily asked innocently.

Was it innocent? Abby couldn't tell. She shifted in her seat, trying to get comfortable, wishing this thing would stop pressing on her bladder.

"It's not like that," Abby said.

"Funny. Wes said the same thing."

Abby was convinced that Lily would have more questions about Wes, but instead she laid her head on Abby's shoulder and closed her eyes. Abby relaxed. Sitting beside Lily, matching the rhythm of each other's breathing, she leaned back and let her eyes close.

Abby startled awake. Lily was still dozing beside her. How long had they been asleep? Five minutes? Two hours? It was definitely too long. Abby's body ached all over. She stretched, careful not to wake Lily. Across the room, Wes was huddled with Sheriff Rogers and the FBI. Abby's stomach dropped. She was skilled at reading body language, and judging from Wes's, things were bad. Really bad. As if she could sense trouble, Lily sat upright, brushing her hair out of her face and blinking rapidly.

"What did they say? Is there news? Did they find them? Are the girls all right?" Lily asked.

"I don't know. I just woke up," Abby said. "I was asleep when they came back."

Lily was on her feet, heading toward the sheriff's office. Abby struggled to follow, her legs still half-asleep. Ahead of her, Lily burst through the office door.

"They're okay, right?" Lily asked, her voice high-pitched. "Tell me they're okay."

Sheriff Rogers cleared his throat. "Shaina, the fourteen-year-old victim, was in bad shape. Beaten, dehydrated, and disoriented, but she's alive. She's at the hospital with her folks."

"And Bree? How is she?"

Abby winced. Lily asked about the girl as if she knew her, as if they were family. *Brace yourself, Lily*, Abby thought. She could read the news in Sheriff Rogers's eyes before he ever said a word.

"She's..." He cleared his throat again. "She suffered a great deal of abuse. And well...she didn't make it."

"He killed her?" Lily whispered.

"Not exactly. I'm afraid she took her own life."

Abby heard her sister's pained exhale, but she couldn't look at Lily. Abby stared down at what she could see of her feet, and willed herself not to break down.

Beside her, Lily was motionless, absorbing the news like a boxer absorbs blows to the head.

"How long did he have them?" Lily asked.

"A month or two. We're not exactly sure."

Lily grimaced.

"Hanson had grown bolder. Gotten overly confident. That's probably why he screwed up, and you were able to escape."

Lily didn't appear to be listening.

"I want to see her. I want to see Shaina."

What the hell was Lily saying? This was crazy. Enough was enough.

"Lily, no. We're leaving. It's time to go!"

"I need to see Shaina. I need to tell her I'm sorry."

"Sorry! Why are *you* sorry?"

Lily ignored Abby's question. "I'll walk there if I have to."

"Lily, you don't have to walk," Wes said. "I'll drive you."

Abby had almost forgotten Wes was even there. For a fleeting moment, all she wanted was to wrap her arms around him and let him hold her. She shook off that feeling, blaming her exhaustion and hormones for making her so needy. But Abby wasn't going to let Wes be the hero. Abby took her sister's hand in solidarity.

"I'll go with you, Lil. We'll do this together."

Deep down in her gut, Abby knew this was a bad idea. That Lily had been through too much, that she'd been pushed too far. But they'd already been to hell and back. How much worse could it get?

LILY

At the hospital, Lily received a hero's welcome from Shaina's parents. They wrapped their arms around Lily, tearfully thanking her for her sacrifice, for helping bring their girl home. Shaina's father Bert was a city bus driver in Philly; her mother Tina worked as a receptionist at the local Toyota dealership. They were an ordinary family, Tina kept saying over and over again, as if horrible things didn't happen to ordinary people every single day.

"We aren't perfect. Bert works so hard and so do I. But we love our girl. The last few months, she was so darn moody. I thought the terrible twos was hard, but the teenage years are something else."

Bert choked up when he spoke about the last night they'd seen their daughter.

"She'd wanted to go to a homecoming party, and we said no. Her grades were slipping, and I wasn't going to let her wind up like me, driving some damn bus for peanuts for the rest of her life. I thought she was okay with it. We had dinner and Tina's homemade strudel. We all went to bed, and the next morning, she was gone. Vanished."

Their daughter had been gone for forty-seven days. Forty-seven days since they'd seen her, and now here she was, alive. Tina's mother was emphatic. "Tell me, what can we do for you? Please tell us."

"I'd like to see her. Would that be okay?"

Tina hesitated but Bob insisted that it was fine as long as Lily went in alone.

Lily agreed, asking Abby and Wes to wait in the hallway. She followed Shaina's parents. Shaina couldn't understand now, but two months with Rick was nothing. She'd still have a childhood. She'd still fall in love. She could still be a normal person. She wanted to tell Shaina all of that. She also wanted her to know that she was sorry. She thought she'd been enough for Rick. She'd tried so hard. She couldn't have known he'd take someone else.

Lily stood at the entrance of the room, taking in the young girl's battered face. Shaina was fourteen but could have passed for twelve, a child really. Lily couldn't stop staring at the girl's heart-shaped face and the dark bruises covering her cheeks. Both eyes were blackened. She had a busted lip. One of her arms was in a sling, and the other was covered with scrapes and burns. *Rick's training period*, Lily thought. She took several deep breaths, trying to calm herself.

Tina leaned in closer to Shaina, who lay staring up at the ceiling with hollow, pale eyes. "Shaina, honey, this is Lily. She's the girl who saved your life. The one who made sure that horrible man wouldn't hurt you again."

Shaina's eyes darted toward Lily, then her parents, then the door. She was scanning the room, Lily realized. Waiting for Rick to arrive. Waiting for whatever punishment he might inflict next.

Lily moved over to Shaina's bedside, reaching out to console her. "He's not here, Shaina. He can't hurt you. I know what he did to you, and I'm so sorry, but you're going to get through this."

Lily reached for Shaina's hand, and the girl slapped Lily's hand away, letting out a guttural yell.

"No! No! No!" Shaina sat up straight and began screaming, grabbing at Lily, pulling her hair, tearing at her clothes. "He's going to punish me. He's going to punish me. Please tell him I'm so sorry. Tell him I love him and I'm so sorry." Her cries turned to sobs as she flailed at Lily like some wild animal, unused to human interaction.

Lily accepted the blows, ignoring the pain as Shaina's nails dug into her cheek. She understood the girl's rage and terror. Nurses stepped in, struggling to restrain Shaina as her parents tried to help. Lily was ushered out into the hallway. She watched the medical team descend, sedating Shaina until she finally grew still and drifted off.

Lily knew what Shaina had endured; she could never

forget those early months when the brutality was at its worst. Abby reached for Lily again, a tissue in her hand as she attempted to dab at Lily's bleeding face.

"We're done. That's enough," Abby demanded.

But Lily couldn't leave. She ignored Abby and moved back down the hall toward the waiting room. Sheriff Rogers and Wes were watching her, but Lily ignored them. She sank down onto one of the waiting room chairs, and then she spoke, mostly to herself.

"I'll see her again when she's calmer. Once she's had a good night's sleep."

"She doesn't want to see you, Lily. Let's go," Abby said, her voice louder and more demanding than before. She took Lily's arm, and Lily instinctively jerked away.

"Don't touch me."

"I'm sorry, Lil. But you can't—"

"I said I'm not going anywhere."

Abby took a deep, angry breath. Lily always knew when Abby was angry. Her face got red, and her cheeks puffed out. With her weight gain, she resembled a sunburned seagull.

"What are you going to do here, Lily? You think you can fix that girl? Well, you can't. You have to fix your own life."

Lily absorbed Abby's words. She took them in, thinking about her own life, the fragments of her life. She leapt to her feet, tired of being rational.

"What life, Abby? What life? My father is dead. He

died, and I never got to say good-bye. My mother is sleeping with God knows who. The entire world knows I'm having a monster's baby. And if I don't have the baby, they're ready to label *me* a murderer. A monster. Me!"

Abby was backing away from Lily, as if driven by the force of her stinging words. But Lily couldn't stop herself. She kept getting closer to Abby until they were almost nose to nose. "But you know what the worst thing is? You know what that is, Abby, don't you? Tell me that you see it. Tell me you understand why I can't go home with you and *fix* my life."

Abby was crying. "I don't... I don't understand."

Wes stepped forward, holding up his hand as if refereeing a fight. "Lily, stop it. Come on, Abby. I'll take you to Eve's and I'll come back for Lily."

"I don't need you to come back for me," Lily spat at him. She glared back at Abby, her fury building. "I asked you a question. Tell me, Abby, do you know why I can't go home?"

Abby was crying even harder now. But Lily kept at her, not an ounce of sympathy on display. "I don't have a home, Abby. I don't have a life. Not anymore. You stole *my* fucking life."

The look on Abby's face was exactly what Lily wanted to see. Devastation, sorrow, regret: all of these emotions crashing into her. The instant Lily said it, the instant she saw Abby's look, Lily's legs gave out and she tumbled to the floor. She heard someone calling for a nurse, but all Lily could do was sit there on the scratchy carpet and stare at Abby, her body contorted as she sobbed, eyes haunted and swollen and clutching her pregnant belly. Wes moved to Abby's side, whispering something to Abby that Lily couldn't hear.

This is what he did, Lily thought. *This is what Rick did. He found your weakness and then he pushed and pushed at you until he broke you down and destroyed you.* That's what he'd done to her, and now she'd done the same thing to Abby . . . and it couldn't be undone.

Abby pushed Wes aside and almost crawled over to Lily.

"You think I wouldn't give up all of this? You want Wes, you can have him, Lily!" Abby's voice was barely a whisper. "Take him. It's always been about you. It's always been about us. We're the twins. Me and you. That never changed. When you were gone, I was gone too. Three thousand one hundred and ten days, Lily. All I wanted was you. I'm sorry I blamed you for stealing the sweater. I had it. I had it all along. And I'm sorry I'm fat and gross and I've wasted my life. And I'm so sorry I can't take all this pain away. I can't change the past. I can't change what happened to you. I can't change what Wes and I did. Or what Rick did to you and these girls. But I would, Lily. You have to believe me. I'd do anything to change it."

Lily began to cry. How could Lily help that child when she was so broken herself? Ashamed, Lily stood up and headed for the exit. Bursting out of the hospital doors, she started running. She owed Abby an apology. She owed Wes one too, but she wasn't strong enough for that right now. The only thing she cared about was getting back to Sky. It had been the two of them before. It'd be the two of them against the world now.

RICK

He'd miscalculated. Rick had looked into Lily's eyes and he'd listened to her make him a promise. And she'd lied. She'd flat out lied to him without even batting an eye. Once Lily was gone, he'd lost his cool completely, giving the officers the chance to pounce: pepper spray to the face, kicks and punches to his lower extremities long after they had him subdued. He kept thinking about ways he could stop Lily from killing his child, how he could ensure that his baby was protected. He'd hoped that when Missy came to visit him, he might convince her to help him. He was sure they could file some kind of an injunction. Missy could even raise the baby if she wanted.

But the minute she sat down, Rick realized that he'd lost Missy. It wasn't her appearance. Her makeup was now flawless, her black pantsuit tailored to perfection—icy and untouchable, a perfect Southern belle in fluorescent light. It was the vindictive gaze in her eyes that told him everything he needed to know.

"So, I heard the news," Missy said from behind the

glass, carefully cradling the phone in her hands. "It appears one of your *other* girls killed herself. They're charging you with manslaughter."

He wondered which girl it was. He'd bet it was the older one. She'd been a hassle from the moment he grabbed her. He'd been aware of the risks, how brazen it was to keep all three girls. It was a little greedy; he knew that. And it wasn't that he didn't still love Lily. She was his baby doll after all, but he needed someone younger, a new challenge. He'd liked both girls, figured he'd train them both and then pick his favorite. Which is why this was so ridiculous. They'd barely even gotten to know each other. It wasn't his fault that weak-minded twit had taken her own life.

"You're going to rot in prison for the rest of your life," Missy said, the hint of a smile on her face. She was enjoying this. Damn. He hadn't seen this side of Missy before. Her vindictiveness was starting to turn him on.

"Mother and Daddy put the house on the market. The realtor said it would sell in no time because people are so screwed up and would find living in a monster's home a novelty. I thought about moving back to North Carolina with them, but people would never stop talking about how dumb I was, wondering how I could live with you, how I could go to bed with someone like you and not know what you are."

Her voice dripped with hatred. Rick almost felt sorry for her.

"Tell me, Rick, did those other girls trap you too? Did that fourteen-year-old hitchhiker tell you that she loved you? Or that sixteen-year-old girl, the one who hanged herself with a bedsheet, was she also madly in love with you?"

Really, what more could he say? Maybe Missy was dumb enough to buy his story about Lily, but even she was smart enough to see what kind of person he was. He shrugged and leaned back, giving her a dismissive wave.

"Lily was a wonderful companion, a brilliant mother, and a generous lover. The others demonstrated potential, as well. They were all better than you. All of them." His words were hollow and revealed who he really was. He owed that to her. To show her that part of him. It was the truth, and she deserved the truth. He expected her to fall apart, to lose it. He was proud that she didn't. Instead, she leaned in closer, cradling the phone to her ear.

"I hope you burn in hell, Rick." She paused, then laughed. "What am I talking about? I *know* you'll burn in hell for what you've done."

She hung up the phone and walked out of his life. He was disappointed. Not because he had lost her, but because he was pretty sure he'd lost the three-hundred-dollar-an-hour attorney her parents had been financing. Now he'd be stuck with some pathetic public defender. He really should have demanded that Lily sign something instead of trusting that bitch. He should have never put himself in this situation. But love blinded you; it made you do foolish things.

All this meant was that he needed a new plan. Over the past few days he'd focused his attentions on Angela, the pig-faced guard. He'd seen her watching him, sizing him up, wondering if everything she'd heard and read about him was true. She kept her distance but he'd been breaking the ice, starting casual conversations about meaningless things like the weather. He'd asked her why she'd intervened that first day when he'd been arrested. Why she stopped his beating.

Angela shrugged and said, "Because that's not what we do."

He appreciated her integrity but he hoped that it was tenuous. He needed to figure out an angle, find some way to get closer to her. He'd heard from the animals in this place that she was a single mom, which was good. They were easy targets: vulnerable and desperate for affection. He didn't know why exactly, but he had a good feeling about her. He sensed something familiar in her, a darkness lurking under the surface. If he played his cards right, she might just be his ticket out of there. He was still trying to assess the situation properly. It wouldn't be easy, but he was formulating a plan. That was his specialty: planning. One thing he was sure of was that once he escaped, he was going to pay a visit to Lily. She was in need of serious punishment for her transgressions. *Don't get too comfortable*, he thought. *I'm coming for you, Baby Doll.*

LILY

"Please just leave me alone."

That became Lily's mantra. For twenty-two days she camped out in her bedroom, perfectly content to stay locked away, perfectly content to shut out Rick, the media, the other victims, or anything else that might come her way. At least that's what she told her family. Truthfully, after her behavior at the hospital, the things she said, Lily was too ashamed to face anyone. She'd crafted a long e-mail apology to Wes on Eve's laptop, telling him what he'd meant to her, telling him that she wanted him and Abby to be happy. In the end, she'd deleted the entire thing and simply wrote: *I'm sorry. Lily.*

She'd tried to talk about it with Abby, but her sister didn't want to discuss it.

"It's already forgotten, Lil."

But Lily couldn't forget that night. She couldn't forget how much she'd wanted to punish her sister. What if she did it again? What if Rick had ruined her? No, it was easier to stay in her room. She had Sky to cuddle with, to make her feel normal. Mom delivered her meals morning, noon, and night. The flat-screen TV was equipped with endless cable stations. Lily hadn't seen cable TV in years. They'd had a black-and-white set with basic channels that worked sporadically. Lily was amazed at how much mindless entertainment there was. She was obsessed with reality TV and the inane problems of even more inane people. She enjoyed watching fights over meaningless things. Who got a rose? Who wore it best? What housewife was the most real? It was all so ridiculous that she couldn't look away. It was easier to watch this mindless crap than think about Rick or the other girls or to think about the thing that was growing inside her. She'd found the perfect place to hide from the world and the terror that lurked in her subconscious.

And then she woke up one day, the house still dark, to find Sky gone. Terror coursed through Lily's body. Where was she? Maybe Rick had sent someone for her. It was possible. Anything was possible when it came to Rick.

Lily bit back a scream, scanning the room, trying to keep her breathing steady. Sky never left Lily's side without permission. Sky never did anything without making sure Lily gave her approval. She'd wait patiently for Lily to say yes, often trying to lure her out of the room. But this morning she was gone.

Lily leapt out of bed and was almost out the door when she spotted the edge of her grandma's knitted blue quilt sticking out of the closet. She swung open the door and found Sky curled up in a ball, fast asleep. Relieved, Lily knelt down and wrapped her daughter in her arms. She'd picked Sky up and put her back to bed, telling herself this was an isolated event. But soon this became their routine, night after night, Lily waking from a deep sleep to find Sky dozing in the closet. Lily tried to ignore what was happening, tried to tell herself that Sky would be fine after more time had passed.

On the fortieth day of Lily's self-confinement, she woke with a stomach ache, her body racked with cramps. She found Sky in the closet and raced her back into bed. She felt something wet staining her legs and looked down to see blood.

She raced into the bathroom. Lily didn't need tests or doctors to tell her that the baby was gone. She wanted to mourn the loss, but this baby had never been real to her. It couldn't be. Lily stared down at her thin, angular frame, surveying the scars, the souvenirs he'd left. Her body was hers again. All hers. Lily began to cry, deep, heavy, heart-wrenching sobs. Rick no longer controlled her emotions. She collapsed onto the bathroom rug, her crying growing louder and louder. Lily didn't know how long she lay there. She heard yelling, saw Mom and Abby staring down at her.

Mom grabbed a towel and moved beside Lily, ordering Abby to get help.

"Call 911. Right now."

But Lily stopped her.

"No. Don't. Please. Just wait."

She reached out for Abby and Mom, and they held Lily until her tears were all cried out. When she was finally able to speak again, Abby brushed Lily's hair aside.

"Lil, you tell us, what do you want us to do? What do you need?"

Lily thought about Sky, about the sharpness of the memories that were seeping in day by day, and she forced herself to say the words she'd been so afraid to say since she'd returned home.

"I need... I need help."

EVE

"Have Yourself a Merry Little Christmas" wafted from the speakers of Dr. Amari's private practice, a plush office located a few miles from Lancaster Medical Center. Eve sat beside Lily, waiting for her appointment to begin.

"I haven't heard you sing in so long. I forgot how pretty your voice was," Lily said softly.

"Good Lord, I must be losing it. I didn't even know I was singing," Eve said.

"You'll have to teach Sky all your favorite carols."

"I can't wait. She'll be our little Christmas songbird in no time."

Lily squeezed Eve's hand just as Dr. Amari appeared at the door.

"Lily, are you ready?" Dr. Amari asked.

Lily nodded, putting on a brave face. Eve knew that it was difficult for Lily to come here, to discuss all that she'd endured. But Dr. Amari had been a lifesaver. There was a part of Eve that actually believed one day they might all be whole again. Lily reached out to Eve for a hug. There were always hugs now. Eve hoped that wouldn't change.

"Abby will pick you up, but if you need something, you have my cell."

Eve watched as Lily disappeared into Dr. Amari's office. Over the last few weeks, they'd settled into a comfortable routine. Eve would bring Lily to therapy while Abby looked after Sky. Then Eve would do whatever errands she had, following up on her hospital lawsuit or stopping by to visit with Bree Whitaker's family. She'd been lucky to get Lily back but the Whitakers' daughter was never coming home. Eve would sometimes drop off food, but most days she'd just sit and listen. Listen to Mrs. Whitaker talk about Bree, who she was, who she might have been. While Eve was busy, Abby and Sky would pick Lily up from therapy. Some nights they'd go out to dinner; other nights they'd all meet back at the house and Eve would whip up one of her specialty dishes.

It was still early days, but Lily was making progress. She spent less and less time in her room, instead choosing to hang in the den with Eve or Abby. Sometimes she'd slip out the back door with Abby and Sky and take a walk around the neighborhood. Eve would never be able to thank Dr. Amari enough. She'd been there with Lily, Abby, and Eve every step of the way, dealing with the press and the protestors. Eve had been convinced that news of Lily's miscarriage would be met with skepticism, but Dr. Amari took charge. After consulting with the police, she'd been able to release Lily's medical records, which contained explicit details of the abuse Lily had suffered at Rick's hands. It was easy to assume that those injuries had led to her pregnancy complications. Even if the public hadn't believed her, a mass shooting at a middle school in Texas resulted in the death of six children, and just like that Lily's sorrows were old news.

Eve tried not to think about Rick Hanson, his other victims, all the damage he'd wrought. She was determined to put him out of her mind and focus on the future. In just three days, they'd celebrate their first Christmas together. For Eve, holidays had always been the personification of everything she'd lost. But now, they would build new traditions. Her parents and Meme were returning. Abby had even called a truce (or so it seemed) and invited Wes for Christmas dinner. Eve was cooking a turkey, and Lily and Abby were making enough desserts to open a bakery. And if Eve had her way, there would be so many presents in the house she'd give Santa a run for his money. It was safe to say that all her Christmas wishes had come true.

Of course, she still had a million things to do before she headed to the mall. Eve pulled into the motel and quickly made her way up the stairs. She'd seen Tommy's car in the parking lot and quickly picked up her pace, knowing they didn't have a lot of time. She'd told him they'd wait to see each other until after the holidays, but he'd insisted on one last night together before he went to Boston with his family.

Eve slipped the key in the door, pushed it open, and gasped. Inside were dozens of red poinsettias, her favorite holiday plant. White lights hung from every conceivable surface, and a miniature Christmas tree was proudly displayed on the makeshift desk. But the biggest surprise was Tommy, sitting on the bed wearing a ridiculous green Christmas sweater with a fuzzy kitten on it, holding a sprig of mistletoe.

"Merry Christmas, Eve," he said, beaming.

Eve could barely believe her eyes.

"What... what is this?"

"Our first Christmas together."

Tommy reached for her and kissed her gently. There was still passion but she felt the shift, the promise of something more. She'd tried to tell herself that this was temporary, that the stolen moments they had together were enough. But maybe things were changing for both of them.

Tommy pulled away first.

"We'll get back to that in a moment. First, your gift."

Eve playfully swatted him.

"That's not fair. We said no gifts," she reminded him.

Tommy laughed. "*You* said no gifts. I made no such promises."

He handed her a tiny package, and Eve carefully undid the gold and red wrapping. From a tiny box, she pulled out a delicate gold locket.

"I figured you'd find the right picture to put in it."

Eve felt tears well up. She leaned in and kissed him, wanting him to know what this meant to her, wanting him to feel everything she felt. He wrapped his arms around her and held her, the two of them sitting side by side on the bed, the twinkling lights casting shadows on their faces.

She knew they were headed down a dangerous path. That at the end of this road more people could get hurt. But Eve didn't care. After all she'd been through, after everything, she deserved to be selfish. She deserved this. She deserved him.

LILY

How do you feel? Overall how would you describe your mood? What color is that emotion? Apparently, there were hundreds of ways to express yourself, and Lily had been forced to suppress them all. Dr. Amari asked difficult questions but never pushed Lily to answer when she wasn't ready.

The holidays had been more difficult than she'd imagined.

"Tell me why," Dr. Amari said.

Lily was quiet. She wasn't quite sure. There were so many things she'd loved. Watching Sky come downstairs to a Christmas tree stuffed with presents, her tiny body vibrating from excitement as she tried to choose her first gift to open. Late-night wrapping sessions with Abby, and helping Meme make her famous pecan pie. But there was something lurking beneath the surface, something she still hadn't told anyone.

"It's about Sky, isn't it? That's what's troubling you?"

Lily hated that she'd given herself away. She wasn't going to discuss Sky.

"She's doing fine now. She's making great progress. Her tutor says she's reading at a third-grade level."

"Lily, you can't deny your daughter's suffering."

"I kept her safe. I told you—"

"You did. You've raised her well, brilliantly, in fact. She's incredibly smart and intuitive and kind. But she's not clueless. She knows something wasn't right about her life down there. She has to be experiencing some kind of after-effects. Or am I wrong?"

Lily tried to deny it, but Dr. Amari kept pushing and pushing until Lily confessed about Sky's night-time activities.

"I don't know why she'd want to sleep in the closet. I did everything I could to make sure he didn't hurt her."

"But she knows that Rick hurt you. She knows something. She has to."

Lily cried, knowing it was true. No matter how hard she tried, Sky had to know that Rick had harmed Lily. Dr. Amari moved to sit beside her, handing over tissues.

"As much as you want to protect her and move on with life as if none of this happened, Sky lived with the same terror and anxiety you have, even if she was too young to properly communicate it to you. She needs therapy just like you, Lily, and she needs it soon."

Lily left the office, Dr. Amari's words ringing in her ears. The last thing she wanted was for Sky to suffer. That night, after they'd said their prayers and kissed

Mom and Abby good night, Lily curled up in bed with Sky, wrapping her arms around her, breathing in her perfect scent.

"Baby, do you understand why you can't see Daddy Rick anymore?" Lily asked, bracing herself for the answer.

"Because he made you sad?"

"Yes. But he also hurt me. You know that, don't you?"

"I know."

"And I know it's hard to understand, but Daddy Rick kept me away from Grandma and Abby and all my friends and family."

"Why did he do that?"

That was the million-dollar question, wasn't it? Lily didn't understand, so how was it possible to explain to Sky? Lily's inquiries seemed to give Sky permission, and she unleashed a torrent of questions. Did Daddy Rick still love her? Could she love him? Was she bad because he was her father? Lily realized Dr. Amari was right. She wasn't equipped to answer these questions. How do you explain to a child what evil is when you don't understand yourself? She pulled Sky in for a hug. She'd make this right. She'd help her daughter get answers.

With Dr. Amari's support, Lily and Sky began working with a top-rated child psychologist. There were other things besides Sky's sleep issues, phobias Lily hadn't realized: large crowds, public spaces, food hoarding, suppressing her emotions. Sky thrived in therapy, enjoying the games her new "friend" Dr. Dobson taught her each week.

Dr. Amari was working with Lily, trying to prepare her for the day when Sky would go to school, something she constantly talked about. Dr. Amari stressed the importance of allowing Sky to have a real childhood, which meant interacting with children Sky's age. Lily wasn't ready to send Sky to school, but she hoped that one day soon she would be.

Initially, Lily dreaded her sessions with Dr. Amari, but slowly, she began to look forward to them. If Lily wanted to spend forty-five minutes talking about how much she hated driving by the high school, Dr. Amari let her. Lily found herself opening up more and more about Rick's "training," about her sadness over the death of her father, and her worry about what Abby had been through. She still never mentioned her feelings about Wes.

Some days she wished he'd just go away. Just walk out the front door and never come back. She knew that was wrong, especially when he treated them so well. Sometimes he'd stop and drop off dinner; other times he'd bring ice cream from Friendly's. Lily might have been uncomfortable around Wes, but Sky adored him. He gave her piggyback rides and told her outrageous fairy tales that made Sky giggle uncontrollably. Lily reveled in those joyous moments. She'd taken a ridiculous amount of pictures and video on the cell phone she'd gotten for Christmas, recording all those "normal kid" things so she could review them later. Sometimes, Lily would lie awake for hours on end, staring at those images, freeze-framing them as if she might forever capture that happiness and remind herself she'd done something right. But inevitably, Lily would find her gaze drifting over to Wes, watching his dimpled smile and effortless nature. She'd force herself to shut off the video or leave the room, determined to forget about Wes and any fantasy that he would ever be hers.

As spring made its arrival, Lily grew stronger. She'd also gotten a new pair of running shoes for Christmas, and while she wouldn't run alone, sometimes Mom would come along with her or she'd recruit Trisha to go for a run. She spent a lot of time staring at the garden, hating to see it so neglected. Something in Lily stirred, a desire to restore the yard to its former glory. She realized how strange it was, considering how much she'd resented her father's devotion to the garden. He'd spend hours and hours on his days off, wearing his ratty U Penn med school T-shirt and shorts, his stupid gardening hat tilted to the side, digging and pulling weeds while educating the girls on the best times for planting. But now, Lily could pass hours in the sun, the moist dirt in her hands, the space transforming day by day. With her hands working the soil, she'd find herself feeling closer and closer to Dad, often waking up at dawn to pull up weeds or begin planting blooms and vegetables.

Lily loved being outside during the day, soaking up the sun. It was only at night that Lily began to see shadows that weren't there, to hear noises that weren't real. She knew it was irrational. She'd been kidnapped in broad daylight, but all those years in darkness had taken their toll.

It was one of those gorgeous spring days that Lily decided to stay home while Abby, Mom, and Sky went into Philly to do some shopping. Lily had been determined to plant her remaining tulip bulbs and had sent them off with her blessing. It was almost six o'clock that evening when Abby called.

"Lilypad, there's a total cluster on the highway. We'll be at least another hour. Maybe two."

Lily tried to fight her rising panic, staring at the sun as it began to sink into the horizon.

"Okay. Thanks for letting me know."

"Are you sure you'll be okay?" Abby asked.

Lily hadn't told anyone about this irrational fear of the dark, even Abby. Considering everything she'd endured, it seemed almost silly.

"I'm fine, Abs. Drive safe, and tell Sky that Mommy loves and misses her."

Lily hung up the phone and went back to work. Her hands dug into the dirt, but they were shaking, her breathing coming out in rapid spurts. She could feel her panic growing and she kept glancing out at the street, worried that Rick or some other unknown evil might choose tonight to take her away from all of this. She couldn't take it anymore. Lily grabbed her phone and dialed.

"Wes, it's Lily. I know it's dumb, but it's getting dark, and Mom and Sky and Abby got stuck in traffic, and I'm...I can't be alone. I was just wondering..."

She didn't even finish her sentence.

"I'm wrapping things up here at work. I'll swing by in ten."

She'd known that he would come. He'd do anything for Abby and, by extension, anything for Lily.

Wes arrived ten minutes later on the dot, still wearing his coat and tie. Lily had learned that Wes had his own real estate business, buying and selling fixer-uppers. He stripped off his necktie and jacket, rolled up his shirtsleeves, and clapped his hands, gesturing to the remaining bulbs waiting to be planted.

"Come on, don't make me feel useless," Wes said.

"Let's just call it a night. I'll finish up tomorrow."

"No way. We've got a job to do."

He picked up a tulip bulb, cradling it in his palm. Lily pointed out the order she wanted, and he followed her instructions, carefully organizing the flowers in long rows. He was calm, his brow furrowing as he planted. Lily finished her batch and then sat back on her heels. He turned and caught her staring at him.

"What is it? Am I doing something wrong?"

Without thinking, Lily reached out to wipe the dirt from his cheek. Wes stared back at her, and Lily leaned forward, her breath catching as their lips touched. The kiss began chastely, but Wes's lips were so tender and warm. She moved in closer. She couldn't believe it. He smelled and tasted exactly as she'd remembered. He felt it too. He stood up and pulled her to him. Lily pressed her entire body against his. She wanted him. She'd never wanted anyone more than she wanted Wes right now.

"I love you. I still love you."

Wes jerked back as if she'd struck him. Lily realized she had to fix this. She had to make him see that she was the one he wanted. That it had always been her.

"Whatever you want, whatever you want me to do, I'll do it. Please, Wes, there's nothing I won't do." Lily's voice was desperate as she reached for his belt. He roughly pushed her away.

"No, Lily, Jesus Christ, no. Don't!"

She cowered, her hand blocking her face before he could strike her.

Wes stepped forward, stricken.

"I'm not...Jesus, Lily, I wouldn't hurt you. You have to know that. But I can't...We can't..."

Lily heard the pity and the judgment in his voice. What had she done? What was wrong with her? The thoughts of that night at the hospital came rushing back. Horrified, Lily stumbled and almost toppled over into the dirt.

Wes reached out to steady her, but she pushed him away.

"I can't believe . . . I shouldn't have . . . I wanted to remember what it was like. What it could be like."

"Lily. I understand."

But he didn't. Lily didn't want to hear anything else. She pushed past him and fled upstairs. She stayed in her room until she was sure Wes had left, and then she texted Dr. Amari, requesting an emergency session.

An hour later, Lily sat across from the doctor and haltingly confessed what had happened. When she was done, she let out a sigh.

"I'm an awful human being."

Dr. Amari leaned back, her gaze probing.

"Why do you say that?" Dr. Amari asked.

"I kissed Wes."

"And that's wrong because?"

Her tone held no judgment. No condemnation.

"He's Abby's now. She's having his baby."

"That's true. So, why do you think you kissed him?"

Lily inhaled, her confession tumbling out. "I think about him all the time. When he's in our kitchen and he pours Abby a glass of water, I want it to be me that he's pouring it for. When Sky's sitting on his lap and he's reading to her, I think, 'I wish he was reading to our daughter. I wish we were a family.'"

"But he's not. You're not."

"I know."

"And how does that make you feel?"

"It makes me feel like a horrible person. He's been so

good to me and to Sky. But I liked kissing him. I wanted him. But he's Abby's now. They're having a baby together. And—"

"And you made a mistake. You're human. You're an ordinary person who makes mistakes."

"No. No, it's not that."

"What is it, Lily?"

"It's Rick. He's made me this way. Turned me into someone who takes what I want, without thinking about the pain it causes the other person."

"Is that really what you think? Why do you feel that way?"

"Don't do that. Please don't do that."

"Don't do what, Lily? We all know that Rick Hanson is a depraved individual. You could never be like him. You know why? Because your daughter is a wonderful child, and you are a wonderful young woman."

Lily's chest tightened. She stood up, worried she'd explode if she sat any longer.

"Don't you see that I've thought about seducing Wes? I think about it, what I could do, what I'd let him do to me. Anything he wants, so he'll love *me*. Not her. But she's my sister..."

"And Wes was your first love?"

"That doesn't matter."

"It absolutely matters, Lily. How could it not? You were a child. A helpless child. And Rick Hanson stole that. He stole your sexuality and your innocence and all those years with your family and even your life with Wes. But, Lily, if you were like Rick, you wouldn't be sitting here in my office, talking about what a bad person you are. You'd be in bed with Wes or you'd be figuring out a way to steal him away. You're not like Rick, Lily, and nothing you do will make you like him. It's simplistic but it's true. Good people make bad decisions. It happens all the time. That doesn't make you a sociopath; it makes you human. Listen to me when I say you're not like him. You can *never* be like him."

You're not like him. You can never be like him. Those words echoed in Lily's head as she left Dr. Amari's office. She promised herself that would become her mantra, and she'd keep saying it until one day, she'd finally believe it.

RICK

The bitch was a murderer. There was no way around it. Rick still couldn't believe that his baby was dead. As he stood under the leaky faucet in the jailhouse shower, icy cold water drenching him, he still felt that same sense of fury as when he'd heard the news. A miscarriage, that's what they'd said. He'd never believe that. He'd hoped to deal with this tragedy in private, but Fred and the other guards had latched on to it, taunting him by leaving newspaper articles and decapitated dolls in his cell.

What really bothered him wasn't the loss of the baby itself. What bothered him was that disobedient cunt and her lies. Didn't everyone see that this was proof that Lily simply wasn't capable of caring for herself?

"Rick, time's up."

Rick heard Angela's voice and he shut off the water. He grabbed his towel and dried off, and he slipped into his jail-issued uniform. Angela cuffed him, her hands gently stroking his wrist. Rick smiled back, playing up their "connection" for all it was worth. Things had definitely heated up in recent weeks.

He'd been right. It was almost too easy earning her trust. Rick was kept in constant isolation, away from other inmates due to his "high-priority" status. Angela worked the late shift, or the "shit shift" as it was called, given to all the newbies. The other guards hated his guts, so it fell to Angela to escort him to the showers, his lawyer, or outside for his hour of recreation.

Rick's trick to winning people over was simple— shut up and listen. Most people want to be heard, but they're always just waiting for their turn to talk. Ugly women craved attention more than anyone. All it took was asking Angela about her life and she came alive. Each night she'd go on and on, venting about her mother, who thought Angela was a loser. Or her drug-addicted ex-husband Nick, who was withholding child support. Or her three-year-old son Caleb, whom she was convinced she was failing. Rick cataloged each name and issue, inquiring about them daily.

"How was Caleb's first day at daycare?" "Did Nick keep his word and buy diapers?" "Did you tell your mother to go to hell?" Before long, Angela forgot who he was and the crimes he'd confessed to, and she began treating him like a trusted confidante. She'd fume about the ongoing abuse Rick endured at the hands of the guards, wondering how she could rat out her coworkers without losing her job. Rick told her not to bother.

"Maybe someone like me deserves this. Maybe they're right."

Angela would grow serious, and quote some bullshit Scripture about forgiveness. Rick never paid attention to religion. It was for mindless sheep, people so weak they couldn't make decisions without written instructions. But he'd thanked Angela and mentioned that reading Scripture might be a useful way to pass the time. The next day a King James Bible appeared on his cot.

As the days passed he tested Angela, mentioning a novel he wanted to read (generally something pedestrian he knew she'd like, some inane romance novel or self-help book), and like magic it would appear in his cell. Before long there were chocolates and other home-made treats. He'd always thank her profusely, continuing to feign interest in her mundane life.

Now that he was fully dressed, they made their way around the corner and away from the camera's view. He stopped, pushed her against the wall, and began kissing her passionately. Her desire was obvious, her tongue practically excavating his mouth as her roly-poly body clung tightly to him. He let his hands graze her body. He was really scraping the bottom of the barrel, but he'd been planning this moment. Their first kiss. When he finally pulled away, she was breathless.

"I've been wanting to do that for weeks. You're all I can think about. But it's not safe. If you got caught..."

A hesitant expression flashed across Angela's face.

Rick wondered if he'd misjudged her, that her sense of duty might outweigh her desire. But she clung to him, her voice a throaty whisper.

"You're right. We'll be careful."

He grinned, lifting up a cuffed hand to stroke her cheek. Angela leaned into it.

"They're wrong about you, Ricky. I know it."

He winced. *Ricky?* But he forced a smile and put his cuffed hand in hers. He let it rest on the front of his pants. Even if she was disgusting, he still had needs and he'd been without female contact for far too long.

"You've made me very happy, Angie."

"I'll look out for you. Whatever you need, I'll do it."

She'd leaned in for one more kiss, and then led him back to his cell. Her hands trembled as she took off the cuffs. By the time she slammed the door shut and disappeared back down the hall, Rick realized that he finally had an ally.

As he settled into his bunk, his mind was racing with ideas and strategies about how Angela would be most useful. With his baby gone and Rick locked away, he knew that Lily was out there celebrating with that pathetic sister of hers, the two of them convinced they'd outsmarted him. He'd have to plan carefully but he hadn't come this far to let anyone get the best of him. He'd make sure Lily and her entire goddamn family would regret ever underestimating him. He'd make them all pay.

ABBY

The rain poured down in steady, relentless sheets as Abby leaned against the porch railing. Movers drifted in and out of Wes's house, their arms weighed down with boxes. Her boxes. Since Abby had been living at her mother's, Wes had moved back into his house. Abby had decided to move home permanently.

Why wouldn't it rain on moving day? she thought. *Just so fucking typical.*

Abby sighed, a sharp pain shooting through her back. It was aching so badly it was as if tiny spikes were digging into the muscles. The alien invader was killing her, literally killing her. That nesting instinct or whatever they called it made her restless. She'd been putting this off, but the baby would be here soon and she needed to extricate herself from Wes in all ways.

She saw Wes watching her. He was covered in sweat and drenched from the steady rain, his black hoodie covering his hair and part of his face. For once, she wasn't annoyed. A wave of sympathy coursed through her. She was leaving this house, the house he'd tried so hard to make their home. These days—and she blamed the hormones—but these days, she was grateful for his steady presence. Wes had a knack for entertaining Sky, making all of them laugh, including Lily. Abby knew her sister was wrestling with the reality of what they'd been through. Lily had tried to apologize, but she had nothing to be sorry for. They'd moved past that night at the hospital, and for Abby, it felt like they were getting closer to where they'd been. But she worried it would never be the same.

Lily tried to put on a good show, but there were times when Abby saw the darkness consume her sister. One minute, Lily would be gardening, or teasing Sky while she cooked breakfast, or they'd all be in the den watching *The Bachelor*, or one of the dozens of DVD sets Abby had bought to improve Lily's pop-culture IQ, and then Lily would vanish into her room, into her books, into the abyss Rick Hanson left behind. Every time Lily disappeared for the day or even the evening, Abby was on edge, waiting for Lily to break down again. But the next day, Lily would reappear, as if nothing were wrong. Abby knew that couldn't possibly be true, but she had to follow Lily's lead.

Everyone was trying to move forward, trying to forget about Hanson. Some days it almost felt like things were normal again. But Abby couldn't seem to shake the anger and rage that still consumed her. She wanted to be like Lily—her sister seemed so kind and hopeful and optimistic—but for Abby, keeping up that facade was so much work. Still, she tried. She'd made serious progress with Wes, accepting that he wasn't the enemy. She was just as "guilty" for pursuing their relationship. But Wes was still there, an outsider trying to get in.

"Ma'am, we're all done here. Should we meet you at the new house?" one of the movers asked.

"That would be great. Thank you."

They went to leave and Abby turned to Wes, offering up a weak smile. He moved beside her, trying to act cool, but there was pleading in his tone.

"It's not too late, Abs. Let's tell these guys to stop what they're doing. We'll unpack it all."

Abby's stomach did a flip, an emotional pull deep inside that she blamed on the alien invader. Why was Wes saying these things? They'd already been through this.

"Lily needs me." Abby turned to go.

"I need you." He grabbed her.

"Wes, please don't." She tried to push him away.

But he came back, as he always did, like a goddamn gnat, holding her tightly to him. "You've given up the last eight years of your life. Shutting yourself off to me and Eve and all your friends. When are you going to have your own life? When?"

"I don't know."

"And what about me?"

"You're this baby's father. My moving out doesn't change that."

"Wow. Thanks. That's great. A sperm donor with visitation rights. I appreciate that."

"We've talked about this. I can't be with you. I can't do that to Lily."

Wes's eyes flashed with anger. He shook his head and laughed, but there was something else in his expression. Something so smug and knowing, as if he had a secret he couldn't wait to share.

"What? What is so funny?" she asked, hating that look.

"Lily kissed me. Did she tell you that she kissed me?"

Abby stared at him, at his anger-filled eyes.

"So what, Wes? It doesn't matter."

He grabbed her arm again. "So, you're okay with the fact that she kissed me? That her mouth was on mine and our bodies were *this* close, and I liked it. No. I loved it. We were all alone and I thought, why not? I could so easily be with her. I remembered *exactly* what it was like back then. She was my first love too. I remember how excited she was to be around me, how easy things were. When she kissed me, I thought, maybe I should pick her. She'll laugh at my jokes. She'll be grateful for everything I do for her. Most importantly, she won't punish me for loving her. But don't you see, Abby? You're not interchangeable. I can't pick and choose one

295

of you at random. I love *you*. I love you even though you're a total bitch, even though you make me crazy. I love *you*. Not Lily. And maybe you'll keep punishing me. Maybe you'll keep punishing yourself, but don't tell me it doesn't matter. This matters. *We* matter. And I'm not letting you go until you say it."

She stared at him, his hand on her arm, holding her, clutching her. Abby pushed him away and headed down the sidewalk, feeling nauseated and dizzy. She needed to get away from him, to get away from the image of his lips locked with Lily's, bodies pressed together. She slowly made her way to the street, but a sharp pain in her abdomen nearly sent her tumbling to the ground. She reached out, grabbing onto a nearby car to steady herself. Wes was by her side in an instant.

"Abby? Are you okay? Is it the baby?"

A contraction crashed into her, and she gasped. "Yes! Oh shit. Call Mom and Lily. I want them at the hospital. Please, get them there."

"I will, Abs. I swear."

Wes put his arms around Abby and carried her to his pickup. He held on to her, whispering about how much he loved her and about how much he was going to love their baby.

Abby couldn't believe he was still here. After all the horrible things she'd said and done to him, he was here. A contraction crashed into her, and Abby closed her eyes. This pain was almost welcome. She wanted to say something, to make him understand why she did the things she did. How it had nothing to do with him. Instead, she took his hand in hers and held on for dear life.

"Don't leave me, okay? You won't leave me?"

"Not a chance."

LILY

"Breathe, Abs. I know it hurts, but if you breathe, it's not as bad." Lily was coaching Abby, calmly clutching her hand, wiping her sweaty forehead, and feeding her ice chips. "You're so brave. So brave."

The contraction passed and Abby laughed. "I'm in one of the top hospitals in the state with the best doctors and lots of drugs, which I will be demanding very soon, and you're calling me brave? *That* is crazy."

Lily took the wet cloth and wiped Abby's brow again. Wes had gone to check on Sky and their mom, or at least that was the excuse he'd given her. Lily was pretty sure he knew they needed some time alone. Now it was just the two of them, waiting for Abby's baby to arrive.

"I can think you're brave if I want to. You can't stop me."

Abby smiled but then quickly sobered. "When you had Sky... how hard... how did you do it?"

Lily was quiet. The day Sky was born was the day Lily was reborn. Lily knew when the baby kicked that something was changing, not only physically, but emotionally. Her desire to survive blossomed with each passing month. She'd still challenge Rick, refuse some of his wishes, but her recklessness lessened. It made her reassess everything. If he wanted an obedient doll, that's what she would become.

The day Sky was born, Rick had left for an annual teachers' conference in New York. In the middle of the week, in the middle of the night, her contractions began, slamming into her body, the pain overwhelming her. After eleven agonizing hours, her water broke. Lily remembered the moment so clearly.

"The pain was nothing. In fact, I welcomed it, because I knew I wouldn't be alone anymore. I kept pushing and crying and telling her I was ready for her. When she landed on the bed of blankets and towels I'd arranged, she cried so loudly. It was the first human sound I'd heard—other than his voice—in so long. Her eyes were so wise and knowing. It sounds crazy now, because she was this innocent little baby, but she'd been sent to keep me going."

Abby squeezed Lily's hand. "You are the brave one, Lilypad. You're so fucking brave."

Lily smiled, wiping the tears from Abby's cheeks. "We're twins. It's genetic."

They were quiet then, Abby doing her Lamaze breathing, Lily rubbing Abby's back, feeding her more ice chips, coaching her.

As the night wore on, Wes returned, taking a spot on the other side of Abby. It should have been awkward, the three of them in one room, all the history between them. Instead, they took turns coaching Abby, calming and soothing her nerves. At dawn, the contractions increased, and the doctors and nurses descended. It was time.

Lily and Wes held Abby's hands, her breathing ragged and shallow as she pushed and pushed, screaming and crying and begging for it to be over. She'd refused the drugs. Abby insisted on being clear-headed for this. The baby arrived, just as the sun peered over the horizon. He was wailing loudly, his tiny body contorting as the doctors tended to him.

"It's a boy, Abby. It's a baby boy," Lily said.

Wes wiped furiously at his eyes, smiling so brightly he could have powered New York City.

Abby stared at the baby, and Lily recognized that overwhelming look of love, a love that surpassed all else. Lily realized that at last they were identical yet again, connected by something wonderful. They were both mothers.

The doctor placed the newborn on Abby's chest. Wes leaned down to kiss the baby. Then he kissed Abby so tenderly Lily thought her heart might break. For a moment, Lily hated her sister with everything in her being. She hated that Abby was fortunate enough to deliver a child in this warm, safe hospital room surrounded by love. She hated herself for hating her sister.

She hated a world in which this child might one day be a victim of some sick freak. Lily forced herself to shake off the darkness. He'd programmed this into her, day by day. But here she had a choice—let those feelings overcome her, or fight to keep them at bay.

She kissed Abby and the baby, gave Wes a quick congratulatory hug, and then Lily left the hospital room. She'd told them both that she wanted to see Eve, to let her know that she had a healthy, adorable grandson. But really, Lily needed distance. She needed to see Sky, to remind herself of all the progress they'd made. Abby, Wes, and their baby were a family now. The jealousy still remained, but Lily would fight to overcome it. She had Sky. Sky was her family. That was enough. It had to be enough.

ABBY

He was real. Seven pounds, three ounces, with a pair of lungs that could break the sound barrier. He wasn't an alien invader. Not anymore. He was so damn real and breathtakingly gorgeous Abby almost couldn't bear it. She didn't want to love him. She'd tried so hard not to love him. Life would be easier if she didn't. Life would be easier if she never loved anyone ever again.

But he was here, and he was…fucking perfect. Tiny pink toes. Tiny pink fingers. Those miniature fingernails. Bright gray eyes like Wes's and a tuft of blond hair. Abby was like a crazy person, crying uncontrollably. They weren't lying when they said hormones made you spin out of control. She was a mess.

Her mom came by, oohing and aahing over her grandson, but she'd left with Lily and Sky, promising to return in the morning. Abby was secretly relieved when they were gone. She wanted more time alone with her baby.

That wasn't entirely true. She wanted time alone with Wes and their baby. He hadn't left her side, and at the moment, he was sitting on the bed beside her, his arm touching hers, as they stared down at their son. She couldn't believe she'd ever considered giving her baby away. The thought of him being gone for even a second was impossible to consider. The thought of anything ever happening to him was, well, it was the most terrifying thing she could imagine.

"What should we call him?" Wes asked, gently rubbing Abby's back.

She instinctively leaned into his touch. Her back was aching and the slow, repetitive motion soothed her.

"I was thinking David Joseph. After our fathers."

Wes stared at the infant, his tiny hands clenched in fists. He gently kissed the baby, as if blessing him.

"David Joseph it is."

Abby imagined how proud her own father would have been. He'd have marched up and down the halls, telling his colleagues, each nurse and doctor he passed, about his grandson, taking endless photos and posting them for his entire social network to see. He'd have loved being a grandfather. Abby closed her eyes, fighting back the sadness that had washed over her. Wes leaned in closer.

"I want David to have what I didn't have. I want him to have a family. We can do it, Abby. I know we can. We can move away from all the shit and the pain and the sadness that Rick Hanson caused, and we can be happy."

David began to wail, as if in agreement. She turned to Wes, staring at him, searching and seeing what she had missed all these years. She had been so blind, ignoring his devotion, his complete and total devotion. He loved her. Why had she never noticed it? He loved *her*. Abby leaned over and kissed him. It was crazy, but maybe he was right. Maybe they could be happy. *I tried everything else*, she thought, *why the hell not try this?*

LILY

"Let's hire a fucking firing squad and call it a day," Abby said.

Lily gave her sister a stern look. *Shut it.* Abby didn't even bother to look contrite. When it came to Rick Hanson, Abby refused to hold her tongue.

They were sitting in District Attorney Elijah Foster's office, Eve on one side, Abby on the other. Wes had agreed to watch the kids, but Lily was starting to think that was a mistake.

"Abs, give it a rest, and let him speak."

Frustrated, Abby shifted in her seat but kept her mouth shut.

Elijah was a quiet man with a powerful presence. Almost six foot three with a bald head, he reminded Lily a bit of Mr. Clean. He was actually a former Notre Dame linebacker and All-American. His college playing instilled in him a furious desire to win. But his gentle nature and sweet demeanor calmed Lily every time she met with him. She'd talked a lot with Elijah over the last six months. He said the most important thing was that she know exactly how Rick's case was progressing. Rick's lawyers kept filing ridiculous motions. All stalling tactics, Elijah had reassured her, but it meant that the case continued to drag on. But today Elijah had called them to his office because he had big news.

"After a lot of back and forth, Rick Hanson has agreed to forgo a trial and accept a deal of life in prison without parole. He's accepted the plea, which means a trial isn't necessary. Even with a great deal of evidence, going to trial has its risks. Not to mention Rick's cult status and the media's obsession with this case. But this isn't my call, Lily. The decision is yours. I've already spoken with Bree and Shaina's families, but I won't accept his plea unless it's unanimous."

"Fuck him. Why is he calling the shots? Doesn't anybody think it's weird that he's finally deciding to take the plea? Why? It doesn't make sense."

Lily ignored Abby's outburst, busy contemplating what it would mean to accept a deal. How it would feel to know that he was locked away for good.

"He'll never get out, right?" she asked.

"Not until he draws his last breath."

Lily turned to Eve. "What do you think, Mom?"

"I think you've got to do what's right for you, Lily. We'll support you, no matter what."

"I don't have to testify?" Lily asked. "I won't have to get up on the stand and talk about what he did to me?"

"No. You can make a victim impact statement at the sentencing if you wish, but it's not required."

Lily's decision was made. "Life in prison is good."

Abby exhaled loudly, and Lily took her sister's hand. "It's good, Abby. He'll spend the rest of his life in a cage. It's exactly what he deserves."

Lily turned back to Elijah.

"What's next?"

"I'll meet with Hanson's lawyer, and we'll let them know we've accepted the deal. Then the judge will schedule the sentencing. Hopefully things will move quickly from there."

The three of them left the courthouse. Her mother drove, all of them caught up in their own thoughts. They'd almost reached the subdivision.

"Mom, can you look after the kids this afternoon? I want to take Abby somewhere."

"That's fine, Lil. Whatever you need."

"Where are we going?" Abby asked.

"You'll see."

They returned to the house. Lily scooped up Sky, who was almost too heavy to carry. She'd turned seven last month and filled out, her tiny frame transformed into a budding athlete. Sky loved sports, especially soccer. Some evenings it took almost thirty minutes to get her inside. When Wes stopped by, he'd spend hours in the backyard, kicking the ball around with her. It was clear that she was a natural. Lily covered Sky with kisses until she slipped out of her embrace. These days Sky was more interested in playing than hanging out with her mother. It wasn't easy letting go but it was the only way for them all to move forward.

Abby was sitting on a blanket next to Wes and David, covering the giggling baby with kisses. David was squealing with laughter as Wes stared at Abby with unabashed devotion. Lily looked away and focused on Sky. That's what she'd forced herself to do over the last few months. After hours and hours of soul searching and endless sessions with Dr. Amari, Lily realized that it wasn't Wes she wanted. She didn't know him, not the man he'd become. No, what Lily wanted was to recapture that high school love: the optimism and simplicity that made everything so special. But Lily's longing and disappointment over Wes and what might have been was ever present. She hoped it would fade, as time went by.

As far as she could tell, Abby and Wes weren't officially "together." There were no hugs or kisses, no obvious displays of affection, but their body language and looks didn't lie. Whenever she asked Abby about the status of their relationship, her sister changed the subject. Lily thought about pushing for information, but figured they would both come around when they were ready.

Lily knew it was getting late and she didn't want to be out after dark. She clapped her hands. "Come on, Abs. Let's rock and roll."

Abby gave David one more slobbery kiss and told Wes they would be home later. He gently squeezed Abby's hand and turned his attention back to the baby.

Lily climbed behind the wheel of the SUV, and Abby rode shotgun. Lily headed down Highway 12. Abby stiffened and sat up straighter in her seat.

"Lil, I don't think this is a good idea," Abby protested, having guessed their destination.

But Lily wanted to see the cabin in daylight, to see the place she'd called home for so long. The cabin was only a place, she told herself. A building that had no control over her. She'd heard that it had become a local tourist attraction, drawing sick and twisted weirdos that were eager to catch a glimpse of the famous "sex basement." She wanted to see it one last time, and then she'd never come back here.

She pulled into the driveway, turned off the engine, and climbed out of the SUV. She couldn't go inside. She'd never be that strong. Instead, Lily sat on the hood, leaning on her knees and staring at the cabin. Abby sank down beside Lily.

"You were so close. So close and I didn't know it," Abby said.

"I didn't either, Abby."

Lily wished Abby had known. That their bond had brought them together earlier. But that was silly. Just wishful thinking. Lily closed her eyes and was transported to that spectacular day when they'd passed their driving test, sitting on the hood of their car at the Dairy Queen, eating chocolate-covered-cherry Blizzards.

"What does a spectacular day look like now, Lilypad?"

Lily smiled. Their connection was growing stronger. It was as if Abby were reading her mind. Lily seriously pondered Abby's question. Each day she was free from Rick was spectacular on its own. But she'd been seriously considering her future, thinking about all the possibilities that were available.

"In a perfect world, Sky is healthy and happy and has no memory of Rick or the early years. Mom's found something that fulfills her. You and Wes would be married and—"

"Lily—"

"Don't interrupt me. It's my spectacular day. You two would be married and David would have a sister or brother. I'd go back to school and start running competitively. And Rick Hanson would be gone. Poof." Lily snapped her fingers. "It would be as if he'd never existed at all. That would be a pretty spectacular day."

"I want that for you, Lil. More than anything."

Lily knew there was no escaping Rick. She also knew that she was tired of giving up her power.

"I'm going to speak at the sentencing. Not for me. But for Shaina and Bree."

"I'll be there, Lil. I'll be right there beside you."

Lily gripped Abby's hand tightly. She couldn't stop

staring at the cabin. Someone had boarded up all the windows. Police tape still surrounded the perimeter, and graffiti, mindless scribble, covered almost every surface.

"Everything's going to be all right, isn't it, Abby?"

It was an unusual thing to say considering how far she'd come, but Lily was overcome with a sense of foreboding she couldn't quite explain.

"Listen to me, Lil. There are nothing but spectacular days ahead for the Riser twins."

Abby sprang to her feet, standing up on the hood of the car.

"Do you hear that, world? Are you listening?" Abby's voice echoed out into the distance. "Come on, Lily. Let me hear you! Look out world, here we come!"

Lily let out a joyous yell. They kept shouting over and over again, their wishes drifting up into the sky, like prayers.

RICK

Rick continued doing bench presses, trying to appear focused on his workout. The yard was empty and he was finally alone with Angela. She kept a professional distance but her eyes never left his. She inched closer to Rick as he began to lift the weights.

"You feeling okay?" Rick asked her.

"Yeah. I'm good," Angela said, trying unsuccessfully to hide the tremor in her voice.

Shit. Rick could tell she was unsettled. They hadn't had enough time together this week with all the bullshit transfer paperwork. He'd have to fix this quick before she got cold feet.

"If you're having second thoughts, tell me. I'll understand."

"No. I'm not. I mean..."

"It's okay to be scared," Rick said.

"I'm not scared," Angela said. She tried to laugh but it had a strangled quality. "Well, maybe a little."

"As long as the plan is set, we've got nothing to worry

about. Everything's in place, isn't it? As soon as the sentencing is over, they'll transport me. Your cousin can't be late."

"Brian won't let us down," she said.

"He's got the weapons?"

Angela nodded. "Brian's got it covered."

"And the money?" Rick asked.

"It was in the safe-deposit box just like you said. Once I give Brian his cut, we'll have about sixty grand."

Rick was glad he'd put some money away for a rainy day. Missy was so used to Mommy and Daddy handling the finances that she'd let him manage everything. This had certainly worked to his advantage. A small percentage of everything they made he'd squirrel away, using some on Lily but saving some just in case. Thank God he'd thought ahead. The one unknown in Rick's plan was the third party: Angela's cousin Brian, an ex-con with a long list of felonies. He was going to crash into the transport vehicle that was bringing Rick to the prison, take out the guards, and deliver Rick to Angela's family's hunting cabin in the mountains. They'd spend a few months lying low, and once things cooled down they'd head to Mexico. Rick was still trying to decide whether it might be easier to get rid of her and Brian before then, but that was something he could improvise. He actually didn't mind Angela. What she lacked in looks, she made up for in her enthusiasm. He'd at least keep her around until he could find a more suitable replacement.

He studied Angela intently.

"You did good. I'm proud of you."

Positive reinforcement was crucial at this stage. He needed Angela to feel valued and respected. It was clear that his encouragement was working.

"It's all set, Ricky."

This Ricky business was out of control, but he forced himself not to correct her. He'd finished his workout and he moved over to Angela, allowing her to shackle him.

"Ang, I can't wait to hold you. Can't wait until we can be together without these bars and shackles. You know that, don't you?"

He knew she wanted to believe him. She was imagining a life with a man like him, someone who would ease all her burdens. Any rational woman would have thought about the things Rick stood accused of, the things he'd pled guilty to. They'd have asked questions about his crimes. They'd have wanted answers. But Angela wasn't rational. She was an uneducated woman, lonely and unfulfilled, and waiting to be saved.

She led him back inside, unlatching the gate that would take him back to his cell for one last evening. As they walked down the dark, gray hall, Rick whispered, "I love you, Angie. Don't forget that."

She faltered. He'd been saving the big guns for this moment, wanting to leave her with those words ringing in her ears, to remember them in case she had second thoughts.

"I won't let you down."

Angela picked up the pace, opening the cell door and leaving Rick alone. Rick couldn't sit. Not now. He began shadowboxing, thinking about tomorrow's sentencing and his impending freedom.

After Lily betrayed him, Rick realized that he couldn't sit around and wait for a reprieve. He'd thought about escaping, maybe taking a guard hostage, but every scenario he worked out involved him winding up dead. He'd realized that Angela was exactly the person who could get him out of this hellhole. He'd eventually had sex with her. The showers were convenient and as much as he'd been dreading it, it wasn't too bad (as long as he kept his eyes closed).

It was during one of their encounters that he'd enacted Phase One of the Plan. Angela was still breathless when Rick told her they couldn't be together anymore. That this was their last time.

"Please, Rick. Please don't say that. The only thing that keeps me going is being with you."

"Angie, I'm never getting out of here. Once I'm sentenced, I'll be transferred to a maximum-security prison. You can't visit or write. Not if you want to keep your job. There's nothing you can do."

"What if there was?"

Rick knew in that instant he was golden. All he'd had to do was orchestrate a plan and make sure Angela didn't screw things up. It was difficult entrusting details to someone else, especially a high school dropout. But he had no choice. While Angela worked on things on the outside, Rick did his best to slow down the judicial process, which was easier than he'd expected. He made all kinds of crazy demands, firing two lawyers and filing a motion demanding that he be allowed to represent himself. But it was all just smoke and mirrors. Once Angela had all the details set, he'd finally agreed to the plea.

His overworked public defender—a slick-haired twentysomething clearly using this to pad his résumé— couldn't hide his relief.

"This is the best possible outcome."

Rick agreed with him because what was he going to say? *I'm escaping. Go fuck yourself.*

No, the plea was his only choice. All because of Lily's betrayal.

He thought about her every day. All the hours they'd spent together laughing, reading, and listening to music. The times he'd spent brushing her hair, how she'd laugh at his jokes, the eager way she responded to his sexual desires. He still couldn't get over the depths of her deceit.

That's why initially Rick's first order of business when he escaped was to punish Lily. Murder wasn't really his thing. He liked them alive, liked the challenge of pushing women to the edge and bringing them back. But Lily deserved to pay for what she'd done. There was no question about that.

He'd kill her entire family, starting with her mother, then her bitch sister, and then Sky. He'd make Lily watch and then he'd take her life. It was an appropriate punishment.

But the more Rick worked through the details, the more he realized that going anywhere near Lily or her family following his escape would land him right back in jail. No, the best option was to simply vanish and wait for things to cool off. He'd come back for her, months, maybe years down the line when she'd grown comfortable. In some ways it would be better. Every day Lily would wake up and wonder where he was. She'd constantly be looking over her shoulder. He'd still own her. She'd always be his.

He'd made a lot of mistakes over the past few months, mistakes that he'd have to live with. But he was getting back on track. He couldn't wait to have a cold beer, to bask in the sunshine with some good tunes playing. He'd find himself a lovely new girl, someone better than Lily, a girl who'd appreciate everything a man like him could offer. Rick smiled and finally felt tired. He sank down onto his cot and closed his eyes, preparing himself for a good night's sleep. In a few short hours, this place would be a distant memory. *Freedom, here I come.*

ABBY

It was midnight, the night before Rick's sentencing, and Abby was still awake. The tension in the house that evening had been off the charts. Weeks before, reporters had started calling. News reports about Rick and Lily and the other girls dominated the TV and Internet. Everyone was nervous but Abby was especially on edge. Glancing at the clock, Abby sighed and quietly crawled out of bed. She moved over to David's crib, where her little monkey was fast asleep, his tiny arms splayed out, his chest moving up and down. Leaving him tonight was especially difficult, but she had to do this for Lily. She touched David's soft, smooth cheek, whispered, "Mommy loves you," and then she slipped into the bathroom.

Abby carefully dressed, curling her hair, putting on her makeup. She wrote a note for Lily and her mom saying she'd gone for a drive but hoped she'd be back before they ever knew she was gone.

Abby gave herself a final once-over in the car mirror,

feeling pleased with her appearance. She'd dropped the baby weight and then some. Her cheekbones had reemerged. Her green eyes were bright, and her face was flushed. She almost looked like her old self. Abby drove straight to Wes's house and knocked on the door. He was a night owl, always awake until dawn, tinkering around in the garage or binge watching Netflix. The hours he kept used to drive her crazy, but tonight, she was glad that he was up. He opened the door immediately, worry flashing across his face.

"Abs, what's wrong? Is it David? Or Lily?"

She kissed him. They hadn't kissed since that night in the hospital when David was born. She'd wanted to kiss him a million times since then. She hadn't been lying to Wes that night in the hospital. She wanted to make a go of it; she just didn't know how. Not with Lily living with her, not with her guilt over having created her perfect son with Wes. But that didn't stop her from wishing she had the courage to just go for it. On their walks in the park. On nights when he'd stay for dinner and they'd bathe David together, leaning over the bathtub, arms and legs touching but never really touching. Wes had made it clear that he wanted to be with her, that he wanted to be together, but he'd refrained from any displays of affection. She understood that. She'd pushed him away for far too long. Now he was waiting for her cue.

"Abby, wait."

But she wasn't waiting. She continued kissing him, but this kiss was different. She'd always held back; she didn't even realize that's what she'd been doing until tonight. For eight years, she'd loved this man and hated herself for it. Tonight all of that was gone. To Abby, *this* was their first time. Free and clear.

She pushed him inside the house.

"I've been awful to you, and I'm sorry. But I love you. I love you and I love David. I need you to know that."

He pulled her close, kissing her until she was breathless. They quickly stripped, leaving a trail of clothes throughout the house. They fell into bed, discovering each other's bodies the way they had when they were teenagers, except now there were no ghosts haunting their bedroom. It was just the two of them.

Hours later, exhausted, Abby lay in Wes's arms as he shared his dreams with her.

"I put a bid on some land. For a house. I want to build us a house. And I want us to travel. We'll take David to Disneyland for his first birthday. And if you play your cards right maybe you and I can take a honeymoon."

This was the first time Abby had ever let herself think about the future, and it made her feel alive. She wanted to do all of those things and so many more. She hoped it would be possible but she couldn't be sure. Not yet.

Wes dozed off and Abby found herself studying him, wondering what she'd done to be loved by someone so good and kind. She got up and scrawled a note. She kissed him and then she quickly dressed. Abby slipped into the garage, pulled out a gas can from the back of Wes's pickup, and headed out.

Moonlight illuminated the highway as Abby drove. It was a crisp winter night, but she didn't notice the chill. She was too focused on the task at hand.

Abby climbed out of her car and grabbed the gas can, pouring gasoline all over the outside of Rick's cabin. She was careful to avoid the brushy areas. She wasn't out to destroy the land, only this horrible, horrible place. She kept pouring and pouring until the can was empty. She took a book of matches from her pocket and struck one. The match ignited, and Abby flung it at the building that had held her sister captive. *Whoosh!* The match ignited with the old, dry timber and began to burn.

Flames danced, a joyous movement to them. Abby wished Lily could see this, that she could see the wood splintering, the frame slowly beginning to crumble. In Abby's mind, every degradation Rick inflicted upon her sister was burning as well. Abby wanted to stay until there was nothing but ashes and embers left, but she couldn't get caught. Large plumes of smoke were rising up into the sky. She was going to have to call the fire department soon if she didn't want a massive forest fire on her conscience. She'd already purchased a pre-paid phone. She climbed back into the SUV and drove, dialing as she hauled ass down the road.

"911, what's your emergency?"

Abby kept her voice low.

"I saw flames out near Highway 12. I think there's a fire."

"Okay, ma'am, where on Highway 12?"

"Right off the interstate. I can see the fire."

She quickly hung up and tossed the phone into the woods.

It was nearly five o'clock in the morning when Abby returned home. She tore up the note she'd left and checked on everyone, including David. All still fast asleep. Abby showered and slipped back into her pajamas. She stopped to look at David one more time and she found him wide awake in his crib, staring up at his circus mobile, happily playing with his feet as if they were the best invention he'd ever seen.

"Hey, little man, you're up early."

He squealed, reaching out to grab her, his tiny hands and feet flailing. Abby picked him up and settled back into bed. The sun wasn't up yet, but the birds were chirping, signaling that night would soon be coming to an end. She held David close, inhaling his sweet, fragrant baby oil scent, and drifted off.

At some point, she woke, searching for David. She glanced up and saw Lily at the changing table, putting a new diaper on him.

"Rise and shine, sleepyhead. It's almost seven thirty."

Abby shot up like a jack in the box, not wanting to be

late. But she stopped, doing a double take as she stared at Lily. Her sister's beauty wasn't showy. Lily's red bob was sleek and smooth, a silver barrette holding back her bangs. Her tailored gray pants and white silk blouse gave her a polished, confident appearance.

"I must have missed my alarm. Can you get David fed? I'll be quick like a bunny."

"I'd be honored."

Lily tickled David, who giggled happily.

"Come on, handsome. Let's get you some breakfast."

As they headed downstairs, Abby fought to control her nerves. She stood in front of her closet, trying to decide what to wear. She scanned her wardrobe, dozens of options to choose from, but in the end she chose a similar pair of gray slacks and a black V-neck sweater. It was a sweater she'd considered burning a million times. A sweater that had, in her mind at least, caused so much of their suffering. She hadn't worn it but she'd kept it as a reminder of what she'd lost. Abby slipped it on, realizing that she had lost so much weight it fit perfectly. After all these years, she told herself, this sweater would be her armor. Today it would protect them all.

Abby made her way downstairs and into the kitchen, and found Lily and Mom glued to the morning news.

"Abby, did you hear? Someone burned down Rick's cabin last night," Lily said in disbelief.

Abby stared at the TV, watching the news report as they showed the charred remains of Rick Hanson's "torture den" and speculated on who might be responsible.

"Can you believe it?" Lily asked.

"I guess someone got tired of it being a tourist attraction," Abby said.

She moved toward the fridge, trying to keep her expression neutral. Mom wore a troubled look.

"If that bastard uses this to get out of the plea deal, God help me, I'll kill whoever did this."

Abby stared at her mother in disbelief. Leave it to Mom to say the *one* thing Abby hadn't thought of. Abby quickly moved over to Lily.

"Don't listen to Mom. They've got video of the cabin, the physical evidence; they've got your statement, Shaina's statement. No fucking way he's getting out of this now."

"Aunt Abby, language."

Sky was looking at Abby with disappointment in her eyes.

"Swear jar, Aunt Abby."

Abby went over to her purse and pulled out a five-dollar bill. She handed it over to Sky.

"At this rate, you'll have college paid for by the time you're twelve."

Sky giggled, and Abby grabbed the remote and flipped off the TV. They'd had enough of that nonsense. The cabin being gone was a good thing. She'd done a good thing.

The rest of the morning flew by in a blur. Wes arrived at eight thirty. He'd agreed to look after the kids, which Abby was grateful for. She needed to know they were protected. As Lily and Eve made their way to the car, he pulled Abby aside.

"Last night was unexpected."

"I know..."

"I got your note and it meant everything to me."

"I'm glad."

She went to leave but he pulled her close to him.

"I want you and David to come live with me. I want us to have a real discussion about making that happen..."

"We will. After today, we'll talk about everything."

He smiled, and then he kissed her. Abby sank into him, wishing she could hold on to him like this forever. But she couldn't lose her mojo now.

After a quick drive through light traffic, they parked underneath the Lancaster courthouse and were ushered through the back entrance, avoiding the throng of reporters and onlookers who'd gathered on the steps, eager to hear the sordid details of the sentencing.

Not a single seat remained open in the courtroom. Family members, reporters, and true-crime fanatics sat squashed together. It was still a spectacle, Abby thought. Even after all these months, people were still absorbed in their story, reveling in the tawdry details of what Rick Hanson did. Abby saw Missy slip into the court-room, along with her Brooks Brothers parents. The DA had told them that Missy wanted to speak out against Rick. There was a part of Abby that thought she wouldn't come, but she had. Missy appeared years older than the last time Abby had seen her. She was gaunt and her dark hair was cut short and streaked with gray. She wore all black as if she were in mourning.

Lily leaned over to Abby. "She looks terrible, doesn't she?"

Abby shrugged. "She's proof that guilt will destroy you. Don't feel bad for her, Lil. She's got to live with her choices."

Lily didn't say a word. They'd argued about Missy and the fact that even if she suspected something was off, she could never have truly known the depths of his depravity. Abby didn't care. If she had even a shadow of a doubt about someone, she'd do whatever it took to uncover the truth. She didn't have a shred of sympathy for Missy Hanson and she never would.

Abby watched as Rick's mother, Agnes—a fragile, broken woman—was led into the courtroom. She kept patting at her eyes with a tissue as she took a seat in the front row behind Rick. Abby had seen her on an episode of one of those true-crime shows. She'd always imagined Rick's mother to be some white trash junkie, but Agnes appeared to be a simple, decent woman; a lower middle-class single mother and dental technician who'd thought she'd raised a wonderful man. In her eyes, Rick had been a dedicated educator and devoted husband. Agnes couldn't deny the evidence, or that's what she'd told the reporters. But when they asked her about Rick, she said she'd always love him.

"I know what he did. He'll have to face his maker and answer for his actions, but he's my boy. I'll always love my boy."

Rationally, Abby understood what Agnes meant. But as much as Abby loved David, she couldn't imagine standing by him if he did something like that to someone. She simply couldn't imagine. A murmur began spreading through the courtroom, and Abby saw the deputies leading Mr. Hanson in. He was wearing a crewneck and a white button-down shirt with a striped blue tie, his jet-black hair freshly coiffed. He could've stepped right out of a J. Crew ad. She remembered him doing his best *Dead Poets Society* impression, leaping onto desks, inspiring them all, making them think— even for fifty minutes—that there was no better place to be than AP English. And even now he was still so smug and so damn shiny, as if he'd just come from the yacht club. His mother began to weep. He shook his head.

"I'm okay, Mama," Mr. Hanson said, his voice calm, soothing. "I'm okay. Please, don't cry."

If you were unaware of the atrocities this man had committed against innocent women and children, you might have pitied him. Instead, Abby was hit with a wave of disgust that anyone cared about this waste of a human being.

A few moments later, the Honorable Betsy Crabtree entered the courtroom, and court was called into session. There was a lot of legal back and forth between the lawyers and the judge. Abby tried to follow what they were saying, but after a moment, she gave up, deciding none of the legal jargon really mattered. She snapped to attention when she heard the judge ask if Mr. Hanson's victims were prepared to speak. The order of the testimony had been decided by Elijah for maximum impact. Missy went first, her voice soft but powerful. Abby watched Rick but he barely even blinked.

"When I met my husband seventeen years ago, I thought I was the luckiest girl in the world. He was intelligent and charming, dedicated to his work and to our marriage. I believed that he was a good man. Sadly, I have come to terms with the fact that I ignored the signs that he was evil, ignored the signs that he was using me for my money. I cannot change my role in any of this. But I am not here for Rick. I am here to apologize. To Lily Riser and her family. To Shaina Meyers and her family. And to Bree Whitaker's family. We cannot escape the past. We're bound by it. All I can say is that I am sorry for all that you've lost. I am so sorry for the wounds that Rick inflicted upon you. I will never be able to escape the things that he did nor my role in not seeing who he truly was. But I am truly, truly sorry."

Missy sat down, sniffling into her tissues, her mother

patting her gently. Abby appreciated her sentiment, but her resolve didn't budge. That bitch deserved every moment of suffering she endured and then some.

Judge Crabtree turned to Bree's mom, Elizabeth Whitaker. She was a tiny woman, drowning in a floral dress two sizes too big. Her Coke-bottle glasses could not hide her haunted eyes or ravaged expression.

"My daughter Bree was an honor student. She was a cheerleader who loved making people happy. She didn't have to get a job, but she wanted to pay for her own prom dress and her senior trip to Europe, so she decided to wait tables. She is…she was such a special soul, and that man; he stole her from all of us. The only comfort I have is knowing that she's with her Savior. The only other comfort is that Rick Hanson will have to pay for what he's done."

Silence reigned in the courtroom for several long minutes. The judge cleared her throat. "Mr. Meyers, would you care to make a statement?"

Shaina's father Bert stood up. He was sweating, dabbing at his forehead with a handkerchief. His hands trembled as he reached into his pocket and pulled out a torn-off piece of notebook paper. He read, each word loud and punctuated with loss.

"My daughter used to laugh. Nonstop laughter could be heard in our house at all hours of the day. I am lucky, because my daughter is alive, but the laughter is gone. Rick Hanson did not kill my daughter but he stole her from us. She doesn't sleep. She barely eats. She may never be that same joyous, happy-go-lucky girl, and I may never . . . I may never hear my daughter laugh again. I am not a believer. It might be easier if I were. All I know is that whatever happens to Rick Hanson will never be enough. No punishment will ever be enough for what you've done to all of our families."

He sat down, his wife holding his hand and leaning into him.

"Miss Riser, it's your chance to address the court. Whenever you're ready."

Abby fought to control her own nerves. She gave Lily an encouraging nod. "You've got this."

Lily slowly stood up, smoothing out imaginary wrinkles on her slacks. In spite of Lily's trembling, on the surface, she appeared completely composed. Lily stared right at Mr. Hanson, and still he didn't blink or show even a hint of remorse. Abby gripped her hands, fighting not to lose control. She wouldn't ruin Lily's moment. She couldn't. Lily began.

"I lost three thousand one hundred and ten days. During my imprisonment, my father died. My sister battled drug and alcohol abuse and nearly took her own life. My first love fell in love with someone else."

Abby flinched but Lily kept going.

"I missed prom and graduation. I missed so many things everyone here would take for granted. Sunrises and sunsets. Eight birthdays I had to endure without my best friend, without my twin sister, Abby. A lifetime of moments and celebrations and experiences I can never get back. I thought about coming here and telling you all the things Rick Hanson did to me, physically and emotionally. But I realized that's what he wants. He would want to relive that pain and suffering that he inflicted on me. What I'm here to say today is that I don't care about Rick Hanson. He's nothing to me. He's nobody. And it's funny, because that's what he tried to make me into—a nobody. And he failed. I am glad the courts have chosen to give him the harshest of punishments for what he did to me and to my daughter and to my family, but it won't matter. Because Rick Hanson is a man without a conscience. For those of us he hurt, for myself and for Shaina and Bree, and all of our families, the only thing we can take comfort in is that he cannot hurt us anymore. Do you hear that, Rick? You can never hurt us again."

Mr. Hanson's face remained impassive as Lily sat down. Abby was so proud. She leaned in so only Lily could hear her. "You are the shit."

Lily smiled, tears welling in her eyes, but she didn't cry. Abby knew she wouldn't cry. Not here. Not in front of him. Lily just sat there so strong and courageous. *Go fuck yourself, Mr. Hanson*, Abby thought as she hugged Lily close. *Go fuck yourself.*

RICK

"Mr. Hanson, would you care to address the court?" The owl-faced judge stared back at Rick, her disdain for him on full display. He gazed around the packed courtroom, taking in all these people who'd gathered here because of him. He saw his mother, her tear-stained face studying him. He'd told her not to come but he knew she wouldn't listen.

"You're my boy. I'll be there for you 'til the end."

He felt sorry for her, for not realizing who he was, or refusing to accept it.

Then there was Missy. Talk about a disaster. She looked as if she never left the house: so pale and gaunt, her roots showing, her clothing hanging off her. It was unfortunate but not surprising.

But it was Lily, his Lily that he couldn't stop watching. Her hair was ridiculous. Why the hell would anyone want to be a redhead? It just didn't make sense. But despite that, she still took his breath away. At least until she opened her mouth. Then he wanted to punish her.

He wanted to tell her to stop lying. Why didn't she mention any of the good times they'd shared? What about all the things he'd done for her? The outstanding education he'd provided for her, the books he lavished upon her and Sky. What about Sky? Lily couldn't deny that he was a great father. He'd allowed her to raise their child together and yet she said nothing about it. Nothing at all.

When he woke up this morning, a part of him hoped that Lily would come to her senses and realize that she'd loved him too. That their life was something special no one would ever understand. But she was a lost cause.

He was lucky he'd found Angela. She was really going to come through. She had slipped him a note before he was transported, and everything was on schedule. Her shithead cousin was at the rendezvous spot, she'd left her kid with her mother, and she had clothes and toiletries for him. She'd wanted to come to court but he worried that she might draw attention. He told her just to stick with the plan and they'd be together soon.

Rick had spent the morning ignoring the guards' taunts, warning him about all the new "boyfriends" he'd have in prison, warning him that he'd be lucky to survive a week. Rick had ignored them, dressed in the suit and tie his mother had delivered. Knowing these guards were confined to this hellish existence while he was about to bust out of this place was the best revenge.

Now it was his turn to speak. His moment in the spotlight. He knew that he'd be analyzed, that morning talk shows would dissect every mannerism and nuance in his behavior. At least that's what he hoped. Rick stood, bowed his head, and did his best to project contrite remorse.

"I know that I've been labeled a monster. I do not think that's true. I think...I think I am a sick man. But I know that is no excuse. I accept my punishment and promise that after today you won't hear from me again. I will disappear into oblivion, but I hope that my victims can find peace and happiness from here on out."

Pleased with himself, Rick sat down. He wanted applause and adulation but the silence was pretty satisfying. Lily stared straight ahead, never once meeting his gaze. Her sister, on the other hand, was boring holes into him. Rick hated to admit it but she was actually kind of hot now in her tight black sweater that perfectly hugged her curves. Maybe he had made the wrong choice. Maybe. He looked back up at the judge, wanting all of this to be over. In just a few short hours, Rick would be speeding down the interstate, while all these idiots wrung their hands in disbelief. All Rick had to do was get through the rest of this ridiculous dog and pony show and he was home free.

ABBY

Abby wanted to laugh. *How pathetic was that?* Rick hadn't even tried. She'd heard him keep a room full of bored teenagers engaged for fifty minutes and *that* was the best he could do? He really was a pathetic piece of shit.

Abby listened as the judge read the sentencing, which included words and phrases such as "depravity" and "monstrous acts," "vicious disregard for human life" and "a lack of empathy that made him a danger to anyone who came into contact with him." Then the judge reached the part Abby had been waiting for.

"The defendant will spend the rest of his natural born life behind bars without possibility of parole."

A cheer went up in the courtroom.

Judge Crabtree banged her gavel. It was all over. For a brief moment, Abby felt like her job was done. She stood up, celebrating with Mom and the attorneys, all of them hugging and congratulating one another. Everyone but Lily. Her sister stood motionless, staring over at Mr. Hanson. Abby went to take Lily's hand, but Lily unexpectedly broke free, making her way over to him. Startled, Abby quickly followed. A guard stepped forward to block Lily's path from Mr. Hanson. Lily gently raised her hand.

"Please, I need one second," Lily said, pleading with him.

The guard sized Lily up, deciding almost instantly that she wasn't a threat. Abby watched as the guard stepped back and Lily moved forward. Rick gazed tenderly at Lily, as if he'd known she would come to him.

"I need you to know I forgive you, Rick. I forgive you for everything," Lily said, her voice never wavering.

He smiled that smug fucking smile, and Abby could feel the darkness welling up inside of her, the darkness she'd worked so hard to erase.

No. No. No. Why would Lily say that? He didn't deserve forgiveness. In a lifetime of eternities, there could be no forgiveness for what he had done. Mr. Hanson's smile seemed to overwhelm his face.

"I forgive you too, Baby Doll. I'll miss you, and I'll always love you. Take care of our girl."

Lily didn't say a word. She simply turned away. But as she did, Abby saw a look flash across Lily's face. Abby stared at her sister's retreating back. That look...dear God. Lily had said that she didn't care about Rick, that he didn't matter to her. But that wasn't true. Abby had never considered the possibility; she almost couldn't bear to consider it. Could Lily really love Rick Hanson? Could she really love the man who'd done all those hideous things to her? But it wasn't real love. It couldn't be. It was ugly, broken, distorted, twisted love, the only kind of love Rick Hanson knew. But Lily was bound to him, even now. And as long as he was alive, Lily would always be bound to him.

Lily had reached the back of the courtroom, a good, safe distance away. Abby stepped toward Mr. Hanson, clutching the small ceramic blade she'd put in her pocket before leaving that morning. It had always been part of the plan, her gift to Lily. Abby just hadn't been sure she'd be brave enough to use it. But that look, that fucking look on Lily's face, convinced Abby that this was the only option.

She raised the blade and plunged it into Mr. Hanson's chest. Blood spurted out, and he tried to stagger back, but the cuffs made it impossible. The deputy reached out to grab Abby but she was unstoppable, driven by adrenaline and rage, driven to destroy this man who'd taken so much from her.

Her world went mute as Abby focused on the bright red circle spreading across Mr. Hanson's chest. It was so perfect. Abby was a nurse, trained to heal. But this time she knew the bull's-eye, so to speak. For the first time since he'd taken Lily hostage, Mr. Hanson wasn't in charge. He was panicked and afraid, a sick, pathetic freak. He was moaning in pain as he dropped to the ground. Abby leaned over him, still stabbing, wanting her face to be the last thing he saw.

Yes, she hated Mr. Hanson, despised him, but she'd never considered killing him until that day at the cabin with Lily. If Lily needed Rick to be gone in order to have a future filled with spectacular days, Abby realized that she wasn't powerless any longer. *This* was something she could actually make happen. She'd gone to Philly to buy the ceramic knife, knowing it wouldn't appear on the metal detectors. There was a moment after Lily's statement, after the verdict was read, that Abby had considered letting him suffer in prison, locked away in his cell, but then she'd seen Lily's expression, and she realized she had no choice.

She kept stabbing him, blood staining her hands, the metallic smell filling her nose and mouth. Finally, the blade was wrenched from her grasp and she was shoved to the ground. Abby lay on the cold tile floor, a foot digging into her back, immobilizing her. She kept her gaze focused on Rick, his body contorting as he whimpered and moaned. Abby couldn't help but laugh. Watching him suffer was better than she'd ever imagined. Abby wasn't sure how long she lay there before the cold metal handcuffs were roughly fastened to her wrists.

As she was lifted off her feet, Abby locked eyes with

Missy Hanson. *You're welcome, Missy*, she thought. *That is how you take care of business.* The officers hurried Abby out. She caught a glimpse of Lily and Mom, weeping as they clutched each other. Abby hated that she'd caused them pain, but she wasn't sorry for what she'd done. She was ecstatic, in fact. Rick's bloody body lying there, helpless and worthless, was the most amazing sight she'd seen. All she could think as they led her out of the courtroom was *good fucking riddance.*

LILY

The courtroom had erupted in hysterics, screams and shouts of panic. It was pure and total pandemonium. Blood pooled on the floor as Rick gasped for breath. Sheriff Rogers seemed to appear from out of nowhere. He joined the bailiff as they attempted to subdue Abby.

"Please... please, I don't want to die." Lily could hear Rick's ragged pleas. Rick's mother was wailing, trying to get closer to her son as a deputy tried to keep her back.

"Save my boy! Please, someone, save my boy!"

Lily saw the faces of shell-shocked bystanders and she understood their terror. *This is what I endured*, she longed to tell them. *This is what every single day with Rick Hanson was like. A nightmare you couldn't escape. Something so awful it couldn't possibly be real.* Lily couldn't speak or move. She could never have imagined her sister would do something like this. Lily didn't even realize Abby wasn't next to her until she heard Rick's gasp. She turned around a second too late. She saw the knife, the blood, and the hatred on Abby's tormented face as she stabbed Rick again and again.

Seconds, or maybe it was minutes, later Lily watched two deputies drag Abby out of the courtroom. Sheriff Rogers appeared by Mom's side. He wrapped his arms around her and ushered them both toward Judge Crabtree's chambers. Lily saw the guards trying to stop Rick's bleeding. She heard the ambulance sirens growing closer.

Why, Abby? she thought, over and over. *Why?*

Mom was crying and gripping Lily's arm so tightly Lily worried she might fall over. They sat in the judge's chambers. Someone brought them bottled water. Someone else wrapped blankets around their shoulders. Lily trembled but all she could think about was how she'd spent all these months sitting across from Dr. Amari, unaware of Abby's suffering. Something had been simmering inside Abby, something no one had seen. *Not even me.* Maybe Lily hadn't wanted to see it.

Mom shook Lily's arm, her eyes wide.

"The cabin...do you think...?" Mom said. "Do you think Abby...?"

Lily shook her head, motioning to Sheriff Rogers, who stood huddled with Judge Crabtree a few feet away.

"Don't say another word."

Lily knew without a doubt that Abby had burned down Rick's cabin. She knew the moment she saw the knife in Abby's hand. The moment she saw her stabbing Rick. But she wasn't going to help the cops build their case.

Lily couldn't just sit there and do nothing. She stood, directing her questions at Sheriff Rogers. "Rick...Is he...?"

"Dead? Yes, he is. His aorta was punctured. He coded in the ambulance, and they couldn't revive him. He was declared DOA at the hospital."

Lily took in the magnitude of what had happened. Her sister killed a man. Abby killed Rick.

"I have to see her. I have to see Abby."

Sheriff Rogers glanced over at Mom. She appeared nearly catatonic, staring into space. He knelt beside her, holding on to her hand.

"Evie, I'm going to take Lily to see Abby. Will you be okay here?"

"I'll be fine...I'll be right here. And, Lil, tell my girl I love her. No matter what..."

Sheriff Rogers led Lily out and through a throng of police and investigators, all of them collecting evidence, interviewing witnesses. Sheriff Rogers shielded Lily from prying eyes as he led her toward the holding cells, briefing her as they went.

"I can't give you long, Lily. We need to transport Abby to the jail for booking. But please don't discuss what happened. Anything said in here can and will be used against her."

Lily followed him to a row of cells. A deputy stood nearby, hand on his gun. Lily saw Abby through the bars, sitting on the bunk, staring down at her bloodstained hands, which were resting on her lap. She was still wearing her gray pants and a black sweater. Lily stared at the sweater. *The* black sweater, she realized for the first time. Abby had kept it all these years. She couldn't believe she hadn't noticed. Just one more thing she hadn't noticed. One more thing that had led them both here.

Abby's face bore the brunt of her struggle with the cops, bruises from where they'd slammed her down onto the ground. But there was calmness about her now, a peace Lily hadn't seen before. She moved closer to the cell. The guard stepped forward, blocking her path.

"It's okay, Jon," Sheriff Rogers said. "She's okay."

Sheriff Rogers opened the door as the guard stepped back, but remained alert. Abby stood up from the bunk. Lily moved into the tiny cell and wrapped her arms around her sister, clutching her tightly. Lily should have been furious. Abby had David and Wes to think about. But she wasn't angry. All this time, she kept thinking that if she worked hard enough in therapy, if she raised Sky well, if she were able to live a good life, then what Rick did to her and her family would cease to define her. But until she saw blood pooling from Rick's chest, until she heard Sheriff Rogers say he was dead, Lily hadn't realized how wrong she'd been. This wasn't what she'd wanted. It was what she needed, and Abby had been the one to do it.

She stared at her sister, her other half, the person she'd

loved more than anyone. To an outsider, they were now almost identical. Especially if they stood side by side, with their matching haircuts... but there were so many differences. Life had forced them to become different people. From here on out, the world would always see those differences. Lily would forever be the victim. Abby would be the murderer. But it didn't matter what the world thought, Lily realized. She knew what her sister had done and why. She knew that this was the ultimate sacrifice. Abby's freedom in exchange for Lily's.

Sheriff Rogers cleared his throat. "I'm sorry, Lily, but we have to go."

Lily pulled Abby in for another hug, holding on to her. It was impossible to talk, with the police listening to them, but Lily knew this time Abby would understand exactly what she was thinking. *Thank you. Thank you. Thank you.*

ABBY

There were endless questions.

Why did you do it? When did you plan it? How did you plan it? Were you thinking clearly? What triggered such a violent outburst? Do you think about hurting yourself? Do you think about hurting others?

Endless fucking questions. Abby answered them the way she knew was expected. But she couldn't control what they decided, and it really didn't matter to her. Not anymore. Lily had forgiven her. That was enough.

So now Abby was inmate J70621, a resident of the county jail, currently housed in the psychiatric unit. Her lawyer, the same one Wes had hired, told her they were working on a "not guilty by reason of insanity" plea but for now, Abby would remain locked up.

She missed home. She missed Mom and Lily and of course Wes and David, but Sheriff Rogers looked after her, checking in at least once a day. The other guards and even the inmates treated her with respect. She was getting by.

What worried her most was Wes and his anger over what had happened. He'd come to visit the day after the murder. He'd sat across from her, unshaven, anger radiating from every pore in his body...

"That night you came over was like a fever dream. When you showed up at the house, I kept thinking, holy shit, maybe this is the start of something new. But it wasn't, was it? You were saying good-bye, weren't you?"

Abby didn't answer. Their visits were recorded, and the lawyer warned her that she needed to be mindful of that.

"I meant what I said that night, Wes. Every word. I'll always love you and David. And I'm so sorry I fucked up..."

He'd lost it then, slamming his hand on the table. The guard moved over to restrain him.

"It's okay. He's okay," she said. Wes had every right to be angry. She nodded for him to continue.

"You've ruined us, Abby. Don't you see that?" His anger had spilled out, and Abby absorbed it willingly. He'd been too nice and too kind all these years, and he was right. It was possible that she had ruined everything. But it didn't scare her. Whatever happened to her, she would survive. She tried to hug him good-bye, but he'd stormed out. He needed to be angry with her. That was what he needed now.

Time passed slowly in jail. Lily and Mom came every

other day for her hourly visitation. But she hadn't seen Wes for over a month. Abby was beginning to worry that she'd never hear from him again, until Lily showed up and handed Abby a letter. She recognized Wes's handwriting on the envelope instantly.

"He gave this to you? How is he?" Abby asked, eager for any news about him.

"He's hurting, Abs. But he misses you."

Abby could barely speak. She'd missed Wes more than she'd thought possible. This was the longest they'd ever gone without talking, and she was starting to think the silence might actually drive her crazy.

Abby said her good-byes to Lily and returned to her cell. She settled onto her bunk, her hands trembling as she began to read.

It was a Wednesday, April 10th. We'd been hanging out for a few months since I'd moved back to town, and we were at my place and you were wearing that old gray T-shirt and your purple hoodie and we were on the sofa watching Tommy Boy. *We'd seen it a million times, but it was that part where the deer wakes up and rips the car to shreds. You laughed so hard that night, you snorted Dr Pepper all over the place. The look on your face when you turned to me, blushing and embarrassed and so adorable, that look was one of a kind. Classic Abby Riser. That look and a million other looks made me love you. Not Lily. I know you'll find this hard to believe, but I barely remember what Lily and I had. I know that I cared about her but we were so young. We hadn't been through anything real.*

We hadn't lost anything or anyone. I wish I'd known what you were going to do that day at the courthouse, that I could have stopped you. On one hand, I don't understand why you'd throw everything away. On the other hand, it makes perfect sense and I hate myself for not realizing it sooner. I'm furious and hurt and scared. All my friends think I've lost it, that I'm a pushover, that you've put me through enough. They think I should just walk away. God, I wish it were that easy. But I'm telling you this now and I hope you hear it. You're it for me, kid. You're the one. So I'll be here waiting. When you're ready, I'll be waiting.

Abby read the letter six times. She'd barely cried since she'd been arrested, but Wes's letter shattered her. She looked down at the envelope, and that's when she saw it. Her note, the words she'd written the night before Rick's sentencing and left for him. *We matter. Love, Abby.*

She wrote him back, poured out her heart and soul, begging him to come see her, begging him to try to start over. He came the following week and then every week after that. She didn't want him to bring David, didn't want this place to be part of her son's earliest memories, but he'd bring videos and stacks and stacks of photos. Sometimes they'd talk nonstop; other times they'd sit in silence, both of them realizing that after all the fight they'd put up, they were forever bound together.

When their visits ended, Abby was consumed by

sadness, hating that they had to be separated. But once she was back in her cell, once the guards locked her in, she'd curl up on her bed with one of the new bestsellers Lily always brought her. Lately she'd been writing more, filling her journal with long letters to David about how much she loved him.

Abby still had no way of knowing what the courts would decide about her future. The legal wrangling was outside of her control. But whatever happened, Abby knew that for now, she was safe and she was loved. It wasn't the life she'd imagined when Lily returned, but she went to bed each night with a clear conscience. Abby made sure to say all the right things to the doctors. How sorry she was, how she'd snapped, that she went into some kind of fugue state. But she wasn't sorry. She hadn't really snapped. Rick Hanson needed to be exterminated, and no one else was going to do it.

Knowing that Rick was gone, that Lily would never have to worry about him, was what Abby needed. For now, this life, in this room, was enough. Lily was free.

EVE

"This place could go for a fortune. Are you sure you won't reconsider?"

Eve stared back at Amber, the perky realtor who'd negotiated the sale of the property. The house itself would soon be torn down. Eve had decided, along with Abby and Lily's blessing, that they'd rather have it destroyed than let some degenerate get off on living in the Riser home.

"I'm sure." Eve handed over the keys and took a final look around. The demolition was a few weeks away, but Eve knew this was good-bye. She could still see Dave carrying her over the threshold, the two of them giggling as he tripped and went flying in a heap. She could see Dave, the man she'd thought she'd love forever, carrying her baby girls home, five-pound bundles, one in each arm. So many firsts: the squeals of toddlers, the joy of middle schoolers, the exasperated shouts of teenagers. This house had held so many happy memories, but for Lily it was a reminder of what she'd lost. And for the outside world, it was a tourist attraction.

Eve had found a new house across town, with a giant yard for Lily to work her magic on and plenty of bedrooms for the whole family. As difficult as starting over was, Eve knew it was the right decision. She checked her cell phone to make sure she hadn't missed any messages, and Eve made her way outside. She glanced up and saw Tommy across the street, leaning against his police cruiser. Eve momentarily lost her breath. He looked so good. It had been three months since Rick's death, two months since they'd even spoken. She'd ignored his calls and texts that first week but he wouldn't stop, telling her he'd come over and speak with her in person if she didn't message him back. Eve finally texted.

I need some space.

He'd respected her wishes and hadn't contacted her since. It wasn't a lie. Eve simply didn't have the emotional real estate to deal with Tommy and whatever this was. Another bomb had gone off and Eve had to pick up the pieces. There were lawyers to hire, psychologists and mental health evaluations to pay for, therapies to organize, children to look after. But Tommy, it seemed, had waited long enough. Eve knew him well enough to know that he wanted to talk. She made her way over to him. He knew her. He could tell how surprised she was to see him here.

"I didn't mean to blindside you like this."

"No, Tommy, it's fine. It's good to see you," Eve said.

"Is it?" he asked, tension and judgment in his voice.

"Yes. I've been meaning to call you . . ."

"Why do I feel like that's not entirely true?"

Eve forced a smile. "Been a lot going on around here."

"I know. I saw the news in the paper. It's great news, Evie. You'll do a lot of good."

"I hope so."

Eve had just closed escrow on an office space in downtown Lancaster. It was going to be the new home of the Riser Foundation. Eve had no choice in reinventing herself if she wanted to stay in the medical profession. Her career at the hospital was over; her continued legal pursuits against Lancaster General made that clear. Lily had received donations from strangers, people from all over the country. People who connected with her story, with the story of the twins, and who wanted to ease the family's financial burden. When all was said and done, they had topped out at two and a half million dollars. That wasn't counting the repeated book offers and requests for TV interviews that Lily was considering. Or the potential settlement from the hospital. It was more money than they'd ever need. Having spent time with Bree and Shaina's families as well as helping her own girls through this nightmare, Eve wanted to offer help to victims of sexual assault and their families. She wanted something good to come from all the bad. The foundation's task was simple. Organize and fund rescue searches, cover medical expenses, mental health care, and any additional costs for the girls' recovery.

"I don't really know what the hell I'm doing, but I'll figure it out."

"You'll do great, Evie. I have no doubts."

There was an awkward pause before Tommy continued. "I saw Abby. Heard the hearing is next week."

"We're all just trying to stay positive."

The conversation was so polite that Eve could barely stand it.

"I'm sorry I couldn't stop Abby. If I had known..." Tommy said regretfully.

Stunned, Eve shook her head. "You can't possibly think that this is your fault. Any of it."

Tommy didn't answer. Eve realized that's exactly what he thought.

"You couldn't have known. None of us could."

"Then why did you pull away? What changed between us? I thought...I mean, I thought we were going to figure this out."

There it was. The question that had lingered day in and day out as Eve attempted to put her family's life back together. What were they? Were they anything? Could they be?

"Dave and I should have divorced years before Lily was taken. He wasn't happy. He knew I wasn't. By the time she was gone, we were strangers. Then you came into my life. The way you made me feel, our connection, I kept telling myself, 'I can survive this.'"

"I know. And I should've stuck by you after Dave's death. But I was scared. I'm not anymore."

She realized what he was saying. She had to stop him.

"I owe you, and your wife and daughter, an apology."

"Evie..."

"This was never real, Tommy."

Tommy reached out and pulled Eve close to him.

"But it could be." Tommy's voice was low, thick with emotion. "Say the word, Evie, and I'm all yours."

Before that day in the courtroom, before Rick Hanson's death, Eve had spent countless hours imagining what her life with Tommy would be like. They'd travel everywhere. Europe. South America. Asia. They'd take cruises. Eve always wanted to take a cruise but Dave got seasick. She envisioned them as that hip older couple, the one that knew the best restaurants and had season theater tickets. They'd join a country club. They'd take up golf and tennis. They'd forget about all of the crap and build a new life together. Eight years ago, eight months ago, Eve would have said yes. Yes. Yes, I'm all yours.

But not now. Too much had changed since that day in the courtroom. Eve had changed. This was her chance to start fresh, to be that powerful businesswoman she'd once been, a woman her daughters and grandchildren could look up to. She'd spent years hating herself, hating who she was.

Eve freed herself from Tommy's desperate embrace,

worried that she might lose her nerve if she stayed in his arms.

"I can't do that. And if it really came down to it, I don't think you could either."

Stricken, Tommy stepped back. Eve thought about what else she might say to ease his heartbreak, but that wasn't her job. She headed back across the street and climbed into her SUV. Eve pulled away, head held high, refusing to cry. She'd always love him, but Eve had made her decision. She wasn't going to be that woman. Not anymore.

LILY

Five months. It had been exactly five months since Rick's death, and Lily still hated visiting Abby at the Oakwood Behavioral Center. Arriving for her weekly visitation, checking in with security, she'd wait at the designated table, trying to ignore the antiseptic smell as drugged-up patients, eyes vacant and cloudy from medication, shuffled in.

In the aftermath of Rick's stabbing, the media frenzy reached a fever pitch. The news cycle was insatiable, only heightened by the news that Rick had had a new lady love. His fiancée, a guard at the jail, was demanding justice for her slain lover. Authorities launched an investigation and discovered the woman was not a crackpot as they first thought, but that Rick had in fact been planning an escape with her. The love letters written between Rick and the woman revealed that he had orchestrated the whole thing.

The woman, her face plastered on every morning news show, pleaded with the public to rally around her cause. But she was a joke, comic relief. Lily was grateful that no one took her seriously, other than reveling in her delusion. In fact, the public was squarely on Abby's side. But the law was still the law. Abby had taken a life and would have to face the consequences.

Elijah, the district attorney, accepted Abby's plea of temporary insanity, and Abby was committed to a mid-level psychiatric facility for an indeterminate amount of time. Some people who committed violent crimes served a year or two in mental institutions before being released. Others were never ready to reenter society.

Lily was outraged that Abby had to serve any time at all. She'd been on a mission to overturn the sentence and bring her sister home. She was meeting with doctors and lawyers, reaching out to elected officials. Whatever it took. She'd arrived with news—the governor had finally agreed to meet with her.

"Isn't that great news, Abby? I'm almost certain he'll be receptive to my argument. There was a case in California, where a woman killed her abuser…"

Abby grabbed Lily's hands.

"I need you to stop, Lil. Please."

Lily was confused. "Stop what?"

"All of this. The meetings, the interviews. It has to stop," Abby demanded.

"But if I can sit down with the governor, and explain that you're okay, you can come home."

"I don't want to go home."

Lily shook her head. "That's ridiculous. Once you're back home with us, with David and Wes—"

"Damn it, Lily, I'm not fucking leaving here." Abby's voice was shrill as she pounded the table.

Lily knew Abby's look well. It was one she'd worn for eight long years. A look of pure and total terror.

Abby took a deep breath.

"For so long, I was scared of everything, Lil. School and work, even the grocery store was a nightmare. Everything I did filled me with this dread that I couldn't explain. I was so angry and so lonely and so...so lost. I thought you coming home would fix it, but it's all still there. Bubbling inside me. Churning around. I want to get rid of it. I want to be strong and I'm getting there. Some days, I wake up, and I almost feel like my old self, like the Abby I was before you left. I want to laugh again. I want to be able to hold my son and sleep with Wes without worrying that it's all going to go away. I'm learning how to deal with everything. I'm coming to terms with what I've done. I killed someone and I have to live with that. I can't half ass my recovery. I have to be a hundred percent. For Wes. For David. But especially for you, Lilypad."

Lily sat there, not quite knowing what to say or do. Ever since that day in the jail when Abby hugged her, when she realized what her sister had done, all Lily wanted was to make things right. But if this was what Abby wanted, Lily had to honor her wishes.

"Then I'll stop fighting. For now. But you can't give up. Promise me you'll do whatever it takes to get back to us."

"You know I will."

Lily took a deep breath, forcing herself not to cry. "Enough of this," Abby said. "Mom mentioned on the phone that you had some good news."

Lily hesitated. "I told her not to mention it."

"Come on, Lil, you're not holding out on me, are you?"

Lily smiled and reached into her bag and pulled out a letter. Abby quickly scanned the paper.

"You got into Bucknell?"

"A full scholarship. Can you believe it?"

"Hell yes I believe it! My sister's a genius," Abby said, beaming. She held up the acceptance letter, showing it off to the nearby orderly.

"Reuben, my sister got into college. Isn't that amazing?"

He grinned and gave them the thumbs-up. Lily grabbed the letter from Abby, fighting to stop from blushing. Abby was studying Lily. Her smile quickly faded.

"Okay, what's the hangdog expression about? This is great news. You should be jumping up and down."

Lily rarely talked about her troubles. The last thing she wanted to do was waste her limited time with Abby discussing her problems.

"I'm just not sure I'm ready."

"You are so ready. It would be crazy not to go. And we all know that I'm the expert on crazy," Abby said with a wry laugh.

But Lily was struggling, wrestling with this decision. "I'll be older than all the students."

"Who cares? Some people go back to school when they're fifty. This is your chance at having something normal. At being normal. Don't you want that?"

Lily wanted that, almost as much as she wanted Abby out of this place. She'd been discussing it with Dr. Amari, who kept telling her that it would be a big step forward in her recovery. Money wasn't an issue. Lily had more than enough money for tuition. She'd thought about NYU or UCLA—all the places she'd imagined going when she was sixteen and anything was possible. But she had to be close to Abby and Eve, and Sky needed stability and familiar surroundings. Lily had checked out other local schools, but Bucknell University was the closest, and they offered a great sustainable design program. Lily started gardening as a way to remember her father, a hobby to get her out of the house, but it had evolved into a passion. The thought of creating beauty out of chaos as a landscape designer appealed to her.

"Lilypad, listen to me. We can't go back and change things. Not that day Rick stole you from us. Not the eight years we lost. Not that day..." Abby never spoke about what happened in the courtroom, at least not to Lily. "But the future, that's all you."

Lily promised Abby she'd think about it. There was always so much more they wanted to discuss, but visiting hours were over. Lily hugged Abby good-bye, her sister whispering in her ear. Lily always hated this moment, saying good-bye. Even though she saw Abby once a week and they talked on the phone daily, it was never enough. Not when they had to make up for lost time.

Abby kissed Lily's forehead, staring into her eyes.

"Don't let him steal one more thing from you, Lily-pad. Not one more thing." As the orderly led Abby away, Lily still felt uncertain. If she didn't go to school, if she turned down this opportunity, all of Abby's sacrifices would be for nothing. But moving forward meant accepting that this was Abby's life. Could she do that? Could she really leave Abby behind? Leave her *here*? Lily sank down into the chair, paralyzed by indecision. After all they'd been through, all they'd managed to overcome, they were more identical than ever and yet still worlds apart.

LILY

The locker room was empty, and Lily slipped inside. Nerves were bubbling up and she craved the solitude, hoping time alone would calm her. The other girls would arrive soon, and she wanted this time to psych herself up. She sank down on one of the benches and slipped out of her jeans and sweater. She pulled on her blue track shorts and tank top, jumping up and down to loosen her limbs. Her first race of the season was finally here. It was still hard to believe that she'd made it this far.

Abby had been so relentless in her campaign to get Lily to go back to school, Lily almost hadn't had a choice. Lily's arrival on campus initially caused a stir. Reporters camped out to get interviews. Students were bribed in hopes that they might strike up a friendship and get the inside scoop on the famous Lily Riser. Lily was assigned a security escort that first week. But a month into the semester, she was old news, just another college student in the crowd. And now here she was, in the locker room, preparing to run her first track meet of the semester.

When she first considered trying out for the team, she'd been a wreck. She was older than most of the girls by at least four years. She was a mother. There were half a dozen excuses not to do it. Abby called her out yet again.

"Come on, Lilypad, you're not really going to puss out on this. Try out and see what happens."

Lily had shown up for tryouts at the last minute and given it her all, finishing with the second-fastest sprint time. Seeing her name on the roster, realizing that she'd made the team, was one of the greatest accomplishments of her life.

"Hey, Riser, someone asked me to give this to you."

Lily saw Heather, her teammate, approaching with a bouquet of sunflowers. Lily smiled as she took the bouquet and read the attached card.

The faster you run, the faster you see me. It's a win-win. Love, Scott.

Lily burst out laughing. Heather grinned and gave Lily a playful hip check as she made her way over to her locker.

"Someone's a smitten kitten."

Lily smiled, her cheeks flushing. She tucked the bouquet of flowers into her locker before her other teammates, who were now arriving, could join in the teasing. Lily hurried to finish dressing.

If someone had told Lily that she would find love, she would have said that it was impossible. She was focused on being a mom to Sky, helping Wes with David, spending time with Abby. Not to mention juggling a full class load and track practice.

But then one day Lily's Literature and the American Revolution professor assigned partner projects. Their assignment: write a twelve-page research paper and create a presentation, such as a slide show or a video or even a speech. Lily hated partner assignments. She tried to rack her brain, tried to think of any excuse to avoid the assignment. The public was still obsessed with her case. They wanted intimate details about her life, what she was doing, wearing, eating, thinking. Their obsession drove her crazy. She could already predict the questions her partner might ask: How often did Rick rape her? Did he abuse Sky? Did she miss him? Was she angry with her sister for killing him? It was a curiosity she couldn't understand. But she knew that the professor wasn't one of those warm and fuzzy types who'd care about his student's personal life, and she needed an A in this course to keep her scholarship. That's how she found herself paired up with Scott Sandoval.

"Lily's a nice name," he'd said when she'd introduced herself. Lily held her breath, waiting for that moment of recognition regarding Lily's now-infamous moniker. The entire world knew Lily Riser, it seemed, except Scott Sandoval. As they got to know each other, Lily learned that Scott was twenty-three. He'd enlisted in the army at eighteen and had completed two tours in

Afghanistan. He told Lily this class was just as important to him and they should get to work.

Lily tried to focus on the project. But she found herself drawn to Scott. It wasn't just his good looks, dark olive skin, jet-black hair, hazel eyes, and dimples that lit up his face when he smiled. He was just so easygoing and he was rarely serious. He said it was his sense of humor that got him through combat and it would get him through college too. Scott spent their study sessions doing impressions of their teacher or fellow students, and when he ran out of those, he'd do spot-on impressions of famous people. By the time class was over, Lily's stomach hurt from laughing so hard. It was only when he asked her about herself that Lily grew uncomfortable. She said she'd taken some time off to get her life in order and figure out what she wanted to be when she grew up. Which wasn't a lie. Not exactly. Lily had simply omitted the truth.

They'd completed their assignment almost a week early and were goofing off in the student union building. Scott was telling her about his dad's latest fascination with a homeless baby squirrel he'd rescued.

"So, now Dad's trying to find diapers that will fit the squirrel, which is a lot harder than you might think. It's kind of become his obsession."

Lily had burst out laughing, and then she'd looked at him, he'd looked at her, and they'd paused, that millisecond right before a kiss. She'd forgotten about the millisecond until now. She lost her breath when Scott finally leaned in and kissed her. It was different from Wes. Better. Sweet and tender...but more passionate. Lily had pulled away, her face flushed. She'd grabbed her stuff, unable to believe what had happened.

"I'm not just a college student. I have a daughter. She's eight. And I was...I was kidnapped when I was sixteen. This man held me captive. He kept me prisoner...and I..."

She told him because he needed to know, but also because she'd wanted to scare him away. That should be easy enough. What kind of man wants damaged goods?

"I know who you are, Lily."

She'd stared at him like he had three heads.

"You know?"

"Yes, I do."

Lily couldn't believe he knew who she was. "You never asked any questions. You never said anything about my past."

"I wanted to get to know you. Not the person on the TV or the victim they made you into. I have my own stuff to deal with. Things I don't exactly love talking about. It didn't really matter who you were or what happened back then. I just liked making you laugh. I figured if I brought up everything you'd been through, you wouldn't be rolling on the floor."

Lily had been speechless. Scott had taken her hands in his.

"I'm sorry I kissed you without asking. I shouldn't

have done that. But I like you, and I wanted... Forget it. Can we move on? We can still be friends. Can't we?"

There was no malice in his eyes, none of the evil or darkness that she'd seen in Rick. Lily had kissed him that second time. Before she knew it, they were inseparable. Lily was in her first real adult relationship. This was new and uncharted territory for her. If they were hanging out together and Scott got quiet, Lily would worry. Did she do something wrong? Was he mad at her? Would he lose his temper and lash out? Scott was constantly reassuring her that he was fine. "Just because I don't fill every moment with conversation doesn't mean I'm upset. And even if I am, even if I don't agree with you, I'll never hurt you," he'd told her.

She wanted to believe him. It was easier in theory than in practice. Lily had been worried that she wouldn't be able to have a normal intimate relationship, but Scott was patient and kind. It didn't mean that she didn't have trauma when it came to sex. She hated bright lights and she was uncomfortable with her body. Sometimes she'd get moody and couldn't stand to be touched. Dr. Amari reminded her that it was okay, that she just needed space. But like with everything else, Scott displayed infinite patience.

Lily knew what real love was now. Not teenage infatuation. Not Rick's twisted notion. Love was this. Lying in bed with Scott's strong arms wrapped around her. Studying side by side on a blanket in the quad, weekends at the park playing soccer with Sky. Backyard barbecues and late-night stargazing. But everyone knew it was serious when Lily introduced him to Abby. Her sister had given him two thumbs-up.

"He's gorgeous, Lil. And he's head over heels."

When Lily thought about their future, she had no idea what was in store. The idea of marriage and more children made her anxious. Scott laughed when she'd told him she wasn't sure if she was ready for a serious commitment.

"I think we've got time, Lil. Let's enjoy what we have now. We'll take it as it comes."

Taking it as it comes wasn't an easy attitude for someone who'd spent years planning how to survive from one day to the next, but Lily was determined to try.

The locker room door opened and Lily heard Coach Polk shouting.

"Come on, ladies, move your butts. I want all of you out on the track in sixty seconds."

Lily's teammates were focused and quiet as they dressed. Lily was ready. All she had to do now was slip on her jersey—number eight, in honor of Sky. She inspected her reflection in the full-length mirror. Her hair was a little longer now, tied up in a ponytail. The red had faded to a light auburn. Her skin was tan and glowing and she'd put on a good twenty pounds of muscle. She loved each and every ounce. She wasn't a "fatty." She was strong. Healthy. An athlete. Lily reached down and pulled up her lucky blue socks and made her way to the exit.

The track was packed with runners from competing schools and their coaches. Today was the first meet of the season, and there was an excited buzz in the air, the support of friends and family fueling the runners.

Coach Polk stood near the starting line as the team huddled around him.

"Ladies, remember, what separates you from everyone else is focus. Start fast. End first. I don't care about rankings or who you think is better than you. You've all trained and worked to be right where you are today. You've overcome insurmountable odds."

Lily's teammate Heather squeezed her hand, and Lily smiled.

"Winning is here." Coach Polk pointed to his head. "And here," he continued, pointing to his heart. "We've got more heart than any team on this field. Don't forget that. On the count of three. One. Two. Three."

"Go Bison!"

The girls gave each other high fives and began their separate warm-ups. The announcer welcomed everyone and Lily moved toward the starting gate, jumping up and down to loosen her muscles. The sun shined brightly, a crispness in the air.

"Let's go, Mommy."

Lily recognized Sky's voice instantly. She scanned the crowd and found her family in the bleachers. Scott was holding Sky as she waved a sign that read #8 IS MY MOMMY! Scott had her turn the sign around and it read #8 IS MY HOTTIE. Lily burst out laughing, waving to them and blowing kisses. She saw her mom, holding David, his chubby arms waving back at her. Wes was beside her and then she saw Abby. *Abby!* Her sister was wearing a Bucknell sweatshirt and beaming brightly. Lily couldn't believe this. She'd never even considered that Abby might be able to attend, and now here she was, ready to cheer Lily on. Lily knew what this meant, how difficult it must have been for her sister to face the crowds and the noise and the potential public scrutiny. It meant everything to see Abby standing there.

Lily placed her hand over her heart and Abby did the same. She could already feel herself growing stronger, just knowing that Abby was in the stands cheering her on. She didn't know when, but Lily knew that one day they wouldn't be separated by doctors and guards. One day Abby would be her neighbor. They'd take their children to school, celebrate holidays together. *But today is a start*, Lily thought. *Today is a good start.*

Lily forced herself to focus. Her best race was the four-hundred-meter run, and she was up first. She wasn't the fastest out of the gate, but she was skilled at picking up speed and surging past her opponents. Lily made her way over to the starting line. She adjusted her shoelaces, keeping her breathing even and steady. She always closed her eyes before she ran, saying a silent prayer of thanks. She inhaled, breathing in the freshly cut grass, the coconut essence of her sunscreen, always taking time to remember these moments. She could hear the crowd murmuring excitedly, the low whispers of the other runners as they discussed strategy with their coaches. She quieted her mind, listened to the steady beat of her heart. The announcer's voice sounded through the loudspeaker.

"Runners. On your marks."

Lily took her place on the starting mark, staring straight ahead. A hush descended over the crowd.

Bang!

The starting gun exploded, and like that, Lily was off.

She could feel the other runners beside her but Lily blocked them out. She kept running, one foot in front of the other, her arms pumping faster and faster. Her family was chanting her name, and though she knew it was silly, it seemed as if the whole stadium was cheering her on as well.

Lily ran even faster, determined to reach the finish line. She couldn't wait to hug Abby, to wrap her arms around Sky and Scott, to be surrounded by her whole family in this place that she loved so much. Her lungs ached, but Lily surged forward, passing more runners. She didn't know if her efforts would be enough to win, but that wasn't the point. Lily wasn't whole yet, but she would be. One day she believed that all the pieces of the puzzle would fit again. *Keep on going*, Lily thought, as the finish line grew closer and closer. *Just keep going.*

ACKNOWLEDGMENTS

I was nine when I wrote my first novel. Every few weeks I would read the handwritten pages to my mother and twin sister, a captive audience on long car trips. But one day, overcome with crippling self-doubt, I dumped the manuscript in the garbage. Which is why I'm so grateful for the army of people who kept me from committing further crimes against fiction.

To Adesuwa McCalla, manager extraordinaire, you took a chance and never stopped believing in me. I cannot imagine continuing this journey without your tough love and unwavering support. To my agents at WME, Lindsay Dunn and Eve Attermann (whose insightful notes and relentless hustle got people talking), as well as Jo Rodgers and Covey Crolius, who took *Baby Doll* international, a million thanks.

To my fantastic editors: Devi Pillai of Redhook and Selina Walker of Penguin Random House, thank you for bringing *Baby Doll* to life. I knew I was in great hands when your editorial notes were "give us more."

ACKNOWLEDGMENTS

Thank you to SSA Shanna G. Daniels of the FBI's Investigative Publicity and Public Affairs Unit for providing me with your expertise so I could properly depict the work you and your colleagues do in your quest for justice.

To Eduardo Santiago, my writing guru; of all the classes in all the world, I'm so glad I walked into yours. Thank you for believing in this book and for always saying "you can do better."

My Hallmark ladies and early readers; Angie Polk, Jennifer Kramer, Lynnsey Marques, Alex Smith, and Laura Mitten, your killer notes and enthusiastic response gave me the encouragement to keep going.

Big thanks to my Texas crew; Katie Sechrist for your spot-on notes, Nick Chapa, my creative sounding board and tech support (check's in the mail, I swear). Liza "Lizard" Sandoval, no matter where life takes us, your courage and amazing sense of humor keeps me going. Endless gratitude also goes to Matt McArthur, for your friendship and for sharing your criminal justice expertise with me. And of course thanks to Lee Ann Barnhardt, who despite leaving the classroom, never stopped being my teacher.

Sarah Haught, your genius attention to detail and ability to make sense of my time line made me love/hate you (but mostly love you). Ian Michael Kinzle, your in-depth analysis was spot-on and beyond appreciated. Bisanne Masoud, your creative suggestions and proofreading prowess took my first draft to a whole new level.

To my LA hive mind, April Garton, Elena Zaretsky, Shaina Fewell, Jon Levenson, Rochelle Zimmerman, Mem Kennedy, Lindsay Halladay, and Allison Rymer, thanks for knowing when I needed an encouraging e-mail, hike, or a glass of wine and for inspiring me with your own incredible talents.

To my "BB" Shahana Lashlee, you have proven there is nothing you won't do for me. Nothing! Your creativity and quick wit has seen me through my best and worst writing days. Here's to a lifetime of "smidges," together.

Giselle "Chicken" Jones, my beautiful muse and life champion, there is no Dr. Amari without you. You helped craft an honest and poignant look at the patient/therapist relationship. Hope you get to bring her to life!

To Betty Overton, there is no question that I won the Mom lottery. Thanks for choosing us! I will never forget the sacrifices you've made. Even after I destroyed that first novel, even when I denied my destiny, you knew it all along. You were right. I am a writer.

To my UK family, my mother-in-law Linda Boyd and my sister-in-law Rachael Hogg, thank you for your constant encouragement and for raising a man so patient he's able to put up with me... and my twin.

To my husband David Boyd, thank you for enduring my endlessly late nights, for walking Stevie, keeping my chais coming and proving that there are truly good men in this world. Living with a writer requires patience, humor, and a touch of insanity. Thankfully you possess all three (not to mention a great lid!). To quote my favorite Geordie, "You're it for me, kid."

And finally, Heather Overton, my twin sister, my best friend, the Abby to my Lily, not only did you rescue *Baby Doll* from the figurative trash heap but you've rescued me again and again. From paying contest fees when I was flat broke, to giving brutally honest and incredibly smart notes on this book and every script that came before it, you've more than made up for losing that sweater. Through all the struggles, even in my darkest times, you always believed that I had something worth saying. Never ever forget that you do too.